I0604543

Daybreak

Emma Ellis

Copyright © [2025] by [Emma Ellis]

All rights reserved.

No portion of this book may be reproduced in any form without written permission from the publisher or author, except as permitted by U.K. copyright law.

No generative artificial intelligence (AI) was used in the writing of this work. The author expressly prohibits any entity from using this publication to train AI technologies to generate text, including, without limitation, technologies capable of generating works in the same style or genre as this publication. The author reserves all rights to license uses of this work for generative AI training and development of machine learning language models.

This book is written in British English.

This book contains some dark themes. Trigger warnings include death, infant death, and coercive behaviour.

CHAPTER 1

Harriet wasn't born a leader. She was born below ground where people scratch out a living to get by. Or don't. More often it's the latter. She comes from a muffled existence. A lost voice. Her silence was her scream. What she is, is a survivor. Somehow, against so many odds, she's still standing.

It seems all you need to be a leader these days is to shout the loudest, to drown out the rest of the noise. To prove you have the capacity in your lungs like the birds in the morning chorus. Harriet sure as hell never wanted this gig, but the people watching her now need to follow someone. As she stands on the pile of rubble that used to be a skyscraper, they all look to her, expectant, awaiting their instructions as the building is reduced to ash behind her. She should be able to offer some reassurance, to be a show of strength as the steel lintels buckle and the concrete turns to dust.

The heat from the blaze warms the air, sending plumes of ash and smoke in eddies around what's left of the walkway, the wind whipping the fire into a frenzy. Yet still they look to her, awaiting reassurances, judging her performance.

They chant her name, their three-syllable battle-cry comes from soot-covered faces, accompanied by stamping footsteps and air-punching. The whites of their teeth grin through the gloom. They're all high on the adrenalin that comes after an explosion. They survived this one. But then, the bomb wasn't meant for them this time. For once, the destruction comes to those at the top.

She coughs from the dust lingering in the air, but she must find her voice. She must speak for these people. If she doesn't, this has all been for nothing.

Yet, in her heart, she knows it shouldn't be her standing here. It should be Oliver. This is his audience, his applause.

She looks up; there's a clear view of the sky through the gap in the walkways where the building once stood and sees the Hel-Es circling. One of those must be taking her son to safety. In one of those, he lives.

Still, they chant. Their energy is contagious. Her heart pounds as the dust settles; a drumbeat of rebellion.

The encore is moments away. She must get them to safety, to below, where the next round of destruction won't hurt them. They look at her as if she can save them, but it's Oliver who's the protector. Oliver who's the hero.

Step up, Harriet. Now is not the time for stage fright. She raises her arms, quiets the chanting. Up here, on the pile of rubble, she can tell them the truth.

Some have been threatening this for ages, saying the reckoning is here. When humans lose their grip on this world in favour of the bots, humanity will be lost to oblivion.

Based on what Harriet knows of humanity, she says bring it on.

CHAPTER 2

SIX WEEKS EARLIER

Harriet waits on level 6 outside the doors where she first met Oliver. Today she will meet Oliver again for the first time. Only now, he's not going to be her little boy anymore. He'll be fully grown. She's been counting down the weeks, then days, then hours until this moment. She still pines for the six-year-old he was, all fresh-faced innocence, apple-round cheeks, a blank slate with so much to learn. She still remembers their first cuddle, the first time he called her Mother. Time is too linear. She wishes it could curve back occasionally, bend full circle to give her a glimpse of what once was.

It must be like that for every parent. Children grow up too quickly, even MechaniKids, whose growth spurts are exactly that. Two huge spurts from child to adolescent to adult. Nothing in between. As much as she misses little kid Oliver, she's so excited to see the man he has become. And as an adult, he'll be released from the MechaniTeen Institute. Their time together can be spent as they like instead of against the clock. Her son will be free. Five years he's been shackled to the MechaniTeen Institute and now, her son is coming home.

There's more work to do, to keep Oliver and his fellow bots safe, but he is coming home to a world much better than it was a few years ago. The road ahead will still be tough, though she fears, shorter than the road behind her. Her past casts a long shadow. Her future, not so much.

She checks her watch, wiping away the dust from the face before she can read it. She's bang on time. Any minute now. If she had any nails left, she'd bite them, but they all succumbed in the build up to this. She'd pace if it didn't wear her out so much. Her legs ache just from standing. So, she leans against the wall, clock-watches and stares up at the grubby underside of the walkway above. She's seen Oliver most days over the last couple of years as he's battled his teenage troubles and coped with his life locked away. She's loved every second she's spent with him, though she swears the years have passed in the blink of an eye.

She fidgets as she leans on the wall. Weight has fallen off her the last year, leaving her permanently weak and freezing. She has no insulation to the elements however many layers of clothing she piles on. The weight of her clothing adds to her tiredness, her muscles cramping from the exertion as much as from the cold.

She hides it from Oliver, her ill health. The coughs, the fatigue, the weight loss. She'll never allow herself to seem tired in his presence. Her lungs ache and she presses her hands into her ribcage, her breaths rattling against the pressure.

The doors slide open, and she pushes against the wall to stand upright. There he is. Her shrivelled lungs inflate with a gasp, her dry eyes mist with tears. He steps out, her little boy, now all grown up, and takes the final steps towards her.

'Mum,' he says, then wraps her in a hug.

He's so strong and broad, at least a foot taller than her. She leans away and gazes at his face. He's all there, all the signs of her boy, only now he appears about twenty-five, his voice has the depth of maturity, an Adam's Apple pokes from his stubble-dusted neck. He's a strong jaw, yet still those little-boy cheek dimples. He crouches a little so she can reach his hair, and she musses it up like she's always done. It's a shade darker, a kink of a curl.

'Let me just look at you for a moment.' Her thumb traces the contours of his face.

'Have you shrunk?' he asks, wearing that grin she loves so much.

'Cheeky!'

Behind him comes another man who Harriet does a double-take to recognise. Thomas, unmistakably him. An inch shy of Oliver with the same gorgeous freckles he had as a kid. His red hair has darkened to auburn, sleek and tidy. He rolls his shoulders forward as if trying to hide his new height. He's never developed Oliver's confidence.

Harriet's hands go to her cheeks as she looks at him. 'Oh, my. Thomas.' She swallows back the lump in her throat. 'I wish your mum was here.'

He nods and smiles. 'Me too.'

'Come here.' Harriet opens her arms and embraces him. She's never felt so tiny as she does right now, in the presence of these two who used to be so small just a heartbeat ago. She was always short, though, and Oliver's right, she probably is shrinking.

She releases Thomas and backs up a couple of paces. 'You two just stand there for a moment. I want a photo.' Harriet whips up her phone and snaps a few as the boys stand tall and smiling. She puts her phone away and stares at them for a moment longer, her mouth agape until the boys start to fidget like they've been gawped at for long enough. 'Come on then,' she says. 'Let's get a taxi and take you boys home.'

'I thought, well, we could get the lift up to 99 and walk a bit?' Oliver says. His deep voice startles Harriet for a second. 'Thomas has never seen the sky in daylight.'

Harriet really can't manage a walk, but she won't let on. Eventually she'll let Oliver know she's sick, but not right now. Today is all about him and celebrating. 'How about I leave you to enjoy that? I need to get back a little quicker, so I'll see you at home. But you take your time. Theo and Monty will be waiting for you two when you're ready. You sure you remember the way?'

The boys chuckle as they reassure her, like not knowing the way would be ridiculous. She should know better than to doubt their homing instincts.

She watches them walk towards the lift shaft before she steps into the taxi, wheezing her breaths. She's freezing, yet she itches from sweat. The rash up her back is so easily irritated. She has all manner of creams and lotions at home to keep the worst of the symptoms at bay, but she's avoiding the pain relief at the moment. It makes her head foggy, and she has to be alert for her son's homecoming. She wants to be present, not in some opioid-induced haze. She's just pleased her vision lasted long enough to see her son a grown man.

Her breaths steady as she sits and the taxi rolls away, a plume of soot and dust in its wake blackening her view of outside for a moment. One day soon, she'll go up top again. She'd like to feel the sunshine one last time.

In her chapped hands she can still feel Oliver's skin, his hair, in her arms his embrace is still warm. She wipes her tear on her sleeve, a happy tear as she knows whatever happens to her now, most of her dreams have come true.

CHaPTer 3

For five years, Oliver and his friends didn't know what the time was. They worked to the schedule the staff at the Institute gave them, underground, with no sun or clock to guide them. Doing what they were told and when. It's been such a long time since Oliver's seen the sunshine. For Thomas, it's been forever.

Oliver hopes it's a sunny day. A few clouds would be nice, though even if it's raining, he wouldn't mind. He doesn't breathe, but he can tell when the air is humid or dry. The sensors that cover his skin react differently. When he was a kid living up high, his skin felt alive in the freshness. Below ground, it was like his skin would rather fall off.

At the Institute they were always so grubby. This new body is clean but still has a layer of dust from its brief time below. They're dressed smartly enough to fit in on 99, or Oliver thinks so anyway. They're the nicest clothes he's worn since he was a kid. Truly Realistic Intelligence gave them an outfit to wear for their new professional lives. A shirt and new pair of trousers with a crease down the front, and shoes that can be shined, though they're not shiny right now. And a jacket, a plain thing without any buttons, but it lets them fit in and they don't stand out as bots. MechaniBots don't need jackets. Oliver can tell when it's cold, but it doesn't make him uncomfortable. He remembers humans shivering, so it can't be nice.

They alight the lift, and his wish is granted. There's a breeze, unlike any they've known in years. His skin tingles as the fresh air brushes past. The air is lighter, not the heavy dampness of the Institute below ground. It's like he can move more freely, stand taller, and his joints work better. But the best thing is the sun's out. Huge and orange, it sits low in the sky and glints off the high-rise windows. There are more high-rises now, he's sure of it, like the buildings keep extending up and up. One day they'll reach the moon.

Some birds fly in a V across the sky. The few bubbly clouds glow pink in the sun's wake. It's exactly the kind of day Oliver hoped for.

Thomas stares quietly, his hands in his pockets, eyes scrunched up in the glare, a half-smile across his face. He saw the night's sky once, but the daytime sky he's only ever seen in pictures. Oliver holds his hand up to shield his eyes, like his mum showed him when he was a kid, and Thomas copies.

They both stand for a moment, admiring the view. Oliver can feel warmth without knowing what it's like to actually be warm. It's like a hug, like his insides are wrapped in a blanket.

'We're finally free,' Oliver says.

Thomas looks his way and nods. 'We got through it. Now we can have a future.'

Oliver's less excited than he thought he'd be, less delighted. His smile feels forced and fake. Leaving the Institute is all he's wanted for so long, and he is ready to start a proper job rather than spend so much time in crappy classes. Life should be good, perfect. It's everything he'd hoped for. But his shoulders drop readily, his chin goes down. Leaving the Institute is what he's been wanting, but the sight of his mum has cast a dark shadow. He knows she's sick and the fact she hasn't mentioned it makes Oliver think she's really sick. As sick as Josie, Thomas's mum. She looks the same as Josie did, thin and wobbly and out of breath. Not at all like she was when he was a kid and she used to carry him and run around after him. Perhaps it's normal for humans, but he worries.

They stroll through parks, past beds of real flowers. There are so many colourful ones out at the moment with butterflies and bees visiting them. Thomas flinches when he first sees a butterfly, then laughs as one circles around him. The bees are so loud, like they're humming inside his ears. The Institute warned them their hearing would be more acute, and he snaps his head round, looking over his shoulder but spots the bee on the next flower bed over. This new hearing is going to take some getting used to.

In the skies above, some Hel-Es fly. Oliver remembers there being more when he was a kid, but then, lots of things seemed bigger back then. What doesn't, though, quite the opposite, is the amount of space out here. The Institute was often cramped but on the 99 walkway, he can see forever, like it's miles to the walkway fence. He could jump, run, and not even bump into anything. He stretches his arms out to the sides, his shirt billowing in the breeze and lifts his chin to the sky.

This is where he's meant to be. As much as he's going to love living with his mum and uncles on 5 again, the lure of life up top is like a charging point when his battery is low. It's a pull, a need. Down on 5 there won't be much breeze, no real sunshine. He'll have more room than at the Institute but not nearly as much as up here. He looks over one shoulder, then the other, checking out all the people going about their day, getting lifts up even higher to their huge top-level apartments with private gardens. His eyes narrow, his mouth twists, and he folds his arms. What is the word for what he's feeling? He wants what these people have and is bitter that he and his mum will have less. It doesn't seem right that someone as wonderful as his mum shouldn't live up here. He knows how much she loves the sky. Maybe, somehow, he can give that life to his mum again.

'I never imagined it being this spacious,' Thomas says. 'And bright. I don't think I've ever seen colours like this before.'

Oliver faces Thomas and places his hands on his shoulders. 'Let's promise, Thomas, as brothers, because we are like brothers, that somehow, we're going to live up here one day.'

Thomas turns his head and gives him the side eye. 'Is this just because Evie's job is above 100?'

Oliver takes his hands away and gives him a playful nudge. 'No. But then, it wouldn't be the worst thing to see her.'

Thomas laughs and shakes his head.

Leaving the Institute without Evie has created a heavy emptiness inside Oliver he didn't expect. There was a time when he assumed they'd always be together. He never really planned his future, but assumed she'd be part of it. Instead, she's gone to work somewhere else, and they don't have phones to keep in touch. Bots don't need to make proper friendships, the handbook says. Bots will be friends with anyone. But Evie wasn't just a friend. He doesn't know what she was, just that she was special.

They start walking, both stumbling a little. The ground is perfectly smooth and even, but they've been in their full-grown bodies only for a day and they've barely had time to get used to their new dimensions. Oliver has hit himself in the face several times, walked into furniture, and head-butted the walls. He didn't pay much attention to his own challenges at the Institute. He hardly even looked at his new body. At the Institute, he was entirely enchanted with Evie's new body. She was beautiful in ways he simply can't describe.

The idea of bumping into Evie isn't why he suggested a walk up here. Definitely not. Even though she left the Institute yesterday and she could be out up here now. But if they did bump into her, that wouldn't be a bad thing. Is this what it means to be an adult? To wonder about such things all the time? He really wishes the Institute covered emotions. Bots aren't meant to have these feelings, is what they'd say. He always meant to talk to Evie about it, but there never seemed to be the right moment. She was always there and time got away, and then before he knew it, they were saying goodbye, and he was left wishing he had just one more day with her. They never even had a moment alone without all the other teens there. Oliver's not sure what difference being alone would have made, but he'd have liked to have found out.

Some birds fly past and land in a bush to the right of the walkway, cheeping as they go. Goldfinches, Oliver thinks, though he's rusty on all the different types. No one else seems to notice them and even Oliver doesn't for long as his attention is grabbed by children laughing. He stops to watch some playing on a climbing frame, just like he used to. Part of him aches for that life again, so simple and carefree. His job will be great, but he'll have responsibilities. There's so much he's unsure about.

'Hey,' Thomas says when they start walking again. 'I'm worried about your mum.'

'Yeah. Me too.'

'It's a human thing, isn't it, to just get sick? Maybe she's not that sick.'

'Maybe. I hope not.'

The big advertising billboard at the side switches from some new clothing item to a shiny notice from AM Investments. Oliver tenses and glares at the billboard. That's Anthony's company.

There's not a day that goes by where Oliver doesn't relive his hatred for him, his anger. He can still hear the sound of Anthony thumping his mum, the sound of the china plate smashing against the wall when he threw one at her. The happiest moment of his life was when Anthony collapsed to the floor and Oliver thought he was dead. He should be dead. The MechaniTeen Beatrice wasted her life saving him. He wasn't worth it.

Anthony's face is in the corner of the billboard screen, smiling in that awful way he always did before hurting his mum. He looks healthier now, or maybe they've edited the photo. Oliver hopes that's it. He hopes he's on death's door.

The rest of the screen shows inside huge apartments, even bigger and fancier than the one Oliver lived in as a kid, the view even more spectacular. Anthony's voice speaks over the music, and Oliver grinds his teeth.

Get your reservation in now to avoid disappointment! AM Investments are expanding their buildings! Reach for the sky and live at 150!

Oliver's hands clench into fists, and his new bigger biceps press into his sides. His mum's sick and Anthony's company is doing well. The real world is as shitty and unjust as it ever was. Only now he's an adult; now he's strong. He's not a pushover like when he was a kid. He's not trying to hide and run away like when he was a teen. He's free. Maybe he'll have the chance to do something about the unjustness. Maybe now he can finally wipe that smile off Anthony's face.

He'll never let anyone hurt his mum again. He swore he'd take revenge on Anthony. Now he's a man, which means he's capable. And he means it.

CHAPTER 4

Harriet hasn't been able to speak a word since she got back. Part in awe and part out of breath. She sits at the kitchen table, among the clutter of partly finished refurb projects and the pile of broken mugs waiting to be glued back together as she waits for the children—she'll still refer to them as children, however grown up they are—to come home.

'So,' Monty asks, all smiles and wide eyes. 'How was he?'

She nods, one hand pressed to her painful lungs, giving a tearful thumbs up with the other.

Monty sits at the table with her, his paint-and-glue-covered smock bunching up around his neck. Monty and Theo have moved their work out of the apartment to a lockup a few minutes away to save space, but they still bring work home, as if being in a tidy home that doesn't smell like solder and paint would somehow stifle their creativity. Harriet doesn't mind. After years of living in her ex-husband's pristine show-home filled with air and straight lines, she loves the chaos their creativity brings.

When Harriet takes even longer than usual to catch her breath, Monty's expression pinches and he reaches for her hand. 'Maybe you shouldn't come tomorrow, babe. It's a long way and below.'

Harriet's lungs heave, and after another moment, she's able to speak. 'I'm already sick. Going below won't make me sicker. You know Theo wants us there.'

'He'd understand.'

'I'm fine.'

Harriet missed last year's memorial. She hasn't returned below ground since she took Oliver as a kid, not even attending Theo's parents' funerals. She's been feeling tired for years and was in denial she had the sickness already, instead kidding herself that if she avoided below ground and ate enough vegetables, she could keep the sickness at bay.

Now that she has the sickness, it seems stupid not to go. It's a raucous affair, by all accounts, though Harriet has only vague memories of it from her childhood. Celebrating the memory of those who dug the tunnels wasn't something she partook in even then. She had a sick brother to look after and abusive parents to avoid. Clinking glasses to those who built the place she hated so much felt hypocritical even to a child. But now she's an adult and has a better understanding of the achievement. Being the closest thing the below grounders have as a celebrity means her absence year-on-year is met with a little disdain, like she's forgotten her roots. She wishes she could.

There's a stigma about having the sickness, but maybe coughing with pride will let the other below grounders know that she carries that life with her always. To the grave.

Theo arrives with bags of groceries and starts putting them away. More than a niggle of guilt inches over Harriet. She's not contributing financially much at the moment, and Theo has bought enough to feed them all for a week.

'How was Oliver? Where is he?' Theo asks as he loads up the fridge.

Theo's always been skinny, but his weight loss of late has reduced him to skeletal. As he reaches the top shelves now, Harriet notices the folds in his trousers as his belt has been tightened a few notches. She fears his sickness is not far behind hers.

'He's perfect and he'll be here any minute,' she says.

For a while, Harriet attributed Theo's weight loss to his grief. He's been in a frequent malaise since his parents passed last year, although recently he seems to be coming out the other side of it bit by bit. He quit his job at the school and now works freelance full-time. She thinks maybe that was a mistake. He loved spending time with the children. He just no longer felt up to it. A dark cloud still lingers over him, but he's smiled a few times, even laughed once or twice. Harriet hopes having Oliver and Thomas around will be the extra kick he needs.

When the front door opens again, Monty does a little excited jump-up from his seat and leaps towards the hallway, and Theo leaves the rest of the groceries unpacked. Harriet swivels in her chair and leans forward to watch Oliver and Thomas from the hallway.

'Great to see you, Uncle Theo and Uncle Monty,' Oliver says.

Theo tilts his head to look up at Oliver. 'Blimey! Look at you.'

Even Monty has to look up a little to meet the boy's eyes, and he's the tallest below grounder Harriet knows.

Thomas stands next to Oliver and the pair of them take up the entire width of the hallway. Harriet's eyes well up again. Her son really is home.

'Let me show you what we've done with the place!' Monty says with a clap. 'Theo and my work stuff is all in a lockup now, well, mostly. We actually have our own work premises, so we can keep this place much tidier. So, we split that room in two, and it's all yours. A side each.'

The boys follow him down the hallway and he opens the door, stepping to one side to show them. Inside, there's a partition wall that runs almost the whole length of the space, except the end where there's a small sofa, reupholstered in dark blue, above which a *Welcome Home* banner hangs. On each side of the wall is a bed, table, chair, and a wardrobe. There's a mirror on the wall along with some family photos. Monty spent ages decorating to make it just right. Clearing the dust out took an age, and Theo rigged up the charging sockets in the rooms and equipped each with a refurbished computer and a collection of books.

Harriet ambles to the room to watch their reactions. Both of them step in and walk around, then back away and wrap Monty and Theo in a hug. 'This is all so great,' Oliver says. 'Thank you!'

'There are clothes in there,' Monty continues. 'We weren't sure what sizes to get, but I can adjust anything. You boys make yourself at home.'

Monty and Theo give each other a pat on the back, and they all walk back to the kitchen. Harriet sits again, rests her chin in her hands, her eyes unfocussed to nowhere as she blinks a few tears away. She's not in pain right now; her inner warmth has rid her of her ails for a moment.

'Wow,' Theo says with a long exhale. 'He's so grown up, the pair of them!'

Harriet smiles a watery smile. 'I know.'

Theo grabs a beer from the fridge and one for Monty. Harriet has lost the taste for it these days; she's lost the taste for most things but sips on her hot tea, for the steam rather than flavour.

'So, just the two of them?' Theo asks, as if reading Harriet's mind. 'No Evie?'

Harriet has wondered about Oliver's girlfriend, or who she thought was his girlfriend, for ages. As a teen, he was always so cagey, like all teenagers she supposes, and she didn't want to pry. She shakes her head. 'I didn't want to ask. Maybe you guys could? You know, man to man.'

'He's a grown-up now,' Monty says. 'It's his business.'

'He's right,' Theo says. 'If he wants to talk, we're here. But I don't think we should push the subject if he's not ready.'

Harriet's never been one to discuss feelings and is aware of her own hypocrisy—that she wants her son to open up, yet has always revealed so little herself. Now they're all under one roof, communication should get easier. She'll find a way to break down that barrier.

There's laughter from the boys' room. The sound makes her chest swell, full to bursting. Harriet wasn't sure if the boys would want to live with them, or if TRI would put them up in some bot accommodation, or even if they'd have jobs local to their house. But their work is a short walk away and having Oliver and Thomas home is the perfect scenario she dreamed of. She takes a moment to relish in that, to enjoy the simplicity of her family being together, under one roof. She needs to make sure she takes this time, again and again, to live in the here and now, rather than dwell about the past or fret about the future. Time marches angrily, its footsteps heavier now, aching strides as her life races towards its finish line.

She lifts her teacup, the steamy tendrils collecting around her face, and she breathes it in.

After all the dangers they've faced over the years, having her family safe is all she ever wanted.

CHAPTER 5

Oliver's never been alone in a room before. It's strange how instantly lonely it is, like he's been shut away in a box. But also, he can be tense and frown and clench his fists and no one will know to ask him what's wrong. The Institute was always so busy, he's barely even had a moment where he wasn't brushing past someone else. Now he has his own room, a bed. How long has it been since he's known the comfort of a bed? There are books on the shelves and he picks one up, flicking through it. It's all words, no pictures—some novel about spaceships. He puts it back on the shelf, then runs his hand over the others. Several novels of different genres, an encyclopaedia, a dictionary, a book on the history of Reading town. He chuckles when he sees the tatty copy of *Charlotte's Web*, his favourite childhood book.

'Oliver! Check this out!' Thomas's excited voice comes from the other side of the partition wall.

Oliver walks around to look. Thomas holds up clothes from his wardrobe. 'All these, for us!'

Oliver smiles. 'It's so great.'

His mum and uncles have all gone to so much effort and he truly loves them for it, but arriving down on 5 from 99 made him feel instantly cramped. He never noticed before how obtrusive the roof of the level above is, how different the air is, how walking outside, everyone is in his space. He was smaller last time he was here.

He pushes thoughts of 99 to the back of his mind. His body is bigger now, that's all it is. He needs time to adjust, and this room is more spacious than he ever had at the Institute. He's a bot, destined for a life of simple work and service, not for fine things. Bots aren't ambitious, they're obedient, that's what the handbook says.

So why is he somehow dissatisfied? It aches and makes him wince at himself to notice this. Ambition is a lack of gratitude, surely. And he is incredibly grateful. He doesn't need fine things. But his mum deserves them. His mum should have the best of everything.

Back on his side of the partition, he inspects his own wardrobe, appreciates all the effort they've gone to. It's nice to have a family that cares so much and does so much for him. He knows not all bots are so lucky.

And yet . . .

He has a sense of disquiet inside. As he inspects each garment, he doesn't only see the effort his family has made but also the holes and imperfect alterations. The wardrobe isn't even full. Not that it should be, yet he's sure Anthony's wardrobe is rammed, sure Anthony's clothes have no imperfections. His mum used to have such nice things when he was a kid. Brand new clothes, jewellery, everything people from the top levels have. Their apartment wasn't cluttered like here. It was so big they could own a million things and it still wouldn't be full. And his mum loved the view. She'd stare out the window for ages some days.

That's what life was like for his mum up there. That's what Anthony's life is still like.

It's not fair.

Oliver shoves the clothes back in the wardrobe, then closes it. He glares at the blank door for a while, screws his eyes up, trying to block out the sight of the chip that's been sanded down, the mismatched hinges, the painted-over crack.

He lies on his bed, running his hands over the sheets. The bed is soft, comfortable, and his own. He hasn't had a bed in years. It's a simple thing, and he needs to remind himself that it is enough. His mum is happier now than she ever was on the top levels. But he can't help imagining how much happier she'd be if she lived her current life, but high up.

He runs his hand over his face and shakes his head. This is a fresh start for him, for Thomas, to finally be a family with his mum and uncles. Thomas is more brother than friend; they've always said this, though he's never known life living high up. Showing him the sky, Oliver thought it might make him see what he was missing but, instead, he was satisfied with a glimpse, as if he really believes that's all he should have.

'I'm glad I got to see it,' Thomas said, past tense when they arrived back down on 5. As if the sky is in his past only, not his future. But Thomas deserves a hell of a lot more than Anthony.

Oliver folds his arms across his torso, his new muscles startling him. He's so tense even though he's lying down. He sits up and shakes his arms out, forcing some relaxation into his body.

He's said goodbye to Evie. Anthony isn't in his life. He has a job to look forward to. That's what life is about now. Dwelling on all the what ifs is a shortcut to misery. He knows this. He has a purpose and he should be focusing on that.

It's weirdly quiet. Not nearly silent like on 99, and his new acute hearing picks up even a fly hitting the window in the kitchen. But there's not the constant racket of the Institute, the buzz of dehumidifiers and air purifiers. He loved standby time, when all the other teens were asleep. That's what it's like now, like the world is sleeping, like conversation has died. His thoughts are too loud in these moments. It's not the tranquil exhaustion when his battery is nearly depleted after hours and hours of lessons at the Institute. Then, his mind would stall to almost nothing. His battery is at eighty per cent. That's way too high to have almost no distractions.

He takes another book at random from the shelf and lies back on the bed. It's the dictionary. Not the most riveting read, but it amazes him how many words there are. Perhaps if he knows all the words, he'll know how to name his feelings. There must be a word for it, this burning sensation, where even his eyes feel like hot lasers, where when he thinks of Anthony and all of his fancy things, he wishes he could make them blow up in Anthony's face.

So, he reads. He can read so quickly now. He hadn't noticed it before, since he hasn't had an entire book for so long. He had instruction manuals, city maps, and role play scripts. The dictionary is hardly engrossing, but he can absorb several pages in one sitting.

Anger. He knows that word, he experiences it often, so he continues. He makes it to *begrudge*, which doesn't sound too far off. He does begrudge Anthony what he has. Then *bitterness*, which reads like watered-down anger. That's still not heated enough for his feelings. Then *covet*. No. That's still not right. He may covet what Anthony has, but that's not enough. He doesn't merely desire what Anthony has; he wants Anthony not to have it.

Envy. Is that it? Envy makes it sound like Oliver is the one in the wrong though, and it dawns on him then, the error in his approach. He's been reading these words trying to discern what's wrong with him, where really, it's what's wrong with Anthony.

He shuts the book and summons his memory. It's remarkably good, better than in his teen body. He sifts through all the words and meanings he just read, trying to label Anthony now.

Arrogant. Boastful. Conceited. Corrupt.

He'll read the rest of the dictionary later. Perhaps there's a word that's more accurate, but he has a shortlist for now. It's as if finding a word validates his feelings somehow. If there's a word for it, it's allowed. It means it's been felt before.

The staff should have discussed this more with the teens, so should his mum. Everyone should have, as it's probably the same for humans too. If they are not able to get in touch with their emotions as children or adolescents, what hope do they have in adulthood? Oliver has only known the awfulness of Anthony and the kindness of his mum. Nothing in between. That's not enough experience. Nowhere near.

He and his mum should have had conversations instead of the never-ending dialogue about trivial things. How was your day? How is so and so? They never talked properly about their inner workings. Was that his fault? He never considered the importance of it when life was so routine and predictable. Now, Oliver isn't sure how to talk properly. He'll have to read and try to figure it out on his own. Maybe some TV show will enlighten him. His mum and uncles are always so damned happy around him, always smiling, even when he's sure they don't want to. How is Oliver meant to know what his feelings are when everyone else fakes theirs?

He won't let on about his confusion, the way his throat clamps up when he thinks about discussing feelings, or the way he wants Anthony to suffer. He can't speak to his mum while she's sick. But he'll protect her from all the bad things in this world. It's his turn to look after her now.

A fresh start. A clean slate. That's what everyone says this is.

But a fresh start doesn't mean all Oliver's old anger has gone. He's sure finding the right word won't make it disappear.

CHAPTER 6

Since Harriet has been posting pictures of Oliver on *Get Level* as a MechaniTeen, he's developed quite a following, from teenage girls especially. It was nothing short of adorable to see posts from girls swooning over him. And rightly so. He's always been gorgeous, even if Harriet is a little biased. She's hoping now as an adult she can convince Oliver and Thomas to help her campaign for bot rights.

Harriet knows ideas catch on more if an attractive person sells them, and she's well aware she is not the starlet she used to be, especially in her poor state of health. She's still using old photos of herself online instead of her current shrunken cheeks and pasty skin. No one wants to listen to an ethics lecture from a zombie and she isn't going to be around long enough to change those millennia-old views. She needs to pass the reins to someone for that, and so she needs to prepare Oliver properly for the real world. She posted a couple of pictures of Oliver last night, as he left TRI: he and Thomas standing side by side, their handsome grins, broad shoulders, looking like they could be movie stars. And the comments have started coming in.

Oh, my God! He's even more gorgeous!

Hands off, ladies. He's mine!

WOW! WOW! WOW!

Eenie, meenie, miney mo! I'll take either and both!

It's a little weird for Harriet, sure, but it's exactly what her campaign needs. If Oliver is loved by many, anyone trying to harm him will be hated by many. She wishes she would be around for years to watch over and protect him, but she has to be realistic, so she needs to use every tool at her disposal now.

Despite all Harriet and other MechaniKid parents have done over the years to improve the public acceptance of bots, some still rally against them. Sceptics still shout how stupid it is to love a bot, and she gets more than her fair share of hateful messages that she ignores and deletes. Despite Beatrice giving her life to save Anthony, proving how useful bots are in the population, there will always be haters. The Flesh Fraternity's reasons are unfounded, mere echoes from a past that doesn't exist anymore or hankering for a present that was tried, tested, and failed. Children looked after by devices, AI programs that were not human-like at all, disabled and elderly cared for by computers, shops staffed by security cameras and self-checkouts, deliveries via drones rather than a hand. People need people, whatever form that person comes in. People add value to a business or profession, even if that person is a bot.

She likes the kind comments and posts another picture, then stands, slowly. Everything today will be done at a snail's pace. She needs to save her energy for this afternoon's trip below. She walks like she's twice her age to the kettle, her bones pulsing with pain as she lifts it to fill, then she sits again, exhausted as she waits for it to boil.

'Are you sure you're up for today?' Monty asks when he comes in and finishes making the tea. 'Because no offence, babe, you look like shit.'

Harriet smirks. 'Yes, thanks so much for the confidence, though.'

He plonks the cup in front of her and inspects her face as if he's looking for something wrong. 'We'll worry about you a lot less if you stay home. Theo's already left to help set up. So, we'll meet him there or not. It'll be busy so he won't even notice—'

'Monty, I'm going. Now, where are the boys?'

The apartment door opens then, a fresh gust snaking its way through the hallway and into the kitchen. Harriet tightens her cardigan, a shiver inching its way along every muscle. Her chill dissipates when Oliver and Thomas walk in with shopping bags.

'Juice, fruit. Sorry, they didn't have a big bottle of milk, just little ones. Hi, Mum,' Oliver bends and pecks her cheek. 'I think that was everything left on Uncle Theo's list.' He opens the fridge and jiggles some other bits around to make room.

They never have this much food normally. It's like Theo forgot the boys don't eat. Harriet can stomach so little these days, a few bites occasionally and that's about it. She watches Oliver and Thomas put the food away. Helpful and caring. They're wearing the clothes Monty fixed up, each in dark blue jeans, some rips remaining as if designed in, and snug-fitting T-shirts.

Neither had thought to put a jacket on, which is fine as they don't get cold, but it makes it obvious they're bots. It's always cold on the shady walkways of level 5. Any human would be wrapped up.

'The weirdest thing, though,' Thomas says. 'Some girls stopped us in the street for photos. They knew our names.'

'Oh . . .' Harriet bites her bottom lip. It seems lack of jackets isn't the only reason it's obvious they're bots. 'That might be my fault. You boys are a little bit famous around here.'

'What?' they both say.

Harriet explains about her photos when they were teens, just to show it's okay to be proud of a bot child. 'And, well, you boys are just so handsome. I think a lot of girls are going to have crushes.'

'Crush?' Oliver says. 'What's a crush?'

'Well. . .' Harriet sips at her tea to bide some time, swilling it around her mouth for a while as she hopes Monty might oblige and give this explanation. She eyeballs him and he stays silent, grinning sweetly back at her, the git. She swallows her tea. 'It's like, when you are attracted to someone, as more than just friends. Like you had with Evie, I think?'

'Oh,' Oliver says, looking at the floor.

'I see,' Thomas shoves his hands in his pockets.

Thomas and Oliver are a whole new shade of scarlet, and they fidget on the spot for a moment. She assumed at the Institute the teens might have figured these things out for themselves, but looking at their shocked faces, the crimson blotching their cheeks, it's clear they're as innocent as they were when they were kids. It dawns on her then quite how unworldly these two are.

Harriet sips her tea and pats the chair next to her. 'Come sit with me,' she says to the boys when it seems like their embarrassment has peaked.

They each sit, shoulders rolled forwards, their red cheeks slowly fading.

'You know the public loves you boys now. There's a lot of support for you and the bots.'

'Yeah,' Thomas says. 'That's great.'

'Have a look.' She loads up *Get Level* and shows them some of the comments that have already come in from her latest upload. Mostly admiration, but there are some who think it's okay to ridicule her son.

Harriet hardened herself to critics in her movie days, or tried to. It's impossible to have a thick enough skin for the worst of them, and some people just love to moan, like those who give a restaurant one star because a corner of the lettuce was discoloured. Some comments can be so vitriolic, she can only imagine they were typed by some loveless crone slamming their fingers down on their phone while snarling like a rabid dog and tutting loudly enough to rip the roof of their mouth.

'That's not nice.' Oliver jerks his head back and points at one of the more vile comments.

Monty peers over Oliver's shoulder. 'Don't let it get to you. To complain is to be human,' he says with a shrug. 'People have an innate need to judge, to ridicule, to feel superior. That's what makes humans human. It's evolution, survival of the fittest, or survival of the bitchiest.'

Harriet is probably meant to take some comfort in that. Instead, hopelessness presses against her lungs, and the smile she wears for her son's sake falters. She leans over the table and stares intently at the boys. 'I just want you boys to know how valued you are, how important. And that most people know that, despite the odd nasty comment. The Flesh Fraternity are a really small group now, but they still exist. So, every day we must keep reminding people of how good and wonderful you boys are.'

'Sure, Mum,' Oliver says. 'We really do appreciate all that you do.'

Thomas nods. 'It seems to be so much safer than when we ran away. I think everything you do is great.'

Harriet's heart couldn't be fuller. If judging and bitching is what makes humans, human, then not complaining for the sake of complaining is what makes bots, bots. That's one of the things Harriet loves about these boys so much. They're never unkind, not without reason. They simply take the whole hateful world in their stride. So those who say it's stupid to love a bot, Harriet can only think it's stupid not to.

She should talk to them more, let them know she's not going to be around forever, and the campaigning needs to continue even when she's gone. She should show them how to use social media and teach them good mental exercises to ignore the trolls. But it's only day one. She can't overwhelm them just yet.

'We're actually going to a bit of a party below ground this afternoon,' Harriet says. 'You two are more than welcome to join us. Would be great if you did, actually. But it's up to you. If you want some time to yourselves, you're grown-ups, do what you like.'

'I'm up for it,' Thomas says.

'Sure,' Oliver says. 'I've never been to a party.'

Harriet clutches her chest at this. How has her son grown up and never been to a party?

'We'll leave in a couple of hours,' Monty says. 'That'll give us plenty of time for the journey. We don't want to be in a rush.' He looks at Harriet when he says this, and she knows she'll take an age to get there.

A couple of hours even to get ready feels like a fast effort. She needs to shower, to try to do something with her brittle hair and rub some magic into her cheeks to make her look less like a walking corpse. She shouldn't care how she looks and once upon a time, she didn't. But her face has been everywhere over the years, and in each photo and film she looked a hell of a lot more alive than she does right now. Harriet hasn't looked in a mirror in ages. She can imagine her reflection. A knotted tree branch, spindly and half-eaten by bugs. She can already feel the pity stares, hear the gossip as people compare her to who she once was, as if the cameras ever told the full story.

But she can do it. One last trip below ground, back to the dingy world where she grew up and managed to escape.

They take a lift and Harriet grimaces through her pain as they alight and descend the final staircase that takes them below ground. She sucks on some sugar cubes, just to give her a bit of energy since the thought of proper food is nauseating. All the time she thinks perhaps Monty was right and this isn't the best idea.

The air gets heavier with every step, damp air forming condensation droplets across her skin leaving it slimy. When she tries to speak it comes out like a scratchy squeak. It's the dampness down here. The humidity is so high it rusts even vocal cords. When they make it to the thick door, they pause a moment while Harriet catches her breath. The humidity helps, she thinks, as her lungs behave better than she anticipated. Perhaps that's what the sickness is. Those born below need to be in dank conditions or else they desiccate. Harriet's ex-husband called below grounders a fungus once, and right now, that seems fitting.

Monty looks at Harriet, raised eyebrows, waiting for her to assure him she's okay. Her lungs heave, but she manages a nod and a smile. He pushes open the door. A whoosh of hotter air hits them and Harriet welcomes it. The sticky soup of below-ground air should at least warm her bones a bit.

They join the crowds and walk towards the market square to find Theo, Monty by her side, his hand on her back just in case she falters. He doesn't have to ask or check on her. He's just there, and that's enough to give her the bit of confidence she needs to make the walk. Harriet is unaccustomed to being worried about, so used to being the worrier. She'd like to shrug it away and tell him it's unnecessary, but she's kidding no one.

A veneer of moisture coats the clay walls. There's the usual squelching sound of soggy footsteps, and the tunnels are as busy as they've ever been.

Harriet hasn't missed the crammed-in feeling. Level 5 is squashed, the ceiling of the level above looming over them makes everyone's shoulders hunch, as if ducking instinctively from the shadow of the upper floors. But down here is a whole new feeling of being squashed. No room even to flex an elbow. She's seen so much death down here and from those who escaped. The tunnels to Harriet are more of a petri dish than a home.

People below today seem happy, cheerful about their lives living in the dirt. Like they're carbon atoms being crushed, compressed so much they'll soon gleam like diamonds. Bunting lines the walls, adding a splash of colour though they're still smudged with the orange-brown clay. All through the tunnels people blow whistles, sing the jingles Harriet used to know the words to so well. Lyrics of hope, of freedom, of escaping, even though below, Harriet always felt trapped rather than free. She was never free until she left. Still, she appreciates the tunnels were a saviour for so many. Anything can be seen as a home when what should have been was taken away. In those darkest moments, there's some light in a cave.

'Wow!' Oliver says as he looks around. He and Thomas are the tallest in the tunnels, towering above the bent backs and bowed legs of the below grounders. 'This is not how I remember it.'

'Me neither,' Thomas says, their voices raised to be heard above the music. Brass instruments and drums fill the air, feet stamping in time as dancing begins.

'Well, it's a celebration,' Theo says as he finds them in the crowd. His face is red and flustered, a string of bunting around his neck and his drill in one hand. 'My parents always loved this party. The people who dug these tunnels saved us when those up top turned the entire ground level into landfill then hiked up rents in the towers. The tunnels let us survive.'

'I didn't know there was such a sense of community down here,' Oliver says. 'Mum, why did you never say?'

Because her parents abused her and her little brother died of the sickness she's now inflicted with, should be her honest answer. But since when do parents ever answer their children so honestly with difficult questions? She wants to cushion Oliver from the perils of this world, not subject him to them. Instead, she says, 'I didn't have a happy time below, so I had to leave. But there has always been a sense of looking after each other, among the below grounders.'

Celebrations like this make people forget, for a night at least, about the substance abuse, child abuse, and robberies that happen down here. Theo's parents accredited their long lives on luck, but Harriet thinks it was probably karma. Not everyone below is as kind as they were.

Some people are now lining up to take Oliver's picture, and Harriet steps away to give them space. She hadn't appreciated quite the level of celebrity he'd have down here. Bots are set to save the lives of so many scavengers who pick up diseases and get hurt or killed pilfering through the landfill. Harriet watches his awkward interactions, his forced smile, how much he has to bend to talk to people. She's put a lot of pressure on him by pushing him into the limelight. He at least seems to take to it better than Thomas, whose blush is bright crimson and looks mostly at the floor. The boys aren't used to life outside the Institute, and this is clearly way out of their comfort zone. They're adults, she should let them learn. Feeling a little awkward isn't going to hurt them. She watches both of them and from the sidelines as they both relax a bit more, engage in some small talk, their blush calming down till it's barely visible in the dim tunnels.

After a few minutes, she approaches them. 'You all right, Oliver?'

That makes his blush ignite again. 'I'm fine, Mum. Go sit down.'

She smiles and walks away. At what point does a mother ever feel ready to simply let her child go? She's been absent for so much of Oliver's life. She could smother him now and it still wouldn't be enough for her.

'Harriet Chapel, as I live and breathe!'

The voice comes from the side and in the gloom Harriet sees little, just an outline of the typical below-ground stoop and skinny frame. When she's closer, she recognises her as an old acting friend from Harriet's early days on the film sets.

Harriet wracks her brain for the woman's name, but her thoughts are like wading through sludge. They embrace and against her torso, Harriet feels the woman recoil.

'Oh, shit,' she says when she flinches, then pulls away and clocks Harriet's rasping breaths. 'So sorry.'

'It's fine,' Harriet smiles and waves her hand. 'It's the way it is.' Nope, still can't remember her name. She'll understand, brain fog is part of the sickness. 'You look well.' She does. Rosy cheeks and more than just skin and bone. She's about the same age as Harriet but appears a lot younger.

'Thanks,' she says, leaning in close to shout right into Harriet's ear. 'You seen Michelle? You guys used to be close, right? She's here somewhere.'

Harriet hasn't seen or thought about her ex-girlfriend, Michelle, not since she helped Harriet find someone to remove Oliver's tracker when he was a kid. She did her a kindness there, which was more than Harriet deserved. Harriet was never nice enough to her when they were dating. Michelle was one of many who told Harriet she was distant and cold, but she came through and helped her anyway. That's the sort of below-ground community Harriet has known. Favours among those who now live above, rather than some sense of togetherness when they all lived in squalor.

Michelle approaches. She's as attractive as always, her relaxed curls pinned back, dressed more like someone from the top levels, tidy and stain-free.

Michelle greets them, and the hug she gives Harriet comes with the same flinch as the previous.

Harriet's smile tightens. She doesn't want this turning into a pity party. 'You remember Oliver?' she asks, and nods in the direction of the boys.

'Of course!' Michelle says. 'The world knows Oliver now. And his friend Thomas. It's like you've a boyband in the making.' She looks the pair of them up and down, eyebrows raised. 'What a strapping man he's turned out to be.' Michelle's eyes still flit to Harriet with that same look of pity.

'It's fine, before you say anything.' Harriet presses her lips together. 'What have you been up to?'

'I'm still working for that family on 101. Listen.' She looks over one shoulder, then the other, then takes Harriet's wrist and walks her away a few paces, keeping her eyes on Oliver. 'Is it true they have really, really good hearing?'

Harriet can barely hear a thing over the music and general hubbub. She follows Michelle's gaze to Oliver and Thomas, who seem to be chatting about something. He hasn't mentioned good hearing, so she shrugs.

Michelle leans in closer to Harriet, her lips almost brush her ear. 'This is just between you and me, but I was sick too, last year.'

Harriet coughs after a sharp intake of breath. A crease etches across her brow, and she pulls her chin in, looking Michelle up and down. Michelle's not out of breath, she appears a healthy weight, her cheeks haven't caved in. She doesn't look remotely sick. 'What? I don't understand. You look so . . . well.'

'I signed secrecy agreements, the whole spiel. But if you still have any links to wealthy people up top, maybe tell them you have the sickness. You understand me?'

Harriet's jaw drops. 'You don't mean . . .?'

'Sh.' She puts her finger to her lips. 'I can't say anything else. Except I am as well as I've ever been.'

Harriet moves her mouth to speak but can't find the words. What Michelle is saying has blown away her mind fog and replaced it with utter bewilderment. Her head is a vacuum of knowledge as everything she thought she knew shrivels to nothing. She can't form a syllable, let alone a whole word. Michelle's claim is just too preposterous. It's absurd.

But then, she looks so well. And the sickness isn't something anyone jokes about.

Michelle presses her finger to her lips again, then walks away, leaving Harriet alone and gobsmacked. She finds an old chair that looks like it could use Monty's magic touch and she sits on the wobbly thing, watching the celebration unravel around her.

Harriet's wide eyes blink, each eyelid grates with a sandpaper roughness, a haze to her vision that she knows will get worse. She's dying. She's known this for a while.

But Michelle is saying there's a cure?

Harriet scans the crowd for Michelle but can't see her now. She coughs and pains shoot up her back. It's stupid to hope. She lives on level 5, has no money, and she has a few weeks left at best. Such a cure now would be something so out of reach for the likes of Harriet. She wouldn't stand a chance. And what does it matter? She accepted her fate a while ago.

Harriet can't see the band from where she's sitting, but their music carries, a rapid beat and uplifting tune. The joviality of it all surprises her, like all the troubles of the tunnels never existed. Despite the fertility issues below, there are children, smiles carved into their mucky faces, bendy legs supporting their frail bodies as they loop arms and dance around, their laughter louder than the music.

If her baby Freddie had lived, he'd be a teenager now, complete with all the hormones of adolescence, those body changes that happen so rapidly. He'd have Anthony's dark hair and eyes, though none of his wickedness, she'd have made sure of that. He was born so early, he never stood a chance. She strokes her stomach, where she once carried him. Her weight loss has stripped that from her. She cherished the roundness that lingered for so long. Sometimes she could imagine she was still carrying him.

The children here now prove that some are born strong enough to survive. Her own bad luck isn't everyone's experience. She watches the children, their happy faces, their parents clapping them along and embracing them and thinks, healthy children isn't all she missed out on. Those special childhood family moments never existed for her. Sitting vigil at her brother's bedside was the only family time she had.

She shuts her eyes and shakes her head. Imagine being able to see the present in perfect clarity, instead of being blinded by the glare of the future, or squinting to see through the blur to the past. She tries then, watching Oliver, her friends, and everyone enjoy themselves. She counts her blessings. On one hand, but still, that's more than none.

The world may not be perfect, but down here, it is improving. Perhaps when the bots have sorted the landfill, the below grounders will do more than just scrape by. It's not Oliver's job to clear up the landfill. He has another posting at the moment, thank God. Bots may not pick up the diseases of landfill, but they can still get crushed. They still have to wade through bodies, since that's what's usually done with the dead. Such a job isn't right for her soft-hearted boy, but some of his classmates will be doing that work. They're really going to make a difference down here. A few years ago, she didn't dare reveal her son's true identity, and now she is so proud and watching him thrive.

It's too late for her, she knows this. To create a safe world for her son is all she ever dreamed of. All she can do is think that maybe those who come after her will have it a little easier.

CHAPTER 7

Oliver smiles while he's below ground. His mum always says how much she loves his smile, even as a kid and teen. It's a rehearsed expression. It doesn't mean it's real.

Below ground, he's not sure he could ever genuinely smile. His body wants to shake and tremble every second down here. He has to stop his eyes bulging, stop from flinching at every sound and movement, and they are nonstop. His battery is whittling down quickly with the effort.

He leans in to Thomas. 'This is kind of intense, don't you think?'

'Yeah. My battery is going down quicker than ever.'

Oliver's a little relieved at that. For a while, he thought his battery must be malfunctioning, but it seems pretend smiles use up more energy than remaining neutral. Oliver thinks even anger is less energy-sapping than all this fakery. How can someone who doesn't breathe suffocate? But that's how it feels, like all his sensors are either overwhelmed or not in use at all. Nothing is just right.

'How long do you think we have to stay?' Oliver asks.

Thomas glances over Oliver's shoulder. 'Probably a while. Everyone looks like they're having a nice time.'

Oliver nods and wonders if maybe he can zone it out, if it wouldn't be too rude to just stand and say nothing. Everyone seems to know his name. They've all seen him online with his mum's campaigning. She did kind of warn him, but he hadn't grasped how daunting it would be. He wishes he could hide in the corner for a few moments and take a break.

'I just keep thinking about those videos,' Thomas says.

Oliver stands a little closer to him then, staying straight but really he wants to lean on Thomas, put his arm around him or shield his eyes from the view of the orangey walls. They watched so many videos at the Institute of people being buried below ground. So much footage of people hurt and suffering. He hated watching them, but he also hated his best friend was forced to watch them. He'd watch them twice over if it saved Thomas from having to watch at all. It's better that only one of them has to suffer with the nightmares, and Oliver is tougher than Thomas.

The Institute was below, but it was nothing like this. It didn't look like homes and life and joy. In the Institute, there was only misery to bury. He hasn't thought about those videos since they stopped forcing the empathetic bots to watch them. His days have been spent learning about shop work and teaching and repairing things instead. But he can recall them now, clear as anything, and all the happy people around him now appear vulnerable.

They're still smiling, people want their photos, ask them questions and say they remember them from when they were teens. But Oliver doesn't know these people. It didn't seem so bad when the people who knew him were only on her phone. In person, it's much more invasive. It makes Oliver feel like his clothes don't look right and he can't think what to say.

When he thinks of all the comments online, he also thinks of the bad ones. What if those people are here? How is he meant to respond to that? The people who have spoken to them seem nice so far, with happy faces and pleasant laughs. When Oliver speaks to them, he tilts his head to the side, blinks a few times, trying to gauge if they're being genuine. They giggle at his expression, but he's not sure why.

'You hear what that woman said to your mum?' Thomas asks when they're finally alone for a moment. Oliver can tell he's trying to sound relaxed but is straining with the effort.

Oliver nods at Thomas, then glances over to his mum. She's not talking to anyone now. Instead, she's sitting on a rickety chair with a glazed face, and he knows she's also pretending to be relaxed, and it's also making her tired. When he looks at her below ground, he recalls when the tunnel caved in and she was half buried. He plays over and over in his mind the day he thought his mum wouldn't wake up.

And now he's below ground, faced with his nightmare, and in this place full of vulnerable cheer, he heard some words that offer him a little hope. Michelle helped them before. He trusts her. She uttered few words but said an awful lot. Oliver's gaze goes to Thomas, and he nods. Michelle said his mum doesn't have to die like Josie.

His mum has this smile that appears resolute, like she isn't even going to try to get help. If there's a way to save his mum, Oliver doesn't care if he has to go to the ends of the earth. He'll get her that treatment somehow.

He walks to her, leaving Thomas chatting to another group of people wanting photos.

'Mum.' He sits next to her as people dance all around. 'Are you ever going to tell me you're sick?'

She faces him, and her smile falters. 'Oh, darling. I don't want you to worry about your old mum.'

'So you are sick? Like Josie?'

She takes his hand and shuffles around to face him. She takes a while to respond. 'Yes. But I don't want to be sad. I just want to enjoy every second I have with you.'

Her hands seem like they're made of frost rather than flesh. They feel like the climbing frame used to, on the days they couldn't spend much time outside as it was so cold. Her fingers are so bony they could be twigs for a tiny bird to perch on. He pulls his hands back. 'That's not good enough. I heard what Michelle said. There's treatment.'

'Not for the likes of me. But that's okay.' She puts her hand on his knee. 'I've had my time. All I ever wanted was to see you grown and settled. And look at you now. I am so content and happy to see you all grown up.'

Her expression is strange: a mixture of happy and sad. Oliver smiles back as he doesn't know what else to do, what else to say. What he's thinking, she probably wouldn't like.

'Why are you so okay with just accepting you're going to die?' he asks. 'Josie died and she seemed peaceful, but it still didn't seem like something anyone would want.'

'I know, darling. It's not that I'm happy about it. It's just that there isn't anything I can do.'

'But Michelle got better.'

'If there's a way to get treatment, I will take it, of course. But it's unlikely, so let's not get our hopes up, okay? There's no point dwelling on the impossible.'

Oliver folds his arms, tensing all his muscles as he tries to push away the heavy feeling he gets when he thinks about life without her. 'I don't want you to die. It means forever goodbye, and I don't want that.'

'I know, darling. Come here.' She opens her arms for a hug.

Oliver stays there for a while, in his mother's embrace. It used to bring him so much comfort as a kid. Now he can feel how thin she is, how many layers of clothing she has on, how weakly she wraps her arms around him. He mustn't squeeze too hard. His core temperature is heating up, all his components on overdrive.

His mum withstood Anthony beating her up for so long, it's like she can't stop anything bad happening.

It's not fair. It's not right.

Their hug finishes and Oliver faces forward, and his mum rests her head on his shoulder. He's so much bigger than her now. It's up to him to protect her. Perhaps that's why she's not trying hard enough. She's too small and weak. But Oliver is neither. He's relieved he's out of the Institute now so he can take matters into his own hands. And he knows exactly how to save his mum.

They stay at the party for hours. It's Oliver's first party and he hopes it'll be his last. He wants some quiet time to read, to listen only the voices he wants to hear. His face is tired from smiling, his brain sluggish from saying the same things a hundred times to different people. There's a tug in his neck like his head needs to coil up into his shoulders. He's been bending down all day, he's too tall for down here. He's so used to looking up at people, he's not ready for that to be switched around.

When they leave, Oliver walks in silence. His thoughts conflict as they bounce back and forth, which only makes him angrier. It's like his head is ripping down the middle. When he was released, he was determined to make Anthony pay for all the horrible things he's done. He was imagining hurting him somehow, and he'd like that. He'd enjoy making him suffer like his mum suffered, like Evie and the girls did when he made them nothing more than toys. To pay him back for all the anti-bot marches where they cut people to see if they would bleed or not. Anthony's done so many bad things and he deserves bad things happening to him.

But maybe the way to make him pay is less violent, more financial. Maybe Anthony needs to be alive and unharmed to make amends.

He knows his mum won't ask him, but Oliver will. Whatever threats are needed to make him agree, Oliver will dish them out. He runs his hands over his biceps and smiles as he imagines using his body to its full ability. He'll make sure Anthony gives his mum the cure.

He'll kill him if he doesn't.

Chapter 8

Harriet has fussed around Oliver and Thomas too much this morning. She knows this. Theo and Monty know this. The boys definitely also know this, but they tolerate it with nods and smiles, Oliver only occasionally batting Harriet's hand away and groaning 'Muuuum, I'm fine!' But it's her son's first day at work. His first day in the real world and she'll be damned if she's not going to drink in every moment of this. She takes photos, and for once smooths Oliver's hair rather than messes it up.

They're wearing shirts Monty found at a salvage sale and re-stitched. They're crisply ironed and almost entirely stain-free, just some yellowing around the collar that's impossible to wash out. They'll have uniforms when they get to work but thought it best to arrive looking as tidy as possible. Harriet has adjusted their collars a dozen times, sprayed them with aftershave, and wiped flannels over their faces.

Normally a mum would feed her children, but Harriet can't do that. After all these years of raising a MechaniBot, she still finds it strange not to pack a lunch or a bottle of water for her son. Brushing any dust off their clothes is the best she can do.

'You excited about starting work?' Theo asks over breakfast.

'Definitely,' Thomas says when Harriet takes her hundredth photo.

'I am too,' Oliver says. 'It's not my first choice of job, but hopefully when we've proved we can be good workers and good with customers, they'll let us do more demanding roles.'

'Don't underestimate the need for good customer service,' Monty says. 'Everyone uses the supermarket, and a friendly face can make or break somebody's day.'

Harriet wishes she could walk them to work. It's not far. She could manage it, but she'd slow them down and they don't want her trailing after them. She's still exhausted after the trip below, and had to massage the cramps from her legs in the night. That was the furthest she's walked in months. And, for the millionth time, she reminds herself, they're adults, allowed to be independent and they don't need her fussing over them. It's not like when they were alone in the world as teen escapees. They know the way and they know what to do when they get there.

When it's time for them to leave and Harriet's made sure not a speck of dust resides on their bodies, she stands at the building doorway and waves them off, wiping away a tear. She's cried so many happy tears lately she resembles a wet rag.

She exhales slowly when they're out of sight, her body crumpling as she sags against the doorframe, then she plods her way back to the kitchen table. Harriet hasn't been able to work in a few months now. She was still coping with her light hours at the Institute while Oliver was there, but she quit as soon as he was released. Even light work was getting too difficult, and giving up her position for another parent whose child was being taken seemed like the right thing to do.

She had to stop her teaching work a while ago. She misses it so much. The laughter of the children, their excitement to hear a new story, become a new character, the applause from the parents as they put on their productions. The drama school she started has been taken over by a new teacher, so the children are still catered for, but her own needs are not.

Now, with the boys out and no work at all, she twiddles her thumbs. Tired, restless, she does what she's done to fill every spare minute she's had over recent years and gets back to campaigning for bot rights. Years ago, she assumed Amber would be here to help her. When Amber's daughter Delilah was murdered and there was no punishment, Harriet promised her she'd try to get *Delilah's Law* passed. But Amber never made it out of prison. Suicide, the official line was. She couldn't face freedom without her daughter.

Oliver's popularity with the girls is continuing, by the looks of the reactions to the photos. He really could be in the movies. Imagine that. Oliver following in his mum's footsteps. Oliver being the first bot on a TV show. She thinks perhaps she'll see if he can act, maybe research some auditions for him. TRI has to approve any work placements. They still technically own Oliver, but if he was to land a good role, maybe earn some money, perhaps it would be enough to do what Michelle suggested.

Harriet blinks that thought away. There are too many variables to have such hope. It's a dangerous thing for a woman in her position to hope. She hasn't had any medical tests, so she's not sure how much time she has left. But from experience, once the rash starts spreading, it'll be weeks before she's virtually blind and bedbound. Nowhere near long enough for Oliver to rise to stardom. Still, she can imagine him on the big screen, walking the red carpet, the cheers from the crowds, his face on posters. She only wants what's best for him.

It's a whim, a silly thing to do to idle away the time, but she does an Internet search, then sends an email to a production manager, asking if they've considered a new reality show about the bots.

'We're off to the workshop,' Theo calls through to the kitchen.

Harriet slams her laptop shut, guilt written all over her face.

Theo views her with narrowed eyes. 'What're you up to?'

'Nothing.'

'Yeah, right.'

Harriet huffs. She can never lie to Theo. A bullshit filter is his superpower, so she tells him.

He sucks some air through his teeth. 'You probably should ask him first.'

'I know, I know. But . . .' Michelle told her not to say anything. However, it's only Theo, so she spills.

Theo's jaw drops. 'Seriously? A cure?'

'I know. It's ridiculous. But that's what she said. In so many words, anyway. It's too late for me, I'm sure of it. But, well, maybe not for everyone.' She still doesn't mention Theo's symptoms. The elephant in the room is looming large. 'And I wouldn't put any pressure on him, obviously. But, well, if he's up for it, it's worth a shot. Don't you think?'

Theo scratches his scalp. He does that a lot these days. Another early symptom. Just watching him makes Harriet's own rash itch. 'I know what you're thinking. I see that look. And I'm fine. Look at my parents. They lived so long.'

'Mine lived a long time too. But you know how it is. Every generation gets sick younger.'

He sits then, taking her hands. 'We don't choose this; we live the hand we're dealt. Whatever Oliver and Thomas want to do, I'll support them. But don't even mention it's for any kind of income to help me. That's not fair. He's had such a tough time. His life should be his to live now.'

Monty shouts for Theo to join him and they leave, to a flurry of promises from Harriet she won't do anything to put pressure on Oliver.

And she won't. Of course she won't.

But the elephant in the room has been discussed. Theo knows he's sick even if he openly denies it. She heard it in his voice, a hint of dissent. There's no way Harriet is going to let her friend suffer. Her sickness is advanced, so she's sure it's too late for her. But she's not dead yet, and if there's anything in the world she can do for Theo, she's going to try it.

CHapTer 9

Oliver spends his days stacking shelves. He's the tallest employee, so he's useful to reach the back of the top shelves. And the boxes aren't heavy for him. He can lug around almost anything. He hasn't used anything close to his maximum strength yet. It startles him how strong he is, stronger than any human he's met. His manager, Jeff, says he'll be doing more customer service jobs when he learns where everything goes. It only takes Oliver half a day to learn the layout of the entire store, but he doesn't want to show off or make Jeff seem inferior. There are lots of things Oliver can do far better than a human, but also a lot of things humans are better at. Like deciphering emotions and people's intentions.

Earlier, some girls came in who recognised Oliver. They asked to take his photo, and he said yes. He smiled, like he knows he's meant to, but the attention made him unsure what to say. He stood awkwardly and his new skin felt even newer. Then Jeff wasn't happy Oliver was wasting time. But Oliver was only doing what the customers asked, which is the whole point of his job, so he didn't think he was doing anything wrong. Jeff wasn't cross, not properly cross, just not pleased. Oliver wanted to ask what he should have done, but Jeff's body language was all closed up, and Oliver didn't think he looked like he wanted to talk.

Thomas has been in the warehouse all day. Tomorrow, they might switch. There are some other humans who work here doing Oliver's job, but not many and Oliver can tell that without him, they would have struggled to keep up.

He works hard, as hard as he knows how, though all day his mind is on how to get to Anthony. He knows he has to get Anthony to give his mum money, but he keeps imagining hurting Anthony instead, the way he used to hurt his mum. Oliver starts working quicker and slamming the tins on the shelf harder, in a way that uses more battery than such a task should use.

Oliver knows Thomas feels some emotions like he does. He remembers how sad Thomas was when his mum died. But sometimes, part of him thinks he must be alone in the way his inner workings function. Surely if all bots felt such things, if all of their insides were the coiled spring that Oliver's are, one of them would speak out. They can't all be going around burying everything, but the fact that none of them talk about what is on their mind makes Oliver think he really is alone in having such tormented thoughts. He thinks about saying something to Thomas, but when Oliver opens his mouth to talk, the words don't come.

'What did you think about work?' Oliver asks instead, keeping the topic easy.

'It was good. I think I did a good job. Jeff seemed pleased. How was the shop floor?'

Oliver opens his mouth to say something vague like fine or good, but actually, his day wasn't any of those things. The shop is almost always busy. Oliver doesn't eat, but he knows what good and bad foods are. He remembers the kind of dinners his mum used to cook for Anthony. The labels all looked fancier than the most popular products here. Down here, they all have white labels and appear basic and unexciting. There isn't much fresh food, it's all in tins and packets with no pictures to show what it's meant to look like. Most people here look like they need to eat more, but there are a lot of people who buy only a little. It makes his chest ache, right down the middle, when he sees thin people with small children buying tiny bits of food. It doesn't seem right. He's sure there's plenty of food to go around.

'It was quite sad, I think,' he says eventually, and from the edge of his vision, he notes Thomas's eyebrows shoot up. 'If you're on the shop floor tomorrow rather than the warehouse, you should know that some people come in buying such small amounts of food when, really, they have children and should be able to buy more.'

'Okay. Thanks for the warning.'

'And the packaging here all looks cheap. I don't think the food is as good here as it is up there.'

'Right.'

Oliver turns his head to look right at Thomas now. He does still appear a bit shocked, but not angry. Such injustices don't rile him like they do Oliver. 'It doesn't seem fair.' He over enunciates every syllable, just to hammer it home.

'No,' Thomas says, his voice quiet and calm. 'I guess it probably isn't.'

Oliver faces forwards again, looking down at his hands. Across his palms are little blue-black semi circles from his nails digging in. Perhaps when Thomas works on the shop floor and sees it for himself, he'll understand. Oliver can't be describing it very well.

They pause in front of the advertising billboard that plays an advert for Anthony's company.

'That's my mum's ex-husband,' Oliver says. 'He lives on 107.'

Thomas has his hands in his pockets and nods. Oliver isn't sure he's made the connection. He steals another glance at Thomas's face. He doesn't seem to have reacted at all. Perhaps in his pockets there's a rock and he's going to throw it at the advert. That's what Oliver would like to do, among other things.

'So, he has to be rich to live up there, right?' Oliver says. 'He had this huge apartment with a view over the whole world. When we lived there, we had so much stuff. Clothes and games and everything.'

'That must have been nice,' Thomas says. 'But your mum and uncles do loads for us.'

'I know. I know. I'm not saying they don't. What I'm saying is that Anthony could get the medicine for my mum.' Thomas is such a dimwit sometimes.

Thomas's face crinkles up for a second. 'This is the guy who Beatrice died for, the one who was really awful?'

'Yes. That's him.'

The billboard moves on to the next advert and they start walking again. Oliver looks over at Thomas, his brows are knitted as he looks at the floor.

'You reckon he'd help.' There's no question mark in Thomas's tone. That intonation is replaced with disbelief.

'No. Obviously not. Not willingly. He's the worst man in the world. But I'm going to make him.'

'How?' Thomas's eyes go to Oliver now, and Oliver grins back.

'Strangle him until he agrees.'

Thomas's walking slows, his eyes widen. 'You scare me when you're like this.'

Oliver lifts his shoulders up. 'What?' It's the most significant reaction he's had from Thomas.

'So angry. Like, I think you really mean it. Like when you hurt that man in the riot, you stabbed him, you could have—'

'Hey.' Oliver snaps. He stabbed one bad man once, and Thomas throws it back at him. They wouldn't have survived the riot if he hadn't hurt that man. And he only stabbed him in the arm and punched him so he couldn't let the other rioters know about Oliver and Thomas and Evie. He doesn't regret it. He's not sorry and isn't going to be made to feel bad for doing what he had to do. 'I did that so we would live. He was going to kill us and Evie.'

'You never talked about it, though. It was . . . brutal.'

Thomas says this like Oliver had a choice, but he never saw Thomas standing up for them. Oliver protected them. Being brutal was necessary. 'Well, what was there to say? I did what I had to do. Like I'm going to this time. I'm going to figure this out. No way am I just going to let *my* mum die.'

He put stress on *my*. He didn't mean to, but it came out like that. Thomas didn't let Josie die and Oliver doesn't want to imply that. When he's cross and tries to talk, his words come out all muddled. It used to happen in the Institute when the other bots would pick on Thomas or Evie or anyone. Oliver just wanted to lash out, to be worse back, so they'd shut up and he'd say things and do things much worse than he intended.

Oliver walks off, dipping his chin, unsure if he's more cross with Thomas or ashamed of himself, and Thomas's footsteps hurry along behind him.

'I . . .' Oliver searches for what he wants to say. 'I'm sorry. I didn't mean to snap.'

'It's okay.'

'No. It's not.' Thomas is so damned understanding about everyone and everything. It's like he never learned how to be angry. It occurs to Oliver then, that Thomas didn't have an abusive man around when he was a kid, so he really never did learn to be angry. Thomas is all empathy and no rage. Anthony was such a presence in Oliver's early years, he can't just scrub him from his mind. Oliver inflates his chest and lets it down again, like he sees humans do when they take a big breath. It helps. 'I know you didn't let your mum die. If this option was around when she was alive, you know I would have done the same for her.'

'Strangle someone? I don't think she'd want that.'

'It won't come to that.'

'Okay. Maybe, just promise you won't strangle anyone?'

Oliver watched Anthony strangle his mum loads of times. He watched her face turn purple and her eyes bulge before he'd let go. He made it look easy. Anthony should know what it's like to be on the receiving end of that and he can't see what the problem is with being the one to do it. Why can bad people hurt good people, but not the other way around?

'Fine,' he huffs to Thomas. 'I won't strangle him.'

Thomas looks at him, cocks his head, and blinks a few times. Oliver knows he's trying to suss out whether or not he's telling the truth, and even Oliver isn't sure if he is.

They walk in silence along the busy walkway for a few minutes. The lights are bright. No one needs torches down here now. Some electric bikes whizz past. They never used to do that. The electricity was never good enough when he was last on 5. Perhaps things aren't so bad down here. The food might not be as good as top levels, but things seem to be changing for the better, albeit slowly.

'Hey, are you Oliver and Thomas?' someone asks.

Oliver groans and his back rounds as if his insides have hollowed out. He's not at work anymore. He doesn't have to be nice to anyone, and he's definitely not in the mood.

He turns around to face whoever spoke. 'What?' he asks.

Oliver stumbles back a few paces, the impact throwing him off balance. The impact of what? He can't understand. His thoughts aren't working properly. Someone asked if he was Oliver and now he can't stand. His vision is strange, swimming and blurred and he reaches for his head, a little blue-black liquid collects on his palm.

His name comes from somewhere. It's like he's submerged, and the voice reaches him murky and distant. It takes him a moment to locate where the voice comes from. He looks up and Thomas stands over him. Thomas's lips are moving, but the sound comes later. His face is pixelated, like a broken TV.

Oliver blinks a few times, the pixels blur, then clear again, and Thomas's voice is back where it should be.

'Oliver! Oliver! Are you okay?'

Oliver stands, slowly. The world tilts each way a few times before he can trust he won't fall. 'Yeah. Yeah, but what the—'

Thomas bends before Oliver and picks up a brick by Oliver's feet. It's stained with the blue black from his head. Written across it in red, it says: *Flesh is Divine.*

What does that mean? Oliver scowls at the brick and feels his head again. There's the outline of a dent.

Thomas takes Oliver's arm. 'Come on. Let's get home.'

CHAPTER 10

The brick sits on the kitchen table where Harriet put it. She glares at it, seething. She has a good mind to go and throw it back at someone. Flesh is divine. What pious crap. She photographs it, plasters *Get Level* with it, along with a photo of her poor son's head.

Someone hurt her boy. How dare they!

She'd love to march the streets and shout on a podium like the Flesh Fraternity used to, declaring war on anyone who would hurt her son, but who's she kidding? She's too sick to walk across the kitchen without coughing.

Every day she still strives to make the world safe for her son, for him to be appreciated and valued. But if people are so incapable of accepting him and being nice, and people still try to hurt him, it makes her wonder what's the damned point?

'I'll go to the police,' Theo says, to which Harriet and Monty snort a laugh.

'They won't do anything!' Monty says.

The boys are in their room. Tonight should be a night of celebration for them. Harriet imagined them all sitting around the kitchen table, listening to how their first day at work went. Harriet thought they could have a movie night, or they would go to the park and she could watch as the men kick a football, or something nice. Instead, Oliver is recovering and Thomas is reading alone. She has such precious time left and this is how it's having to be spent.

'There is literally no justice in this world when there is nothing we can do,' she says. 'We got the teens all properly cared for—well, better cared for—at the Institute, but out here, still, no rights. Nothing.'

'Maybe try a call to TRI?' Monty says from the stove. Harriet's always loved his cooking but she can't stomach any flavourful food these days and, right now with her stomach twisted with rage, it's more nauseating than ever.

'They won't care.' She slouches over the table, her forehead in her hands. 'And if they do, they'll take him away.'

'He'll recover fine, though, won't he?' Theo says. 'I mean, he had loads of scrapes as a kid.'

'That's not the point.'

'Do you think, maybe,' Theo stretches out his words like he's padding for time or bracing for a fight. 'Perhaps, possibly—'

'Spit it out, Theo,' she snaps.

'Okay. Maybe you had the best intentions, but exposing him so much on *Get Level* wasn't the best idea? You've made him a mini celebrity.' Theo's voice is small, and Harriet wonders if he's been meaning to say this for a while.

She lifts her head and meets his pleading eyes. 'But it's drummed up so much support. People love him.'

'Yeah, which means there will be people who hate him.'

'I am not going to allow him to disappear into obscurity. We are not hiding again. We can't run.' Her nostrils flare. Her son deserves adoration, not hate. He's owed every bit of the limelight she has sought for him. He's made for centre stage, not the shadows. What few muscles she has tighten. 'No. What he needs is more fans, more people who adore him. Maybe TV is a good option for him, then we can hire security—'

'Woah!' Monty says, holding up his hands like he's bracing for an impact. 'Harriet, seriously?'

She hasn't mentioned the reply from the TV company. They were keen. A fly on the wall documentary about a bot integrating in real life. She only sent them a two-line pitch along with a photo of Oliver and they fell in love with that. Of course they would. It's impossible not to love Oliver.

'I'll talk to Oliver,' she says, defeated. 'When he's healed. He might be up for it. A bit of fame never did anyone any harm.'

'Well, as long as I don't have to be on TV,' Monty says. 'I stopped auditioning when I lost my hair.'

Theo rubs his hand over his own sparsely-haired head. 'I don't think I'm up for TV either.'

She sees the look exchanged between Theo and Monty, the one that says they think she's crazy. She grits her teeth until her jaw aches, which doesn't take much. She's not crazy. She's a mum, a domestic abuse survivor, an actor, and she's dying.

What will happen after she's gone terrifies her more than anything. She has little to lose and a legacy to leave. What will her legacy be now? Some trashy movies and a part-baked campaign for the bots? Her days might be numbered but her campaign must be immortal. It has to be.

Isn't that the sort of bullshit all actors say when they're ridiculously famous and rich as hell. 'Oh, I just want to be remembered for my charity work and philanthropy.'

Such disingenuous narcissism usually makes Harriet want to heave. When such crap comes from the mouths of people who have known such adoration and wealth, it really does sound like garbage. But Harriet is different and her cause is personal. This is her son, and if she has to seem like some batshit crazy eccentric to protect him, then so be it.

CHAPTER 11

It's late. The kind of late where Oliver should be at home, but he has other ideas. He doesn't have to ask to go out; he doesn't need permission. He just shouted that he's popping out and that was that. Because if he told them what he was doing, they probably would tell him not to.

His head still has a small dent from the other day, so he takes a hat and scarf from the hook in the hallway. It's a disguise as well as covering up the dent. He tries not to think about that. He's angry about enough things already and whenever he thinks about the brick, his whole body goes stiff and his insides heat up. What if that brick had hit Thomas instead? He should have retaliated, but he was too dazed. It shocks him to know that despite his much bigger body, he can still be weak.

He walks towards the lift and pulls the scarf up to cover most of his face. Hopefully no girls will recognise him either. Human girls are weird. They keep wanting to talk to him and take his photo, even when he's made it clear he doesn't want to. He was polite enough to them at work again today, but some actually waited after work. He thought humans could read each other's emotions well. Turns out he was wrong.

He's in the lift and it's whizzing all the way up to 99, up to the top-level walkway where there's fresh air and unlimited sky. Up where his mum belongs. Thomas could visit 99 anytime he wants, and Oliver's suggested it to him, but he doesn't want to. He reads and watches TV, like he's exactly where he's meant to be, like there is nothing in the world that needs fixing. It's maddening.

Oliver alights the lift and strolls out onto the walkway and makes a beeline for Swan View apartments where he used to live as a kid. He knows he can't just walk in. He'd need a key and there are staff at desks who would stop him. And Anthony goes everywhere by Hel-E, so there's no chance Oliver's going to just bump into him outside. These are all the issues he's come to try to resolve.

His happiest memories are from life up here, as a kid, playing on the walkways and parks, meeting other human children. Oliver didn't know how different he was then. He didn't know the concept of being an outcast and hated. He didn't know his mum could die.

Oh, to go back, wouldn't that be amazing! To wipe it all clean, to ctrl:alt:delete his existence and scrub all the badness away. To erase all the trauma he witnessed. To be born anew, fresh, a kid again.

He waits at the park he used to visit most frequently. The climbing frame looks tiny now. When he sits on the bench, his feet touch the floor. He looks up at Swan View. It's even fancier than he remembers. A Hel-E lands on the roof and he bristles as he thinks that could be Anthony.

One of the concierges leaves the building with a sack full of rubbish and chucks it over the fence. A couple more follow with some furniture, making two trips to dispose of all the items. It looks like the kind of stuff Monty would fix up, and it would need a lot of fixing by the time it's landed at ground level. They probably wait for dark to throw away most things, to spare the shame, if indeed anyone up here knows what shame is.

The night sky is grey, patchy clouds blotting out the stars, no moon yet the path is lit by overhanging lights with decent wattage. Uncle Theo would be in awe of the electrics up here.

Uncle Theo should have access to the electricity up here. Everyone should. Even though Uncle Monty diverted some electricity down, the bulbs aren't as good and they blow often. Oliver's sure—looking at the lights here—the top levels still manage to take more than their share.

Oliver kicks some of the tarmac with his shoe. Fucking up top and their fucking horrible greed.

The walkways are fairly quiet, just the odd person strolling past. His attention is snagged by a voice coming from behind, a voice he recognises. He jumps to standing, and she's there. She's on the phone (she has her own phone!) and she's about to walk right past him.

'Evie!'

She stops walking and her pretty face erupts in a smile as she hangs up the phone. 'Oliver. What . . . what are you doing here?'

God, she looks stunning. Her hair is part tied back but with tendrils blowing over her face. She wears a yellow top that's covered in paint, her trousers too. It occurs to Oliver he really doesn't have a reason to be here that he can tell her.

'I just . . . I guess . . .'

'Oh, Oliver.' She walks up to him and gives him a hug. His insides go all spongey, like he could melt. 'I miss you too.'

They've only shared a few hugs before. His arms wrap around her, and he wishes they could stay like this forever. Her body's heat makes his skin tingle, but she pulls away sooner than he'd like. As soon as there's space between them, he wishes there wasn't.

'So, you're working in that building?' he asks, and tries to sound casual. She looks too relaxed for him to convey his desires.

'Yeah. I'm looking after two crazy little boys. We've been do-ing arts and crafts today. I'm just popping out to buy groceries. Actually, the mum just called, and they need even more. Want to come? You can help me carry it all.'

'I would love that.'

They walk in silence. The sort of silence that presses down and makes Oliver feel like he's shrinking. There's so much Oliv-er wishes he could say. His mum had a name for it. What was it again? He recalls and without thinking about it anymore, he tells her. 'Evie, I had a crush on you.'

She laughs. 'Yeah, I know.'

His face gets hotter, his back and palms too. He told her, and she didn't tell him to go away. That's really something special. 'I didn't know the word before. My mum told me.'

'How is she?'

'She's happy to have me home.' There's no point burdening Evie with all of his worries. He wants to make her happy not sad.

'She does a lot for the bots. I see her online talking about us, and pictures of you and Thomas, of course.' She looks his way and smiles. 'Tell her I said thanks. The bots appreciate her.'

'I will.' He grins.

This grocery shop is like a different world to the one Oliver works in. Evie has her employer's credit card and for such few things, the price is really high. All the food is colourful with those fancy labels and the fruit and vegetables are so attractive they could be bunches of flowers. There are jars too, and packets of food he doesn't recognise. The shop is much calmer than his and much more spacious. He'd like to work in this store instead.

They walk back, making small talk. That pressing silence has lifted since he told Evie he has a crush. They laugh a bit, and Oliver doesn't feel so hot anymore. His tense muscles soften. When they get to Evie's building, he leaves her with the bags.

'My employers, the family, they're going on holiday in a few days and leaving me here by myself. Maybe I could come visit you? I could say hi to your mum and Thomas too.'

The surprise makes Oliver back up. 'What? Come down to 5? No, that's nuts. Let me come here and see you.'

Evie's cheeks have a beautiful rosy glow. Perhaps it would be okay if Oliver kissed her now. He decides not to. She's working after all.

She nods. 'Yeah, okay. That would be nice if you came here. How does Thursday sound?'

'Thursday? That's perfect.'

'Great. It's a date. Tell Thomas I said hi. It'd be great to see him. And your mum.'

'I will do. And Thursday! I'll see you then.'

He doesn't kiss her goodbye, as much as he wants to. Instead, Oliver watches her go into the building and waits until she's out of sight before he does an excited little leap. He walks home, skipping more than walking. His new body is as light as a feather. He has a date with Evie. (*date: a romantic appointment,* the dictionary says) and the very thought of being close to her again makes the world spin.

And the best bit is, he'll be inside Swan View apartments. The building where Anthony lives. He'll be within strangling distance.

CHAPTER 12

The apartment is tidy enough but Harriet leaves it cluttered, with clean cups left on the side, some cushion mid-upholstering on the side, a broken fan in bits on the table. Harriet walked around the apartment through the eyes of a set designer and left items where they would be seen in the background but not in the way. She dusted and polished the glass to let as much light in as possible, which still isn't much, and swept the floor. This is a low-level house with five adults, two of whom work in refurb jobs, so it should look exactly like that. Not some polished spacious top floor abode.

When the TV production manager arrives, he introduces himself as Lenny. A stout man with a beard that looks like it could be one of Theo's wiring projects comes to the apartment while Oliver and the others are at work.

Harriet notes Lenny's mid-level accent as soon as he speaks. His assistant, Nathan, doesn't say a word so Harriet assumes he must have the gravelly rough accent of a below grounder. They probably know Harriet for her movie accent voice as that's what she uses on TV, but as soon as they see her, they clock her for what she really is. Nathan's mouth falls open, while Lenny diverts his gaze from Harriet to the floor while he stumbles over his words for a few moments.

'Are the bots home?' Lenny asks when he can string a sentence again, and they sit at the table.

Harriet's actually having a better day today, can walk around without coughing and the makeup she applied a few moments prior has given her cheeks a hint of colour. The pain, well, she's used to that. She can grit her teeth and bear it and she manages to take cups of coffee to the table and sit without a wince or whimper.

'It would be great to meet the charming Oliver and Thomas,' Lenny says.

'They're at work. They should be home—' she pushes back several layers of clothing to check her watch '—in about ten minutes. I thought we could chat a little first. So I can learn a bit more about what would be involved.'

They sip their coffee and ask her all manner of questions, their relationship, how the boys fit in with daily life, any friction . . . 'There really does need to be some friction for a show to work,' Lenny says.

'But then,' Lenny continues after looking Harriet up and down, 'a sob story can work very well and your health . . . Am I right in assuming you've the sickness?'

'My health isn't what's important here.'

'So sorry to be crude, but are you dying?'

'I haven't seen a doctor.'

'I see,' Lenny says, and he and Nathan make eye contact for a moment before Lenny gazes at the ceiling, a grin spreading across his face as if he can see the headlines in neon lights already. 'It could be a great play. Harriet Chapel, ending her days on screen. That could be quite something.' He blinks a few times, then looks at Harriet again. 'Oh, sorry to be so brazen, but you know how showbiz is.'

She dismisses his apology with the wave of a hand. 'I'd much rather focus on the life of the boys, rather than my health. This show should be about them. I'm merely an extra.'

'Right, right, of course,' Lenny says as Nathan scribbles some more. 'Well, we all know the boys are certainly camera-quality. Have TRI approved this?'

'I haven't spoken to them yet. Bit chicken and egg. Thought in the end it's best to wait until I know you're interested.' She sips her coffee. It tastes foul and she hopes that's just her sickly taste buds rather than the coffee.

'I see. I can't imagine they'll have a problem with it. It's only promoting their product. And they would obviously benefit from the financial aspect.'

Harriet chokes a little on her coffee. 'Excuse me, but since my life is being invaded, I would also seek to benefit from the financial aspect. And Oliver. We're not doing this for free.'

'Bot's don't earn money. They earn electricity, which TRI already funds, I assume?'

'Yes, of course. But this is my pitch. My idea. So obviously I get some financial reward.'

'Naturally,' Lenny says. His grin now has a sinister sharpness to it, his chin held a little higher.

If Harriet hadn't revealed herself to be a below grounder, she bets there would be no doubt as to a fat pay cheque coming her way. She attempts to match his posture, so as to sound authoritative rather than desperate. This needs to pay off if she's any hope of funding treatment. It's not just about bot rights, though she can't possibly explain that.

'The stars' wages will have to go to TRI,' Lenny says. 'Unless your contract with them states something different, I believe they are TRI property? But of course, there will be some recompense for you. Is there anyone else in the household who would be involved?'

'Two others live here but they would prefer the focus away from them.'

'Very well. We can email you the details for your approval.'

Harriet winces through another sip of coffee, then gives Lenny a pinched smile. She knows how this kind of pitch works. If she gives them the slightest impression she's worth less than she wants, they'll undercut her even more.

Oliver's voice shouts a hello from the hallway and Harriet breathes a sigh of relief. Her son is home. He sounds fine. That's one commute done without any trouble. He walks into the kitchen, Thomas filing in behind. 'Hi, Mum.' He pecks her on the forehead, then looks at Lenny and Nathan. 'Who's this?'

'He calls you Mum?' Lenny says. 'That's adorable.'

Oliver's smile wavers, his eyes glued to Lenny.

'Darling,' Harriet rubs Oliver's arm and notes his tension. He's still so protective. 'These nice men are from a TV production company. They're interested in doing a bit of a TV show, about you boys and how you settle in.'

Oliver snaps his arm away, his eyebrows lower as he looks from Harriet to Lenny. 'What? Why? We're already all over social media. Is that not enough?'

Lenny beams. 'This is great conflict. You should bottle this up for when we start filming.'

Harriet shoots Lenny a look that wipes the smile off his face for a moment.

'Maybe we can discuss this as a family?' Thomas says as Oliver takes a step closer to Lenny.

'Good idea,' Lenny says, looking up at Oliver, his face more pleading than inspired now. 'Ms Chapel, pleasure.' He holds out his hand and Harriet shakes it. He then offers it to Oliver, who keeps his fisted hands at his sides. 'We'll be in touch. Soon. We won't delay. We want you on the show before . . . well. Anyway! Goodnight all. Fantastic to meet you.'

Thomas walks them to the door while Oliver stares after them. When the door shuts, the tension in the room slices open.

'TV? Seriously?' Oliver raises his voice to a volume Harriet hasn't heard before. It makes her jump. 'I don't want to be on TV!'

'I know, darling, just sit.'

'No. What the hell? Why not at least ask us first?'

'Please, listen.'

'Fine. I'm listening.' He sits, plonking down on the seat with such force Harriett thinks Monty will have to fix it when he gets home.

She takes a breath and looks her son in the eyes. 'He won't admit it, but your uncle Theo isn't well.' Theo may have asked her to leave him out of this, but she'd rather betray his trust than allow him to die. And Oliver is an adult. He should know the truth.

Oliver's eyes bulge, he shakes his head. 'What? No. He's fine. You're sick, I get that. But Uncle Theo—'

'He's just less advanced. Trust me. I know the signs. It's too late for me but if that cure exists, maybe we can earn enough to get it for him.'

'I'll do whatever you need,' Thomas says without hesitation.

Harriet reaches for his hand and thanks him.

Oliver drops his chin and his lips press together.

'Oliver?' Harriet asks. 'I'm not forcing you to do anything. This was just an option I considered.'

'It's all right for Thomas,' he says through his teeth. 'He doesn't get half the attention I do. Three times I had people hassle me at work today.'

Harriet goes to hold Oliver's hands, but he snatches them away. 'I'm so sorry you've had hassle. I won't post anything more, I promise. There is no pressure for the TV show, of course.'

'No pressure?' He snorts a laugh. 'Except that if I don't do this, Uncle Theo dies. Yeah. No pressure. Fuck this. I'm going out.'

Oliver stomps down the hallway and Harriet jumps when the front door slams. She missed out on most of the teenage grumps other parents go through, so she supposes this is the universe's way of making up for that. Her coffee, now cold, smells even less appetising as her stomach swirls. She should have spoken to Oliver first. That was a horrible way to broach the subject with him.

Thomas stands with his hands in his pockets and his neck bowed.

'Thomas, sweetie, I'm so sorry.'

'It's fine really,' he sits now, giving Harriet a weak smile.

He's always so docile and amicable. Harriet wishes, as she does so often, that his mum, Josie, was still here to see how he's turned out.

'And he'll calm down,' Thomas says. 'I think . . . I don't want to gossip, but he mentioned he's seeing Evie.'

That cheers Harriet right up. 'Oh, that's wonderful!'

In the space of a second, she pictures Oliver holding hands with Evie, Evie sitting at the dinner table with them, Oliver and Evie giggling at a film, taking walks in the park, perhaps getting a MechaniKid of their own. And it explains so much. Oliver isn't cross with Harriet. He's stressed with the blossoming of his relationship. For a fleeting moment, the chill that is permanently wrapped around Harriet's bones thaws as she imagines her son's future.

Then she remembers Thomas sitting opposite her. His face is a little pale, his smile appears forced. 'And how are you, Thomas?'

'Me? I'm fine.' He gives a one-armed shrug. 'Work is okay. My battery is lasting well.'

Thomas is such a sweet and handsome boy. He must feel a sense of loneliness if his best friend has a partner. 'You'll meet a special someone one day. I'm sure of it,' she says, hoping it doesn't come out condescending or too mumsy. Because she's sure she's right.

'Nah, I'm all right,' he says, a little too breezily. 'I'm enjoying the computer games Theo sorted. And the books. I just want Oliver to be okay. He's so angry.'

Harriet sighs and realises Thomas is right. 'He gets that from Anthony. I never considered it before, but being a kid around my ex-husband was bound to affect him.'

Anthony left his mark on her life in so many ways. Her own physical scars as well as the nightmares that still claw at her throat when she does manage to sleep. She's lost count of the times she's woken up, slick with sweat and gasping for breath as images of Anthony come to her in her nightmares. His foetid breath on her face, his nose an inch from hers, her lungs fighting for air as he tells her she's worthless. Her panic attacks are much less frequent these days, but she sometimes still needs to escape those doubts that nibble at her when she tries to take control of her life. Her neck, her breath, her voice, all choke in Anthony's grasp.

Is it the same for Oliver? Her trauma isn't hers alone. She brought a son into a household brimming with violence, and now it shouldn't surprise her that Oliver is riddled with anger.

As much as she worries, Harriet can't help but buzz with a hint of excitement. She'll talk to Oliver about the TV show and his feelings. But none of that seems important right now. What's more important is he's seeing Evie again. Her son has a proper, grown-up girlfriend.

CHAPTER 13

In all the time at the Institute, Oliver never felt so suffocated as he does when strangers approach him and want to take his photograph. At least at the Institute he could tell people to leave him alone. He could fight or swear and no one gave a shit. Here, it's all fake. He's on show all the time. The Institute never told him how to pose for photos. His mum took photos when he was a kid, but he was hanging upside down on a climbing frame. It was easier to smile then. He had less to worry about. And fewer bad thoughts circulating in his head.

His date with Evie might involve even more smiling and small talk, but at least the thought of it brings a genuine smile to his face, but he frets too. His hair doesn't look right, his clothes don't fit properly. They do usually, but now everything is too tight or too loose. He's sure he has a grubby face even though he's washed it a hundred times. As he looks in the mirror, he thinks it would be better to be taller or shorter. Whatever he is isn't quite right. He practises facial expressions, making his eyes convey words the way that humans do, and he imagines Evie's doing the same. That makes his temperature spike and his head dizzy. For tonight could be the first time he's alone with Evie.

He's seen TV shows and films about what adults do when alone. It all seems so abstract, so primal and somehow mammalian. The things he's seen people do on TV weren't detailed enough. He needs diagrams and instructions. He doesn't have the instincts humans do. All he knows is a hug isn't close enough, but there's no bot guide to this. Maybe if Evie could take the lead over everything, that would be great.

He realises as he approaches her building, he's empty handed. He should bring Evie a gift. That's what he saw on a TV show, something to show he cares and would make her happy. He doubles back and picks some of the yellow dandelions out of the flower beds. There aren't many that haven't gone to seed, and he doesn't want to spoil the display, so he only takes five.

He gives his name to the concierge, and they check their computers. For a fleeting moment, Oliver thinks they're going to stop him, that it's a cruel joke and Evie wasn't really inviting him. But they welcome him through, and he makes his way to the lift. He knows the way; he's done it a hundred times before as a kid. Evie lives on 105. Just two floors below Anthony.

When the doors ping open, she's standing there to greet him. She's tidier than last time, no paint splatters, her hair loose over her shoulders. He could run to her, embrace her, put his hands under her clothes and hope she does the same to him. But he doesn't. He holds back, hoping she'll take charge.

'They're pretty,' she says, looking at the flowers. 'Are they for me?'

Oliver looks down at them. On the mantle there's a much bigger bunch in a vase with huge blooms. His appear pathetic in comparison.

'Yeah. Erm, there are five. One for each year I've known you.'

'Nice.' She chuckles and takes them, putting them to her nose as that's what humans do, then plops them in a cup. 'Where's Thomas?'

Oliver knits his eyebrows. 'Thomas?'

'Yeah. Is he not here? I thought we were having an old Institute get together.'

'Oh.' His voice comes out too high-pitched, a squeak that unmasks his surprise. 'His battery was low. He didn't charge properly and he was all sleepy.'

She was expecting Thomas, too? Why? Oliver's mind goes to some dark places. He imagines betrayal, laughs behind his back, Evie and Thomas, holding each other the way he should be holding her.

'Okay. Well, never mind,' she says, as breezily as that.

Oliver clenches his jaw a moment, then tells himself to relax. Evie was probably just testing the water, and she's as nervous as he. If there was something going on with her and Thomas, she wouldn't have invited Oliver. It shocks him how quickly his mind went to a dark place and assumed the worst. Anthony used to do that. If his mum even mentioned another person he'd snap. But there's no need for Oliver to think such things. Evie invited him. He said he had a crush. She called it a date.

She walks away from Oliver and down the hallway, Oliver following close behind. The apartment is huge, similar to Anthony's, with high ceilings, chunky furniture and fancy light fittings. No clutter anywhere. Unlike Anthony's, the walls are filled with pictures of the happy family—two little boys and a mum and a dad. A complete unit. Evie must be so happy working here. Why is it that this family gets so much space and such nice things when his mum doesn't? He strains his forehead as he tries to think why. It doesn't make sense.

'I've got some games here,' she says as she stands by a large coffee table piled with boxes. 'They actually have an entire cupboard of old board games, so I chose some that sounded fun. I like the sound of all of them, so you choose. Thomas said how he used to play board games as a kid, so I thought this could be fun.'

Oliver stiffens, his shoulders tense. Board games. Among them, Uno, which he used to play as a kid. But he can't think of happy kid times now. All he can think about is Thomas.

'I'm sorry,' he says through his teeth. 'But why did you invite me here?'

Evie's eyebrows shoot up. 'What do you mean?'

'I'm here to spend time with you, like alone, us two, and you're on about Thomas and board games.'

Evie looks to the side, then the other side, anywhere except at Oliver. 'Oh. Well—'

'I said I had a crush on you.'

'*Had*. Past tense.' She looks at Oliver now, and she makes a face like she's trying not to laugh. 'I mean, we're grown-ups now. With jobs. Don't you think that all sounds rather . . . teen?'

Oliver tries to understand what she said. He scowls, blinks, turns his head to the side to try to make sense of it. 'I . . . I don't understand.'

'Oh, come on, Oliver. I've had no one for company except my bosses and children for ages. You have Thomas and your family. I have no one else here. I just thought we could hang out.'

He narrows his eyes. She still looks so pretty but, right now, he wishes she didn't. He wishes she looked like a horrible hag. 'Yeah, well, I only came here because your rich and fancy apartment is just below where I used to live.'

'You used to live here?'

'Yeah. And my mum's ex-husband lives right up there. And I need to speak to him.'

She folds her arms. 'Right. So, you didn't want to just hang out with me?'

'No. I never wanted to see you at all.'

She gasps, but he turns around and stomps away back down the hallway to the lift. He won't let her see his face. His body wants to fold in half, but he won't do that in front of Evie. She means nothing to him, or that's what he wants her to think.

He gets back in the lift and punches in the code for Anthony's apartment, hoping it's the same as it was years ago.

It is. Sums Anthony up about right. He's too dumb to change it. He probably left it the same in case his mum ever went back. The desperate old prick. That's what men are who pine for a woman who doesn't want them. Desperate. Sad. Fuck that.

Oliver sniffs a little, then blinks that emotion away. He's not pining for Evie. Sure, it hurts, but it's probably just a dodgy connection inside him, a loose wire. That's all it is.

The lift doors open into a dark apartment and Oliver enters, walking straight to that window he used to stare out of so much as a kid. He takes a seat and waits in the belly of the beast.

✿ ❀ ✿ ❀

There's a part of Oliver that worries he'll be home late, that makes him watch the time carefully at the clock that ticks loudly from the wall. That part of Oliver is concerned about upsetting his mum and uncles. Humans transition gradually into adulthood. For Oliver, it's a bump. He needs to shake off the institutionalised feeling. He's a fully grown MechaniBot and he can do as any adult would.

He has fifty per cent battery and should still have plenty of time to charge. He's more concerned about Evie alerting security, but he's almost sure she wouldn't. He may have been a bit harsh back then, but she knows how awful Anthony is. She'll support whatever Oliver does, even if he was mean to her. He shuts their conversation out of his mind. He has bigger things to think about now.

He goes to his old room, and it's exactly the same as when he was last here. There's an extra layer of dust on everything, the shelves on the wall, the box in the corner with the unbuilt cot inside, all undisturbed as if no one has entered the room in years. He remembers every last detail. The wardrobe still has his kid clothes, his old toys are still in a box. It's like Anthony shut the door and never opened it again.

Up on a shelf is a picture of a little boy who looked so much like Oliver when he was young. His mum's little brother, Tipher. He picks up that photo, brushes the dust off, and puts it in his pocket. Anthony won't miss it.

The lift pings and Oliver walks out and into the dark hallway, then steps towards the living room. The lights switch on and there he is, walking in a straight line rather than the drunken swagger he used to have. That image on the advertising billboard wasn't edited much at all. Anthony really is slimmer with a healthier complexion than the last time Oliver saw him, though to be fair, he was literally having a heart attack then.

Oliver sneers as Anthony steps closer. 'Hello, Anthony.'

Anthony stops, jaw hanging open at the sight of Oliver, and he drops his bag. That healthy complexion pales. 'Who the fuck are you? Security will be here in seconds.'

'No need to call them. We're family.'

Anthony screws his eyes up and, without moving his feet, he leans closer. 'Oliver?'

Oliver steps forward. 'That's right. We need to talk.'

There's a hint of fear around Anthony, a slight tremble to his chin and limbs that he's trying to hide. He's not even tall. Those arms Oliver used to think were such huge meat hammers when he was a kid now hang to his sides like deflated balloons. His face sags, pitted and lined with crevasses. His eyelids hang low, pink rims, grey bags underneath. His gut has gone, a flap of skin where it used to hold much more presses against the bottom of his oversized shirt. Oliver must be half a foot taller than him, his shoulders broader, and he still hasn't maxed out his strength. He knows he could pummel him to the ground if he wanted to.

Oliver stands straight, and it's the most manly he's felt his whole life.

'Sit,' Oliver commands. For once, he's the one in control.

Anthony gives him a small nod and sits.

Oliver glares at Anthony awhile, just to make him cower. It takes a second, but Oliver notes the moment Anthony's neck retreats closer to his shoulders, his head shrinking lower. Oliver smiles.

'My mother, your ex-wife, is sick.'

Anthony pulls his chin in, revealing an extra one. 'Harriet's sick? Well, that's a shame.'

'There's a cure. For the below-ground sickness. I know this for certain. But it's only available for those with money. You must arrange this. I won't let her die. I'll kill you before she dies.'

Anthony shakes his head and folds his arms. 'Now, I don't know anything about that.'

Oliver slams his fist down on the table, the same way he saw Anthony do so many times. Anthony jumps. The vase on top of the table wobbles. 'I wasn't asking if you knew anything about it. I know it exists. And I know it's a secret. I am telling you to sort it for her.'

'Or what?' Anthony stands now. The weasel that he is. Oliver doesn't back off, not one inch. 'You're going to kill me. Me! Do you have any idea who you're threatening? They'll destroy you before you've even had the chance to say goodbye to her. Imagine how that will crush her if her darling little boy Oliver is gone forever.'

'She's dying. Crushing her is the least of my worries. Have you no heart?'

'Have you?'

Oliver grits his teeth. Fuck this. He'll kill Anthony anyway.

'But . . .' Anthony says, dragging out the long word, a stalling tactic. 'I don't see why we can't help each other out. I'll find a way to get this medication for her. On one condition.'

'Go on.'

The corner of Anthony's mouth twitches up. 'You come work for me. I'll clear it with TRI and you can still live with your precious mummy. But your working day is with me, doing the jobs I need doing. I'm short-staffed and this would help me out. I think that sounds more than fair.' Anthony holds out a hand. 'Deal?'

Oliver is almost disappointed. He was looking forward to wringing Anthony's neck. But he did promise Thomas he wouldn't, and if he got in trouble that really would upset his mum. His aim was to get his mum the medicine, yet it seems a little too easy. He eyeballs Anthony's hand, then his face, chewing the inside of his mouth for a second.

'You mean it? You'll truly get her the treatment?'

'I'm a businessman. And good businessmen stick to their deals.'

Oliver hesitates. The thought of the word *good* being associated with Anthony gives him a moment of pause. His gaze leaves Anthony and scans the apartment. He is a good businessman, most definitely. No one could have his level of financial success if they were dishonest on deals, surely. 'One more condition.'

Anthony takes his hand back and looks Oliver up and down. 'Go on.'

'She's not to know you're the one arranging the treatment. Make it anonymous. Say it's because she's a celebrity or something. She can never know I was here.'

He watches Anthony think about this. No doubt Anthony wanted to play the hero, but she'll never accept help from him.

Anthony holds his hand out again and this time Oliver shakes it. 'Deal.'

CHAPTER 14

'Talk to me, darling,' Harriet says before Oliver goes to work. He's halfway down the hallway already and she had to call after him. He and Thomas leave earlier than Theo and Monty. The bot working day is a minimum of ten hours, TRI said, longer if needed. She feels like she catches mere glimpses of her son, an afterglow, but it's better than when he was away, when his face was disguised by distance rather than scorn. They've barely spoken since she mentioned the TV show and she needs to break through the barrier he's put up. A mother's love surely can soften such sharp edges.

He walks back towards the kitchen doorway, brow furrowed, and looks at her like she's just spoken a foreign language.

'What about?' he asks, his tone curt.

Harriet would have thought if he was back with Evie again he'd be lovesick, all giddy and vacant with a permanent smile, but he's not like that at all. She wants her son close, but he's pulling away from her. He's worried about her health. She knows this and thinks perhaps that's why. He doesn't know how to process that. He saw Josie at the end. He knows what death means.'

He was out last night, on his date with Evie. Thomas told her, so perhaps she isn't meant to know. But she does and she wants to know how that went, for her son to open up to her just a little bit.

'Anything at all. How was last night? Thomas mentioned Evie?' She winces at her own voice, knowing full well she's sounding like a nosy mother.

He flinches. 'Well? I'm an adult. I'm allowed to see her.'

'I know. I was just wondering how it went. Did you have a nice time?'

He shrugs. 'I don't know. I guess.'

'Why don't we sit down for a moment?'

He holds her elbow as she shuffles the few steps towards the kitchen table. He holds her like he's worried she'll fall to the floor if he doesn't. His grip is too firm, but she doesn't say, relishing any contact with her son.

'So?' she asks when they sit. 'Did you and Evie talk about much?'

'She just wanted to play board games.'

'Oh. So, nothing romantic?'

'Mum!'

'Okay!' She holds her hands up. 'You don't have to tell me. I just want to know that you're all right. And you know that you can talk to me.'

He jerks his head back. There's that scorn again, twisting his features. 'Why would I know that? You do stuff without talking to me first. I came home to find some weird TV guy here and you've said more to him than to me.'

His words cut like rubbing salt in a wound. But it's deserved, and Harriet feels the shame in her actions. The shower is running in the bathroom and, with it, the extractor fan. With that and the spite in Oliver's tone, it's all too loud for Harriet. She rubs her forehead, a splitting headache already setting in for the day. She squeezes her eyes shut and pushes it away, still not wanting to give in and take strong painkillers. She walls in her pain, like a dam, only letting the floodgates open when she really can't take anymore. In her mind she tells herself that a pain threshold is exactly that, and when she reaches it, she can pass it and be free of it. Her threshold then becomes a target rather than something to dread.

She rubs his arm. There's so much tension there. His hands are on his lap, fingers curled like talons.

'I am so sorry about that. I really am. It was inconsiderate of me.' She's put too much pressure on Oliver. She knows this now, but she can't undo it. How hard is it to be a proud mum? She's walking on a tightrope, balancing his feelings and hers. 'Maybe Evie would like to come round here one evening?'

'No!' That taloned hand makes a fist and he slams it on the table so hard, a plate rattles and cracks down a recent repair. Harriet jumps and a yelp escapes. She leans back away from him.

His hand unclenches, and he squeezes his eyes shut. 'Sorry. I'm really sorry. I didn't mean to break the plate.'

Harriet takes a moment to respond. She fights to still her breaths and racing heart. 'It's . . . it's fine, darling. It's just a plate.'

His face now is etched with the kind of anger she used to see in Anthony. An inconsolable rage born from indeterminate cause. Thomas mentioned he was angry and she wasn't aware of quite how consumed he is. All the attention, the good and the bad, is overwhelming him. She puts her arm around him and he's trembling, the vibrations trickling up her arms. She attempts to draw him in for a hug, but his taut body barely reciprocates.

'You need to let your anger go, Oliver,' she says. There were anger management techniques she looked up years ago for Anthony. She only remembers the highlights. 'Imagine all your rage is filling a balloon, then let it go so it can float away. Just let it go, darling. Let it go.'

Thomas calls from the hallway and Oliver faces Harriet and kisses her forehead. 'I've got to go to work. I'll see you later.'

'Love you,' she calls after him, but he's already out the front door.

Harriet slouches against the back of the chair, the broken plate on the table some symbol of her failure. Did he register what she said at all? Some abstract coping techniques might be nonsensical to a bot. Oliver isn't without imagination, she's sure of that. But ridding trauma from a mind is no easy task, Harriet should know.

Oliver is nothing like Anthony. But he made an impact, like Oliver is in his shadow, trying to break free. For almost five years Oliver witnessed Anthony's rages. Somehow, in whatever time she has left, Harriet needs to undo Anthony's influence. At least he's far away from him now. Being surrounded by good people, Oliver is surely going to let his trauma go.

She wraps the plate in a tea towel and stores it in a cupboard for now, hoping Monty won't notice. If she can conceal the evidence, it's like the whole episode never happened.

CHAPTER 15

Oliver knows he shouldn't have broken the plate. Uncle Monty had fixed it so nicely. It has a pattern on it, a swirl of colours. And it was only in two pieces when Uncle Monty found it. Most plates are in three or four, but that was a good one. Plates on the top levels never come in pieces. They're always unchipped and whole. But that plate was probably the best one Monty's had in ages. And Oliver broke it.

He'll fix it when he can. He can re-do whatever Uncle Monty did. It's just glue. Maybe Monty will never even know. It wasn't Oliver's fault he broke it. His mum kept pressing and he couldn't tell her about Anthony.

'What was that noise in the kitchen?' Thomas asks as they walk to work.

They're a couple of minutes away from the shop. The dim walkway is busy. It's the time of day when everyone is going to work.

'Nothing,' Oliver says, keeping his eyes on the ground rather than looking Thomas's way.

As much as he tells himself it wasn't his fault, shame claws at his throat, thick, like he needs to cough to clear it. He tries to, making a gurgling sound, but that's all. He still feels awful.

'How did it go with Evie?' Thomas asks.

Again being asked about Evie. It's like everyone wants to remind him she isn't interested in Oliver's crush. Even the sound of her name brings a heavy feeling to his chest. He shrugs it off and tells himself it doesn't matter. He stretches out his neck rather than make a fist this time. At least there's no plate to break.

He achieved a lot more last night than just seeing Evie, so he needs to think of the positives. He straightens his back. 'I got it wrong. She just wants to be friends.'

'Oh. Sorry, mate.'

'It's fine. She's right, it's for the best. She asked about you, actually.'

'Really? She just wanted the old gang together then?'

'Yeah. Yeah, I guess that's it.' Oliver upturns his mouth into a smile. A forced one, like humans use.

Oliver was stupid to ever think Evie wanted anything else from Thomas. Like Thomas said, she was only asking about him as a friend. She wanted the old gang back together. He's read a bit more of the dictionary. *Jealousy. Petty suspicion or fear of rivalry.* That's what he had. Stupid, nonsensical jealousy. Anthony used to be like that. He'd feel threatened if his mum mentioned someone else. Oliver has learned that and somehow he has to unlearn it.

He gets to work and starts stacking shelves, though it's hard to concentrate as he still wants to curl in a ball, sure he has shame written all over him. When he gets home later, he'll fix the plate. That's the only bad thing to come of all of this. Last night was a success. Anthony will do what Oliver said, and all Oliver needs to do is keep on Anthony's good side until his mum is well again. The thought of seeing his mum running around, breathing normally, eating, and not in pain will be enough to make Anthony tolerable for a time. That'll make it all worth it.

But the problem is . . . all his anger for Anthony has nowhere to go. He can't get revenge. He just has to sit on it.

At least for now.

CHAPTER 16

Monty and Theo are still getting ready to leave, the second shower running, as Harriet searches the apartment for glue to fix the plate. It's tiring even standing for that small amount of time and when she doesn't find it after a few minutes, she sits back at the kitchen table. The sofa in the living room would be more comfortable, but she knows if she sits there, it's a lot harder to get up again.

She wheezes a breath, pain pulsating through her chest. Sod the plate. It can wait until later. She pushes it to one side under a tea-towel and instead, finds a pair of reading glasses on the table, then opens her laptop, out of habit more than anything, to scroll through *Get Level*.

Oliver has every right to be angry. She's angry too, at the damned Flesh Fraternity who harmed her son and everyone making threats. There may not be any haters, but even one is too much. There are posts about it online, not just the one she sent. The Flesh Fraternity are still banging on about the dangers of bots, the end is nigh bollocks that got them so much attention last time. But the tide turned since then. They have far fewer followers now. There's still enough electricity in the lower levels since Monty and his friends redirected the electricity from the incinerators. And that's all people ever cared about. It wasn't the Devil-fearing mumbo jumbo that the Flesh Fraternity tout. If she was a little bit fitter she'd have a good mind to—

Ping!

She jumps as an email alert sounds. She clicks it to open it and almost coughs up a lung. Her eyes are still gummy with sleep, and she wipes them on her sleeve, then she reads it again. It's from a medical centre on 90. She knows that hospital. It's privately funded, frequented by top dwellers only. They do cutting edge medical treatments and lead the country in research. She went there with Anthony when they were trying to stop her premature labour. Then they went back a few times when she was trying to conceive.

But that ship has more than sailed. She hasn't been in touch with the hospital since years before she and Anthony split, so why would they get in touch now? The email says little except asking her to call them.

It must be a prank. She doesn't call the number on the email, instead she searches for the hospital details online, and finds the number that way. She dials and when she says her name, the receptionist puts her through to a consultant.

'Ms Chapel. I'm the secretary to Doctor Peterson. I'm glad you got our email. We understand you have the below-ground sickness?'

Harriet's lips move, but words don't come, her mouth too parched. She reaches for some water, sips, then answers. 'Yes.'

'Please understand this conversation is of a sensitive nature. I must warn you that if it is found you have spoken to anyone outside of your household, your treatment offer will be revoked.'

The secretary has a lilting voice, talking like this is such a normal, everyday conversation, like Harriet shouldn't feel an ounce of surprise. But that's all she feels. Her headache not abating, her vision etched with static as she tries to comprehend the simple words. 'Treatment?'

'Yes,' the secretary says. 'Given your high profile, this treatment is being offered to you.'

'But... I...' Her brain is made of treacle, cogs turn too slowly, rusty and scratchy. The secretary spoke quickly, well-oiled and fluent in weirdness. Harriet's thoughts drown her. She picks through them, one by one, as if such dissection will make them make sense. 'I ... I live on 5. I don't have any ...'

'The treatment is being offered, not billed,' the secretary says before Harriet can even think about the end of her sentence. 'Here at Top Towers Medical, we believe people such as yourself should have full access. I can book you in for Tuesday for your first session. How does that sound?'

She counts the days on her fingers. Tuesday is tomorrow. Harriet's words fail her. Her throat constricts, a lump that can't be swallowed back. She's dying. She *was* dying. How can this be real?

'Yes,' she eventually says, feeling foolish as she does. For this must be some mean prank. But then, what if it's not? 'Yes,' she says again, welcoming a little excitement. 'Oh, my. Yes. Of course.'

They book her in, and Harriet hangs up, staring at her phone for a while, disbelief ousting any other sensation. She's too cynical and joy seems too rebellious. She's numb, a tingle, pins and needles as reality tries to barge its way through her thick skin.

The shower stops running. Footsteps pad down the hall. There's laughter from Theo and Monty's room before Theo comes into the kitchen, his robe tied tightly around his thin frame, his face wearing a smile.

'You all right, Harriet? You look like you're drunk.'

'I . . . I can't believe it.' Her rash itches, and she scratches her back all the way to her head. Then, somehow, she gets her words out and tells him.

Theo's hands press into his cheeks, his mouth agape, his eyes brimming. 'You're actually serious?'

Is she? She's still not sure. Still convinced it's a prank.

'Harriet, this is amazing!' When Monty comes in, Theo takes his hands and twirls him around.

Monty doesn't question the motive but joins in, never needing an excuse to dance. When Theo's elation gives way to joyful laughter, Monty is filled in.

Their joy is contagious and Harriet's disbelief crumbles. This isn't a joke, for no one would play such a prank. This must be real. She might not have to die soon.

Harriet smiles, then laughs, as much as her lungs will allow.

She's going to be well. Somehow, luck is on her side. She doesn't deserve such treatment. She's a Z-list, used-to-be actor. She's no one. Hardly famous at all. But she probably is the most famous below grounder. So maybe, just maybe, this is real.

Someone must admire her for her campaigning as much as her movies. She wishes she could trace the trail, to offer thanks as much as quell her curiosity. But Monty and Theo tell her, the whos and the whys aren't important. She's not going to be sick anymore. Whoever made this happen she could kiss them.

Chapter 17

All day, as Oliver goes about his mundane tasks, his mind bounces between Anthony and Evie, how he wants to hurt one and hold the other. Part of him worries about Anthony not keeping his side of the bargain, but he said he's a businessman, and businessmen make good on their deals. Anthony may be a thug, but Oliver can't recall him lying. He's a man of his word, even if that word means bad things.

Oliver wishes he was working in the warehouse with Thomas. He's had more hassle from girls today, and he's still not sure what he's meant to do. One girl recognised him, then came back with her friends later. If all these girls want to spend time with him, why doesn't Evie? Why does he like the one girl who only wants to be friends?

Then again, do these girls hassling him have crushes? He's not sure. His mum told him what a crush is but never told him how to spot it. There should be a sign, a word, or something to make it clearer.

Jeff approaches Oliver while he's halfway through his shift, still stacking shelves. 'I've just been told you're being reassigned.'

Oliver freezes, shock and disbelief stalling his limbs. Then, as those words sink in, he has to force himself to not smile. 'Oh, really?'

'This is a shame. You're a good worker and you know the layout now.'

Oliver shrugs, then resumes stacking the shelf. 'Not much I can do about it.' His grin is really threatening to break through his poker face and he has to bite down. Anthony is keeping his word. His mum is going to get treatment! And maybe as part of Oliver's job, he'll be working high up and get to see the sunshine!

'TRI told me to pass on to you that tomorrow, they'll meet you at the southern elevator on 2.'

Oliver cocks his head; he must have misheard. '2? As in, level 2?'

'That's what the email says. Sounds like you'll be landfill shifting. Sorry, Oliver.'

Jeff walks away and Oliver's back sags. Is this some revenge from Anthony? He's getting Oliver to do shitty labour work on the lower levels? Oliver stays still for a moment, processing it.

Okay, so, he won't get to see the sunshine, he won't be up top, but it's not that bad at all. Anthony probably thinks that's the worst thing ever but now he's thought about it for a second, Oliver doesn't care.

He stands straighter again, continuing with his work and his limbs feel even lighter. He really doesn't care. Sod the sunshine. He's used diggers and done manual labour forever. Stacking shelves is much the same, just easier. At least he can wash now whereas he couldn't at the Institute. He'll sulk about it if he ever sees Anthony again. He'll let him think he's got one over on him. The main thing is his mum is going to get better.

Oliver knew Anthony would keep his side of the bargain. He can reach the top shelves at work, lift the heaviest boxes, all the girls want his photograph. Oliver is more of a man than Anthony, and he's scared of Oliver. He glances down at his arm muscles, smiles, letting his chest inflate. Anthony was scared of him because he's a man now and stronger than Anthony ever was. There's no way Anthony would risk angering him.

He walks home with Thomas and it dawns on him then he won't be walking to work with Thomas anymore or spending as much time with him. That's a shame. He's never been far away from Thomas for long and working will be weird without him.

'So, I'm going to work somewhere else tomorrow,' he says to Thomas. 'Anthony had me posted elsewhere, in return for mum's treatment.'

'Really? So, he agreed?'

'Yep. And no, I didn't strangle him.'

Thomas chuckles. 'That's great. Really great. Sad you have to work elsewhere, but worth it. It's been horrible seeing your mum suffer.'

'I don't want her to know Anthony is paying for it. You know, she might not accept. She hates him.'

'Okay. I won't tell.'

'And we'll still see each other. At home, and we could go to the park sometimes.'

Thomas nods and appears happy, but Oliver worries. What if there's another bot hater with a brick? Thomas will be alone. Oliver glances at him, looking him up and down. He's not much smaller than Oliver, so hopefully he'll be okay, though he decides that as soon as his mum is well, he'll try to work with Thomas again.

His thoughts go to his Uncle Theo, about how sick he might get. Can Oliver force Anthony to pay for his treatment too? He's not sure. For the rest of his walk home, he thinks about this, that he should do the right thing and help. He's unlikely to get hassle from girls working at the landfill, so if he's not getting hassle at work anymore, maybe the slight fame thing won't be so bad.

When he gets home, his mum is curled up on the sofa. She resembles a stick insect, and it makes him feel hollow to imagine his uncle like that too.

'Are you okay, Mum?'

'Oliver, darling. I have some wonderful news.' she tells him about the treatment, and her eyes shine with happy tears. Oliver knows that however bad the job is, it doesn't matter. He can tell she's excited about getting better even though she can't move much. And there is nothing more important than his mum being well.

'That's wonderful, Mum,' he says as he crouches by the sofa. 'And you know what, I've been thinking. The TV show probably wouldn't be such a bad thing. If it'll help Uncle Theo, too.'

'Oh, darling.' She stands, which takes her forever, and gives him a peck on the cheek. 'You are my sweet boy.'

'Also, well, I've got some other news. I've got a new job.'

Her face lights up. 'A promotion?'

'No. They're sending me down to 2. Landfill, I guess.'

'Oh,' she slouches, her knees wobbling. 'Oh, that's awful. Maybe the TV company—'

'Mum.' He holds his hand up. 'It's fine. It'll be fine. If that's where I'm needed, then I'm pleased to do it. I want to be useful.'

She sits back on the sofa. He can tell even that short time standing has worn her out.

'I am so proud of you. We really do have luck on our side at the moment.'

Oliver needs a full battery for work tomorrow, so he goes to his room to charge. He plugs in and lies on his bed, trying not to think about how bad work will be, or the TV show. He can bear whatever it'll be like.

Luck, his mum said, and as he ponders that now, he tenses up. It's not luck. It was him and his initiative. He doesn't want praise, but luck is a stupid thing to say. Never will Oliver let his fate be dictated by luck. He's learning that if he wants something, he has the ability to take it. That's what a good businessman would do.

But let his mum believe that. Let her believe whatever makes her happy.

In the dead of night, the house is so still with everyone asleep. Oliver tiptoes out of his room and after a bit of searching, he finds the broken plate wrapped in a tea-towel. There's a tube of glue on the table under a pile of broken cups. He sits at the table and glues along the crack, then presses the pieces back together.

When he goes back to his room, he lies on his bed and finishes charging, and so much of the tension he has had lately vanishes. A spider crawls up his wall and he picks it up, letting it scurry over his hands and he smiles. He always loved the tiny creatures, they're so delicate and complicated. So carefree yet dedicated to their tasks. He puts it back on the wall and watches it make its web, a feeling of contentedness about him. For the first time in ages, he's not angry. His mum is going to be well, he's helping Theo, he's fixed the plate, and he has a job where he won't get hassle from girls.

He has fixed more than just the plate. He's fixed his family and his future.

Chapter 18

Harriet's appointment confirmation email divulges little about the technicalities of the treatment. She reads it several times, distrusting her eyesight, sure that eventually the words will morph into some that make sense or offer an explanation. When doubt creeps into her mind, she calms her quickening breaths by reminding herself it's top-secret, so they don't want a written record. She considers calling Michelle to ask, but would that break the secrecy rules? She's not sure.

She's alone on treatment day. Bots aren't allowed time off work easily. Theo and Monty both offered to go with her, but she knows they're swamped with work. Monty has some commission furniture to upholster and paint to a deadline. Theo has been selected for some big project he knows little about except it'll pay well, so their offer to accompany her was well-intended, but she doesn't need the guilt niggling at her. She's fine to go alone.

The nearest lift to the hospital is a half hour taxi away. With no way to earn money at the moment, her savings are dwindling and she's counting her pennies, so the taxi ride is going to hurt. She hopes if multiple treatments are needed, she'll be well enough to walk soon, and get back to teaching.

Her cold bones warm at the thought. Imagine being well enough to walk!

Surely a hospital treating below-ground sickness would be best placed on the lower levels, but Michelle's revelation whirrs in her head. A rich person is needed to fund treatment. The reality bites as Harriet knows this treatment is ring-fenced for those with the sickness but are the rare few who have defied gravity and crawled up the socioeconomic ladder.

As she sits in the slow and dusty AutoTaxi on 6, food wrappers strewn across the floor and the ambient odour of old vinegar, she wonders also if those who licensed the treatment don't want more below grounders surviving. She strokes her non-existent tummy as it knots and cramps, kneading her skin with her knuckles as if she can soothe the muscle ache and the twisting suspicion inside will unfurl.

She shouldn't allow such cynicism to enter her mind. Gratitude—that's all she should feel.

Yet the questions don't stop.

Despite the mind fog that comes with the sickness, the clearest thoughts are those of scepticism and doubt. She needs to get all her pessimistic curiosities out of her system on the journey as when she gets there, she won't dare ask any questions. She can't screw up this opportunity.

When little tingles of relief about her future filter through, when she feels the buzz of hope, her mind's light is darkened by thoughts of Theo. Her best friend. If she's well again she'll go back to the movies. Christ, she'd do nudes and porn if it would save Theo, although at her age, it's unlikely she'd land any such roles. Maybe it won't come to that, and she'll meet a rich partner who'll treat her right this time.

It's strange to have musings of a future when, just days ago, she was certain she didn't have one.

Part or her, the naive part that still clings on to there being goodness in the world, expects the hospital to be rammed, a queue out the door of coughing below grounders, staff struggling to cope with tired yet happy faces as they save the lives of so many. News crews outside documenting this miracle treatment, journalists clambering to get the exclusive.

Of course, reality hits like a slap in the face when she walks into the hospital, gleaming white, shiny surfaces, and is pushed in a wheelchair down empty corridors to a large room, just for her.

Doctor Peterson, fresh-faced and not at all flustered from being overworked, arrives on time.

Harriet recalls the delay in Josie getting palliative care down on 5. It took two days just to get her painkillers. A sharp twinge inches across Harriet's forehead when she recalls the pain Josie was in, but she rubs away her neuralgia, closes her eyes and refuses to dwell on whether the cure was available then. As much as it gnaws at her, she can't roll back the clock.

Doctor Peterson has the coldest hands Harriet has known, or perhaps that's just because she's so cold herself. The doctor makes light conversation, mentioning Harriet's old movies and her latest stints on TV.

'The weather has been crazy lately,' Doctor Peterson then says. 'Such nice days, then the heaviest rain. They say we're going to have a bad storm season.'

Harriet realises Doctor Peterson assumes she lives up high. No one from low levels talks about the weather. They never even see the sun and clouds.

'Well, looks like you've come to us just in time,' the doctor says when she analyses the results. 'The treatment has a ninety-five per cent success rate at your stage, so I'm confident you'll be back to normal in no time.'

It's not a lot of information. Harriet has to sift through the highlights, and process them individually. Ninety-five per cent rate, back to normal. Her eyes brim, her lungs inflates a little easier. That glimmer of hope warms her chill.

'And what's involved?' she asks.

'It's a cutting-edge blood transfusion with some pre-prepared blood. It'll locate the specific components of the sickness in you. Any side effects are minimal, maybe some bruising and fatigue. Three transfusions are normal, over the span of a couple of weeks. We can do another one or two if you're not in the clear by then.'

Harriet's headache comes back stronger as her brow tenses. It's too confusing. It can't be that simple. Harriet was imagining intensive chemotherapy, bone marrow surgery, lumbar punctures, organ transplants, and chest drains. Surprise rids her of her voice for a moment. 'That . . . that's it?'

'I'll give you some pain relief, vitamins, and some other bits to lessen your symptoms in the meantime. You'll feel a bit better tomorrow, then continue to improve. Even if you feel well though, you must come back for the remaining transfusions. No symptoms doesn't mean you're in the clear.'

'It . . . it seems so simple.' Harriet rubs her forehead, smoothing out the furrows. 'It's a shame it's not more widely available.' She slams her mouth shut. A physical barrier to her cynicism.

'These things filter down, eventually. It just takes time.'

Below grounders don't have time. It should filter up, not down. Harriet's privilege shocks her. Why her, why now?

She doesn't ask, even though it's eating away at her. Don't rock the boat. Her survival is worth keeping quiet for. Below grounders often think she's forgotten her roots. Now if they knew she was having a life-saving treatment they're all denied, she'd be cast aside for sure.

The transfusion is painless, as the doctor promised. An hour later and she's free to go home. She swallows a mild painkiller to take the edge off her headache, then rides the lift back down to the vehicle level. As she alights, a woman coughs, a rash so high it's up to her neck, her eyes misty with the end-stage blindness.

Harriet's felt guilty for abandoning her roots before, but this is a whole new level. She averts her gaze from the woman, her skin tightening and her own rash itching from her cool sweat. As much as her lungs burn, she quickens her pace to step around her. If she can't see the woman for long, maybe she can forget, maybe her guilt will vanish.

As she waits for the taxi, the woman's cough echoes behind her, bouncing off the walls and sounding louder than all the other commotion on the street. It rids Harriet of her joy. She wonders what'll happen if she tells people there's a cure after her treatment, if she gets word out the below grounders don't have to get sick. It's one more campaign, one more way how maybe she can make a difference. They can't undo the treatment they've done, or at least she doesn't think they can.

In the taxi, she messages Michelle and arranges a meet up. There has to be something they can do.

CHAPTER 19

It's strange for Oliver to go to work without Thomas. Besides his date with Evie, they've done everything together. He's rarely even been alone at all. He hopes no one recognises him, as speaking to strangers might be a lot harder without Thomas's calming presence to keep him at ease. As Oliver walks to the lift, he keeps expecting to see Thomas walking beside him. The walkways are filled with people but being surrounded by strangers is an unusually lonely feeling.

He takes the lift down to 2, and he's greeted by swarms of flies as soon as he alights. The buzzing noise they make is like a vibration all around. He likes bugs, but this is too much, and he waves his hand around his head to try to clear them.

Gulls squawk and argue along the walkway, fighting over scraps of mouldy-looking food. Not for the first time, Oliver is pleased he doesn't have a sense of smell. The air down this low has a hazy hue and leaves a tacky residue on his skin.

The office building is dilapidated, with crumbling old brick-work and rubbish piled up almost as high as the roof. It's not a tower. 2 is this building's top level, which is a good thing, since it doesn't look like it's strong enough to hold the birds sitting on its roof let alone another storey. Oliver has to kick some trash out from behind the door before he can open it, and even as he does so, more blows over.

'Use the broom and sweep it out,' someone says from inside.

Oliver spots the broom by the door and nudges the wayward packets and whatnot out of the door before closing it again. A few flies follow him in and now buzz around, lost and aimless inside. One gets caught on a sticky piece of tape hanging from the ceiling. By the looks of it, many have done the same thing before.

The air inside is as dense as out, only a fair bit hotter. External heat doesn't make Oliver uncomfortable, but he's aware of how his battery feels extra charged, a buzz of electricity surging through. He tries to empty his mind of thoughts to conserve it, to pay little attention to the cracks in the walls, the bright lights of the vending machine, or the pictures of women without their clothes on—or not many clothes—that hang on the notice board. Oliver keeps his eyes low.

A thickset man in overalls and a hardhat appears through another doorway. 'You must be the new guy. Oliver, right?'

'That's me.'

'I'm Bret.' He passes Oliver a hard hat. 'You've used the machinery before?'

Oliver nods.

'Great. So, the incinerator is about a kilometre west, we—' He stops when the door opens, takes his hard hat off and stands very straight, looking over Oliver's shoulder. 'Sir. This is a nice surprise.'

Oliver turns around and, removing a face mask and wincing against the sticky air, is Anthony. He's grinning, but not the lopsided, teeth-showing grin he used to do before lashing out. He looks happy.

'Thought I'd come see the new guy on his first day. How's it going, Oliver?' He pats Oliver on the arm.

Oliver blinks a few times, tilts his head a bit, trying to gauge Anthony's greeting. It doesn't seem to fit with any greetings Oliver was expecting. It's hard to decipher.

'I just got here,' Oliver says. 'I was going to begin with the diggers at the incinerator.'

The way Bret addressed Anthony was unusual, in Oliver's experience. Oliver has never seen such a formal interaction. He looks at Bret for a moment and notes his stiff posture and his puffed-up torso. It's not fear from Bret, but admiration, acclaim. There might be another word, but Oliver hasn't got that far in the dictionary yet. No one has ever spoken to Oliver in such a way. Not even his boss at the supermarket invoked such attention from his staff.

'I have a different idea for work for Oliver. A better way to put him to his best use,' Anthony says.

At this, Bret gives a small nod, almost a bow, then backs away. Oliver watches, his mouth slightly agape. Bret is so obedient. He doesn't question Anthony at all.

Anthony walks up to Oliver and puts his arm over his shoulder. 'Now, Oliver, I have a much better job for you.' He's looking out the window into the landfill. A shiny watch hangs from his wrist. It looks heavy. His clothes are pristine. Anthony's tidy shirt makes Oliver acutely aware of the yellowing around his collar and the patched-up hole on the front. Oliver thinks, even with Monty's skills, he's never seen stitching as neat as on Anthony's clothes.

Anthony's touch and his expression tell Oliver he's being friendly. He's addressing Oliver like a companion, not as a boy he hates. Not even as a strict boss. Oliver was worried how lonely he'd be without Thomas, but with Anthony's arm around his shoulder, he worries about that less.

'There's a section of landfill I need clearing,' Anthony says. 'No time to sort it and it doesn't matter where it ends up. It just needs shifting so we can have access to ground level. Then, how would you like to use a drill?'

That doesn't sound too hard. It's the kind of work Oliver did loads at the Institute. 'Erm, sure.'

'Great. This job is reserved for my most trusted employees, you understand?'

Oliver nods. He supposes since he did this kind of work so much as a teen, he will be great at it.

Anthony gives him a pat on the back and Oliver stands straighter, rolls his shoulders back. He's going to be really good and useful down here.

'It's a little away from here,' Anthony says. 'You can get a ride in the truck. It's quite time sensitive, so how do you feel about working right through until you're down to twenty per cent? There'll be a reward in it for you.'

A reward? Oliver tingles at the thought. He's never had a reward for anything. Even when he stacked all the shelves in record time at the supermarket he didn't get a reward. 'That sounds fine with me.'

Anthony walks him out just as the truck is pulling up. It has huge, triangular caterpillar track wheels and a ladder to climb up and get inside. Oliver hauls himself in and Anthony waves him off as the truck pulls away. There are six other bots already in the truck. Oliver recognises them from the Institute. He had some classes with George and the others over the years. It's too loud to have a conversation with the driver or anyone else sitting in there, so he gives them all a nod and sits silently as the landscape of piles of trash passes by.

The ride is bumpy, the huge wheels climbing up and over every pile. All the time, rubbish rains down from overhead, thumping against the roof of the truck. It makes Oliver jump at first, but he soon gets used to it. The truck has metal struts and poles inside, but the occasional bit of rubbish still makes a fresh dent.

They arrive at the site that needs clearing, and the drill is there already. When Anthony said a drill, Oliver imagined a handheld thing like Uncle Theo uses. The drill is nothing like that. It's attached to a truck and is a huge thing, the width of a person and as tall as two storeys.

There are some bots here already clearing the space, and they leave when Oliver and the rest arrive, their shift finished. An area the radius of an apartment block has been cleared. It looks like there once existed a park beneath it as the remnants of a slide and climbing frame are bent and pressed into the earth.

'You probably know some of the other bots, so I don't need to introduce you,' a man says.

Oliver assumes the man is in charge. He shouts over the racket, but that makes Oliver wince. It's already too loud for his hearing.

'You lads look out for each other, be loyal,' the man continues. 'This is hard and dangerous work, so you need to get along.'

'Of course. Fine by me,' Oliver says.

'There's a bit more clearing to do before the drilling, but this is where you'll be for now. Here,' the man says and hands Oliver some ear defenders.

With his ears protected, Oliver can think much more clearly. Everything is nicely muffled.

He works non-stop, using the diggers to clear, or by hand when it gets too fiddly. They erect a roof to protect the area from more rubbish filling it and take turns looking up for the larger items. Occasionally, a whistle blows and they all take cover as furniture or other heavy items come crashing down.

The other bots speak a little. It's hard to have a conversation among all the noise, but Oliver catches the odd bit of small talk, but mostly it's noisy, and they're too busy to chat. There's the odd bit of banter, some laughing when someone falls over or cheering when something really heavy is lifted, all punctuated by lots of curse words. It's good to have something more challenging to do than stacking shelves, without girls hassling him. He doesn't have to worry about how he looks, or smiling, or manners.

When he's near enough down to twenty per cent, he tells the man who's in charge, and they call the truck to pick him up. He's got no idea how long he's been working. There's no daylight on 2, only the strip lights to help them work. The truck drops him off at the office and Anthony is there to greet him.

'Well done, Oliver,' Anthony says. His face still wears that smile, the one telling Oliver he's being friendly. 'I got you something. A gift.' He hands Oliver a jacket. Brand new, designer logo on the cuffs.

Oliver brushes his grubby hands on his trousers before he takes it. 'Wow. Thank you.' The fabric is soft, and the stitching is as good as it is on Anthony's clothes. 'Why? I mean, thank you, but why would you get this for me?'

'You did great work today. You deserve it, don't you think? You've worked so hard, I've no doubt you'll be in line for promotion soon.'

Oliver cocks his head, blinks a few times, then looks again at the jacket. 'Yeah. Great. Sure.'

'And here.' He hands Oliver a mobile phone. 'The top men at the top companies need mobile phones. I may need to call you about work some time. You know how to use one of these?'

Oliver's eyes bulge as he takes the phone. There's not a scratch nor a chip on it. It shines in a way Oliver hasn't even seen since he was a kid. He turns it over in his hand, lost for words for a few moments. 'I've used computers a bit. I think I can figure it out.'

'That's my boy.' Anthony pats him on the back. 'Best not tell your mum where you got this. Just say you found it here. Our little secret. Okay?'

Oliver nods. He still can't take his eyes off the phone. 'Sure.'

He leaves, then takes the lift up to 5 and walks home, wearing the jacket, the phone heavy in the jacket pocket. He has his chin high. With such fine things, he feels less self-conscious, more conspicuous, but in a good way. He feels, somehow, more important.

Perhaps working on 2 is going to be a really good thing.

All the way home he strokes the jacket, his fingers gliding over the fine fabric. He tugs at it, inspecting the seams. They're flawless. Oliver thinks even as a kid he didn't have anything so well made.

It niggles at him though. Despite how luxurious it is, it sits heavily on his shoulders; the phone, a lump on his side. Anthony has never been nice to Oliver before. So why now? He can't think of any explanation besides he must deserve it, since like

Anthony said, he's working hard now, whereas as a kid all he did was play.

Anthony used to buy his mum fancy jewellery, and he never stopped her spending his money to buy fine things for them. So, maybe, for however bad Anthony is with his fists, he can still do nice things. And based on Bret's response, the way he stood so straight and still and called him Sir, Oliver thinks Anthony must reward good employees which makes them behave so well.

Oliver's stiff muscles loosen as he mulls it over. He grew up on the top levels, so it's only right he has a top-level jacket. He bounces his shoulders up and down, and the jacket sits better, feels more comfortable. He deserves it, he reminds himself. There's nothing wrong with having fancy things, no matter where they came from. Someday soon, he'll make sure his mum has fancy things too.

Chapter 20

The day after her first treatment, Harriet gets out of bed without thinking, goes to the toilet and it's only when she's washing her hands that she realises she isn't in pain, not much anyway. She doesn't have to shut away the slight pain she does have. It's so mild, it's bearable without trying.

It's early in the morning. Lately, she's been so tired she's been sleeping in late, but she's awake without the sluggishness and fatigue she's had in recent months. She hadn't realised the time until she hears Theo and Monty getting breakfast ready. She walks unimpeded to the kitchen, sits without any muscle cramps, and smells the food. Her stomach is empty, not knotted, and there's not a drop of bile creeping up her throat. They haven't even put a plate out for her, but for the first time in weeks, her stomach grumbles.

Theo and Monty shout good morning over their shoulders as they rummage for cutlery and drinks.

'What you guys having?' she asks.

'Beans and potatoes,' Monty says.

A simple dish, even with Monty's flare. And right now, it sounds like the most delicious thing in the world.

'Got enough for me?' she asks, her mouth actually salivating rather than scratchy and dry. 'No worries if not.'

They both instantly stop what they're doing, then turn slowly to face her.

Theo almost drops the cutlery. 'You're hungry?'

'I am.' She rubs her tummy. 'You know what? I really, really am.'

Monty does a little jump. 'Oh, my God, Harriet, that's amazing! Have mine!' He puts his plate in front of her.

'No!' She tries to stop him but it's a half-hearted attempt. The food looks like the best meal she's ever seen, and she could eat a horse. 'You need some.'

'Piss off telling me no,' Monty says. 'What else? Juice? Milk?'

She laughs. 'Let me just see how this goes.'

Theo and Monty both share a plate and sit at the table, watching her eat like it's a spectacle. She chews, no jaw pain, the sharpness of tomato sauce lingering on her tongue. Then swallows without retching.

She grins. 'It's good.'

'Tea!' Theo says. 'No, you've had loads of tea. Coffee.'

Theo pours out three mugs for her: one juice, one coffee, one milk.

After her plate of food, though, she's full. Her shrunken stomach is unused to any volume. She leans back in the chair, puffs out her cheeks and enjoys the feeling. 'I'm actually full. Not just no appetite, but satiated.'

Theo's jaw hangs open. Monty has his arm over his shoulder and a glint of tears shine in their eyes.

'I just can't believe it,' Theo says.

'Babe, this is amazing!' Monty says, his grin wider than ever.

Harriet wants to tell Oliver and Thomas. She'd love to shout from the rooftops that she feels so well. The secrecy clause is going to be a bitch, but she can at least tell her son.

'Did you guys hear Oliver come in?' she asks. 'I think it was morning.'

'Yeah,' Monty says. 'He worked right through, but he gets a whole day off now to charge and heal. Different schedule with this new job.'

'I hope they're not overworking him. I feel like I've barely seen him.'

'He had a gorgeous new jacket he found down there. Working landfill has its perks,' Monty says. 'That thing looked brand new.'

'Well, the TV crew are due in later,' she says, 'so it's good he has a day off. Hopefully, we can spend some time together today.'

Especially now she has some energy. The results so far are much better than she thought. She keeps her breakfast down, no nausea, then stands at the door on much sturdier legs, waving Theo and Monty off.

She peeks in at Oliver, slowly pushing his door open and tiptoeing a few steps inside. He's charging, his eyes closed. He looks shattered. Dusty, with blue-black bruising up his hands and arms and his hair full of muck. He smells exactly as she would imagine the landfill does. When he wakes, she'll wash his clothes and give his room a clean for him.

She hasn't told Oliver about the offer the TV company made. The money is more than she ever earned in her movie days, though with inflation that's to be expected. TRI has also approved it, no surprises there. They'll be banking far more than Harriet, so they jumped at the opportunity.

Is her pay enough for Theo's treatment? She's not sure. Probably not. But it's a good start. She keeps it to herself, not wanting to put pressure on anyone just yet.

She shuts the door and tiptoes to the kitchen to get the house ready. She washes the dishes at the sink, scrubbing plates without pain or growing breathless. When she's done, her tiredness returns with a bang, and she lies down on the sofa. A bit of tiredness is manageable and expected. But after a year of envisioning a dark future, leaving her son orphaned in this world, she now truly believes she can be here for him in years to come. When she sleeps, it's not nightmares that plague her, but happy dreams.

CHAPTER 21

Oliver is only partially charged when the film crew arrives, but he can finish his charge later. There's enough time before he's due back at work.

He knows he should smile and greet the film crew, but as they rearrange everything and make so much noise, he wishes he still had his ear defenders. Instead, he stands in the corner, slouching and folding his arms. He has to keep reminding himself that Uncle Theo needs this so he can't be selfish. But he hates the eyes on him, the way they talk to him like they think they know him, like he's a prop rather than a person. He doesn't know any of their names, but they all know his. He wishes he could have a disguise, a second body to step into when it all gets too much. Do humans ever feel like this, like being looked at and spoken to is all too much? His mum doesn't, but she used to be in the movies so she's accustomed to being fussed over. His shift at work was a brief respite from attention, but this is a lot harder to bear than the girls who came into the shop.

He goes to his room to stay out of the way and checks himself in the mirror. All over his arms are blue-black bruising and bunched up skin, not the sort of tidy appearance he'd like if he's going to be filmed. His hair is more of a mess than usual, and his eyes are red from gritty dust clogging them. Anthony's secretary kindly arranged for him to have a *Get Level* account, and she texted him the login details. It's only now Oliver sees the extent to which his mum's been posting. And he looks good in all of her photos, bar the odd one. His hair always looks messy but in a styled way, his face is clean and without bruising. He looks a state now. Not camera-ready at all.

He rinses off in the shower. He could completely submerge himself under the stream, but the idea makes him nervous. As a kid, he fell in a lake and it was horrible, so a light spray and plenty of sponging down gets his body clean enough. He wets his hair and rubs a towel on it. He's never known how to do his hair. His mum used to put some product in it when he was a kid, but how does he want it now? He's not sure. He should pay attention to how other men wear their hair. Uncle Monty has none and Uncle Theo has almost none, so they're no help.

The Institute never prepared them for this aspect of life. They never taught them how to fit in with humans. He has no idea how to dress nicely or do his hair. Being locked away for those years was such a hindrance. Oliver was a child last time he socialised with humans. It's a big jump to adulthood.

Back in his room, he searches through the clothes. There's nothing wrong with them. There's just nothing overly right with them either. A lot of the trousers are a bit short and most things have a stain somewhere. Everyone they saw up on 99 was wearing clothes that fitted perfectly, fabrics that were clean and well-made. They looked like they'd feel nice against the skin, brand new and fresh.

Oliver picks out the top and jeans he thinks probably are the best, but then, what would he know? The one item of clothing he has that he's sure is good is the jacket Anthony gave him. He puts it on over the top of his other clothes and instantly feels more confident, more tidy. He checks the mirror. The jacket looks like something a 99-level person would wear.

The TV crew are having a meeting in the kitchen and Oliver says hello now, smiles at all of them instead of slouching in the corner.

The film crew circle the room, discussing their setup, and give Oliver approving nods. They talk around him as if he's not there, though they look at him often, sizing him up like a piece of furniture.

'We could brighten the lighting in here,' one of the crew says. 'Make sure Oliver sits against that wall to add some contrast.'

'The sound in here will be tricky. Perhaps some vocal coaching for Oliver.'

'The jacket is good,' another one of the crew says, and Oliver tugs on the lapels. 'Keep shots above the waist.'

'Should we get hair and makeup to take a look at him?'

They're talking *about* him, not *to* him, and despite the confidence he's managed to muster, Oliver is unaccustomed to such attention. He feels on show, an object, something to be scrutinised and judged. His face starts to heat from the inside, and he has the desire to slouch in the corner again. Where's his mum? She used to work on film sets. Perhaps she can reassure him that this kind of talk is normal.

Oliver fidgets, his skin not fitting right, as if it needs to shed. The bruising and bunching now tingles, like an itch. He's more of an ornament than a person. He knows he's not a person anyway, but he rarely feels like he's not. Right now, he might as well be a picture on the wall or one of Uncle Monty's craft projects.

Harriet comes to join them in the kitchen and Oliver rushes to help her, then stops in his tracks when he sees she doesn't need it. His mum is walking without effort. Her face isn't that yellowish hue it's been lately. It's pink and her eyes focus right on him.

'Mum!' His hands go to his cheeks, the same face Uncle Monty makes when he's surprised. 'You look so much better.'

'Thank you, darling. I feel great. Best in ages.' She smiles and doesn't even cough. 'Nice jacket. You find that at work? How was it? Tell me everything.'

'It was fine. We were just cleaning rubbish.' He looks over his shoulder at the film crew still pushing furniture out of the way, hears another mutter that Oliver needs to see hair and makeup again. He lifts his shoulders, like that will somehow hide him. 'Mum, I don't know about this. My hair doesn't look right and these people, they talk like I'm not even here.'

She rubs his arm. It's amazing how that small touch makes his nerves lessen a little. Sometimes he wishes he was a kid again and he could sit on her lap or be picked up.

'That's just the way it is,' she says. 'They're still only planning. You won't be filmed yet. But how would you like your hair?'

Oliver shrugs and rubs a hand over his hair. 'I don't know. I never really thought about it before.'

Thomas arrives home from work. Even though he's been stacking shelves or in the warehouse all day, he still looks tidier than Oliver. His hair is always sleek and shiny and sits exactly where it is meant to.

Thomas pauses in the hallway. 'Do they need me tonight? I might go out.'

'Out?' Oliver asks. 'Where?'

One side of Thomas's mouth curls up into a smile. 'Anywhere but here.'

Oliver smiles back but inwardly kicks himself. He should have said he's going out to get away from the film crew, but where would he go? Has Thomas made other friends? That would be nice. The other bots at the landfill just worked, but maybe Oliver should try to make friends. He was so fixated on making a good impression, but surely he's allowed to chat a bit more.

'Can you hang around for just an hour?' Harriet asks, and Thomas agrees.

The hair and makeup team fuss over the boys, trying different hair products and powders. They've never prepped bots before and seem surprised it's really just the same, like maybe they thought Oliver's skin would fall off if they rubbed it too much. They experiment with some creams to hide Oliver's bruising. His head is almost all better from the dent, but they don't seem to be happy until there's not a trace of bruise. The makeup helps, but they play with his hair a bit to cover that more. They ignore the bad skin and bruises on his arms and hands and tell him to keep his hands on his lap.

After a few minutes, Oliver manages to make small talk and laugh a bit with the makeup people. It's good friend-making practice, he thinks. They chat about some memories at the Institute, he and Thomas recalling times when the staff there got mad, or they messed up their work. The crew say they saw pictures of them as teens and comment on how adorable they were. Oliver and Thomas blush. Oliver wishes there were more pictures of him as a kid. His mum only has one, but he thinks these people would like to see that.

Thomas hasn't noticed Oliver's new jacket or, if he has, he hasn't said anything. It is such a smart jacket Oliver expected some sort of reaction. Just some recognition, like his mum gave. As they sit and put up with being talked at and fussed over, Oliver takes his new phone out of his pocket.

'Hey, Thomas, look what my boss gave me.'

Now Thomas looks impressed. His eyebrows lift up and his jaw drops, much to the annoyance of the woman putting make-up on his forehead. 'Woah! Oliver, that's so nice of them.'

Oliver's smile tightens. He continues showing it to Thomas for a moment, then turns it over in his hands. It is nice of his boss, sure, but Oliver wasn't hoping for praise for Anthony; he wanted Thomas to be impressed with him, since he earned it.

'Oliver, darling.' His mum walks over. 'Your boss gave you a phone?' She doesn't look impressed. He's sure he must be reading her expression wrong so he tilts his head each way, but realises she really isn't impressed. She's swallowing, rubbing her chin, her eyebrows knitted. She's confused. Why? Does he not deserve a phone? All other men have them, so Oliver should too.

'Yeah,' Oliver says, and puts it back in his pocket. 'Said in case he needs to get in touch about work.'

She does a slow nod. 'I see.'

'I am allowed a phone,' Oliver says, a little more defensively than he intended.

'Of course you are, darling. You must have really impressed them. Let me get your number just in case, and I'll put mine in there.'

He hands it to her and she puts her number in, and Theo's and Monty's, before handing it back to him. Her phone looks older, the screen has a crack down the middle. That doesn't seem right. His mum should have the best of everything.

'Why don't you have that one, Mum? I'll have yours instead.'

He notes the sheen of tears in her eyes, a smile lifting her face. 'Oh, my sweet boy.' She clears her throat. 'If your boss gave you that phone then you must keep it.' She gives his shoulder a squeeze. 'I'm so proud of you.'

Oliver smiles then, feeling a little taller, broader. His mum is well and she's proud of him. She talks to him like a kid sometimes, which he supposes is normal for mums. It took him a while to adapt to his adult body, so his mum also might need a little longer to get used to him being an adult. He's a working man now and he's protecting his family. They might not know that, but he should be taken seriously as an adult. One day, maybe he'll tell them it was because of him his mum got her treatment. He wonders if she'll be more proud or mad. He's not sure. He can be proud of himself, though.

The man with a scraggly beard stands in front of Oliver now. Oliver met him before briefly when he found out about the TV show. He says his name is Lenny and is a lot more polite this time and doesn't seem to begrudge Oliver's previous outburst. 'So, Oliver, how are you feeling about the TV show? Any concerns?'

Oliver runs his hands over his jacket, stopping briefly to feel the phone in his pocket. He feels the buttons, the slippery smooth screen, and as he does, his body buzzes, his processors in overdrive, and he puffs his chest out, sitting with the kind of posture he has seen Anthony have before. 'Oh, no. I feel fine about it all. I think it's going to be great.'

CHAPTER 22

The TV crew takes ages to rearrange the house and test lighting and sound. Harriet has never done any filming on a set that wasn't ready-made, and hadn't really appreciated quite how disruptive it would be. The furniture is pushed back, revealing parts of the floor she omitted to clean. The extra lighting highlights patches of dust she missed on surfaces, and plumes of particles dance under the lampshades.

The producer, Lenny, inspects every move with pursed lips as he judges and considers whether or not Harriet and her friends' home and possessions are camera-worthy.

When it's not the objects, it's Harriet. They position her by the window, someone declares the lighting highlights her in a bad way, before opting for a shadier corner and shouting instructions to makeup to at least try to hide the bags under her eyes. It's been years since Harriet has been scrutinised in such ways, and this reintroduction only serves to remind her of the brutality of those days. At least she was young and fresh-faced when she was in the movies. Now it's like they are trying to polish a raisin. And they haven't even started filming yet. This is still all just prep. She keeps asking about scheduling, but no one has an answer yet and when they finally pack up and leave, Lenny shouts that scheduling will be in touch.

At least they're gone now.

Oliver tolerated his stint with the TV crew, and he's been charging in his room since. Harriet opens the door and peeks in. He's lying still, his eyes closed, hands clasped at his front. He appears peaceful like this, like maybe he heeded Harriet's instructions, and he really has let his anger go.

His new jacket is laid over his desk chair and she tiptoes in to have a look at it. It's the kind of thing they all wear up top. Lined, quality fabric, not a loose stitch or worn patch at all. It's the kind of thing Anthony would wear when he wasn't working. She shudders at the thought and replaces it.

Monty arrives home, covered in paint with a bag of fabric in his hand, as always. He smells like dust and fabric glue.

'Theo is taking up our entire workshop, so I need to finish this at home.'

'Really? That place is huge.'

Monty leans against the wall and wipes his shiny forehead on the back of his hand. He has slender fingers for such a stocky man. They joked before that he could have been a pianist if he wasn't born below. 'He's got a bunch of tech people there. God knows what they're working on, but there's seven of them and not a square inch of space for me. He's in his element and I love him so much when he's like that, but he's too busy to have me distracting him.'

Harriet smiles and walks through, bouncing on her feet when she's in the kitchen. 'Cuppa?'

'Sure.' He drags his bags through, then dust puffs up in his wake. 'Yikes!' Monty says when he reaches the kitchen. 'Wow, they really moved a lot around. How's Oliver? His head all better yet?'

Harriet fills the kettle, not even noticing the weight of it like she would have done a few days ago and puts it on the stove. 'Much better than it was. He's just charging at the moment. He looks wiped out.'

'I know the feeling.' Monty plonks down at the kitchen table and stretches out.

Any cleaning Harriet did is undone in seconds. These boys are all dirt magnets outside, then repellents inside. A trail of muck collects under Monty as he sits. The cups are still clean at least and Harriet pours the water, the steam re-frizzing the hair the TV hairdresser tamed just moments ago. They only did a quick job, she tells herself as she tried to squash it back down with her palm.

Monty's pile of repair projects are in a box under the table, and he lifts it to sort through. 'Oh, no!'

'What?'

'Dammit. This plate.' He lifts it out and runs his finger down the broken line. 'I glued this, but it's come apart. The edge, it's been covered in, what is that? Paint?'

'Oh, I'm so sorry,' Harriet says. 'The film crew broke it and I tried to fix it. I must have used the wrong product.' The lie comes out at lightning speed. It's a mother's instinct to protect her son. And it's only a small lie to cover up one mild outburst. Oliver would never do anything so thoughtless again, she's sure. She looks at the broken plate as Monty puts it away again and smiles. Oliver must have tried to fix it. Her poor boy would have been riddled with guilt and did his best. She was never worried about the plate and knew Monty wouldn't be; it was more the action that caused it she was concerned about. She sees this as a sign. Oliver's trying to make amends shows what the good man he is and always has been. So kind and thoughtful.

'No worries, babe,' Monty says as he shoves the box back in a corner. 'Looking at how much they shifted around, I'm surprised more haven't broken.'

'Want to show me the right glue and I'll sort it later?'

'No, don't worry about it. I'll get round to it, eventually.' Monty finds a pair of reading glasses on the kitchen table. They're never sure whose they are—Harriet, Theo, and Monty all share—and he scrolls through his phone and yawns when Harriet puts the tea in front of him. He mumbles a thanks before he gasps and sits bolt upright. 'Oh, my God!'

'What?'

He holds his phone out for Harriet to see. It's a news article with a photo of some men. 'This guy? You seen him?'

Harriet screws her eyes up to peer at the photo, then takes the reading glasses off Monty's face to use herself. The image comes into focus and she groans. 'These people are still making the news? The bloody Flesh Fraternity just won't shut up.'

'Yeah, but this guy.' He zooms in and points to one of them specifically. 'I knew I recognised him from somewhere. He's been on TV, right?'

'Yeah. I remember seeing an interview with him ages ago.' She shudders and hands the glasses back.

'He's in our workshop. He's one of the guys on Theo's project.'

Harriet draws her head back. 'Yikes. Wonder if Theo knows.'

'They're working on some energy saving project, apparently. Should we warn him?'

'Yeah. For sure. He needs to know not to mention the boys.'

The lights coming through the window flicker in such a way they haven't done in ages, not since Monty and his friends rigged the electricity so the lower levels get their fair share. Monty and Harriet lock eyes for a moment. The lights go back to normal, then they flicker again.

'You think that's from Oliver charging?' Harriet asks.

'Shouldn't be. TRI guarantees electricity for bots.' He goes to the window and peers outside as the lights flicker again. 'It's across the whole level.'

The lights brighten, and the flickering stops. Monty sits back down and chews on the inside of his cheek a moment. 'They've let us get away with the electric redistribution for years. Maybe up top have finally had enough.'

'Well, everyone who works at ground level and the incinerators knows to keep the electric directed where it should.'

'Yeah, but fewer humans are working at ground level now. Those jobs are being taken over by bots.'

Harriet's hand goes to her mouth. 'You don't think . . .?'

Monty shrugs. 'Probably only a glitch. Let's assume that. Maybe there's just a lot of demand on the grid right now. I'll ask Theo later.'

Harriet starts putting the house back to how it should be, undoing all the arranging the TV crew did. They piled up some things they didn't want in view in the corner, and she starts sorting through it all. It's mostly laundry and some part-finished electrical projects.

Among some bits on the side, she finds a photograph in a square wooden frame. She gasps, and her eyes glaze with tears as she stares. It's an old photo, one of her and her little brother. Tipher was maybe nine-years-old when it was taken; she was about fourteen. It was taken not long before he died. She hasn't seen this photo in years. She's sure she left it at Anthony's when she fled so she can't fathom how it's ended up in her flat now. Unless . . . She scratches her head a moment. Oliver was a kid then. Would he have taken it? Surely he wouldn't have found it at the landfill. Chances of that must be almost zilch.

She sits again and gazes at the photo, unable to take her eyes off it. She remembers how Tipher used to laugh when she read to him, how much he loved to play games, how he hung on, suffering for as long as he could. Oliver reminded her so much of Tipher. That's what drew her to his image when she first went to collect him. If Tipher had survived, he'd be the spit of Oliver right now.

She can't fathom how this picture is here, but she brims with gratitude. Perhaps there's something in luck after all.

CHAPTER 23

Perhaps now Oliver is dressed a little smarter and has a phone, Evie will like him again. He's tried to shut her from his mind, but his thoughts drift to her too frequently. When he's hauling heavy bags around at work or sitting alone in the digger, he'll remember her laugh or her pretty hair and find she's invading his mind, and he can't shut her away. He shouldn't have been so mean before. He should have understood. When he thinks of how he spoke to her, he gets a knotted sensation in his middle, and he wants to undo it, to stop remembering how hard his tone was. It's not her fault she thought Thomas was coming too. And it would have been fun, the three of them together playing board games, even if Oliver wanted more than that.

He decides he needs to see her.

He charges for a few minutes after work, just enough to keep him going, and cleans himself up a bit. He shouts through to the kitchen that he's just popping out and leaves before anyone can ask any questions.

He hopes Evie's home and the concierge will buzz her apartment and let her know he's here. He's not sure how else he could get her attention.

He walks as quickly as he can to Swan View apartments, then checks the time on his phone. It's the middle of the day. Evie looks after children, so she'll most definitely be at home cleaning and sorting food while they're at school.

He almost skids to a stop when passing his old park. Evie's there, pushing a child on a swing. She said she looks after two boys, but this is a little girl, her dark blond hair in pigtails, wearing a frilly pink dress. Oliver stands and watches for a moment as the wind blows Evie's hair about her face. Her curls are looser than when she was a teen, and she tries to tuck some out of the way behind her ear. Evie and the little girl laugh at a passing butterfly. How Oliver used to delight in the butterflies too when he was little. He saw so many up here, and bees, and all manner of birds. Down on 5, it's just pigeons and gulls. At least he sees the occasional spider.

Evie holds the little girl's hand and the two of them crouch by a flower bed filled with colourful blooms, Evie pointing at them, the little girl amazed. Something tugs inside of Oliver, a yearning he has never had before, a kind of need. He wants to hold their hands and crouch by the flower beds with them. Is that how his mum felt when she first saw Oliver?

Evie catches him watching. She appears surprised for a second, her eyebrows raise and she is very still, then smiles and beckons him over.

'Oliver, hi. What are you doing here?'

'Erm . . . well . . . I was hoping to see you.' He can tell his cheeks are reddening, and he prays she doesn't notice.

'It's nice to see you. This is Bonnie. Bonnie, say hello to Oliver.'

Bonnie steps closer to Oliver and looks up at him. Her head tilts to the side, and she blinks a few times. 'Hi, Oliver. I'm Bonnie.'

Oliver's mouth drops open a little and there's a fluttering sensation in his tummy, like those butterflies are inside him. She's a MechaniKid. Quite young, it seems. He kneels in front of her. She has perfect chubby cheeks and sparkly green eyes. 'Lovely to meet you, Bonnie.'

She wraps her arms around his neck in a hug. Oliver gasps, eyes wide as it's not the reaction he was expecting, but then reciprocates her hug.

'Sorry,' Evie says with a chuckle. 'Bonnie is brand new, and she's still learning proper ways to greet people.'

Oliver enjoys the hug so much, he doesn't want it to end. He never knew his arms were so empty before. 'It's no bother,' he says when Bonnie lets go.

There's a heaviness in his chest, but a lightness in his body. A sensation he can't describe. He wants nothing more in the world than right now than to stay with Evie and Bonnie, to look after and care for them both.

Oliver is lost for words. A silence envelops the three of them, but it doesn't seem awkward. There's a warmth to it.

'How about we have a go at the climbing frame?' Oliver says to Bonnie.

She does a little jump, almost stumbling when she lands. 'Yay!'

She takes Oliver's hand, and he has to stay crouched as he walks to keep hold of hers. At the climbing frame, he shows her how to hold on and pull herself up. Just the first rung. Her coordination is stiff and unsure, and it takes her a while to understand everything he says. From the edge of his vision, Evie watches, smiling and laughing. Inside, his tummy still flutters, and he has a sense of completeness he's never known before.

After a while, Evie comes over. 'Hasn't this been a lovely treat? Bonnie, say thank you to Oliver.'

'Thank you, Oliver.' She hugs him again.

He wishes he could have daily hugs like this, that he could help Bonnie reach the second rung on the climbing frame. He wonders what stories Bonnie would like to hear at bedtime. Oliver's favourite was *Charlotte's Web*, and he thinks she'd like that too.

'We have to get back,' Evie says. 'I've got a lot to do before picking the children up from school.'

'Wait!' The word is out of Oliver's mouth before he's had time to think about the next one. But he can't let Evie go without making amends. 'I really came, well . . . thing is . . . I wanted to apologise. To say sorry, for how I spoke to you before. I didn't mean any of the nasty things I said. I really did want to spend time with you.'

Evie leans in and gives him a peck on the cheek. 'Apology accepted.'

Oliver smiles. Could it be as simple as that? He feels so much more grown up. He made a mistake, and he's apologised, and he and Evie are friends again. Although, he still wants more and hopes his thoughts aren't written all over his face. But with Evie standing so close, he wants to hold her tightly and be alone with her. Some hair blows over her face and he wants to brush it to the side, to kiss her like he did only a couple of times before.

He pushes away those thoughts. He's messed it up with Evie before, and he knows he needs to be patient now. 'It was so nice to see you and meet Bonnie. Maybe . . . well, I've got a phone now. Maybe I could text you? Or message on *Get Level?*'

'Okay. Of course,' she says.

Oliver hands her his phone and she types in a number before handing it back. 'Nice to see you again, Oliver. Come on, Bonnie.'

Oliver watches them walk away, hand in hand, and he imagines walking with them, back to a home they share, watching TV together or playing a game. He imagines how wonderful that life would be, if he had his own family.

CHAPTER 24

Harriet walks along 99. How long has it been since she walked up here? So often she didn't dare, terrified life would tempt her back, terrified she'd miss the sky so much she'd knock on his door and beg forgiveness or, more likely, she'd get back to her life on 5 and feel overwhelming dissatisfaction. Better to forget. Better to pretend she never felt the sunshine.

When death was imminent, she thought one last walk up here would be nice, then felt too sick to enjoy it. Now with a second chance at life, she grabs that one last time, because even though she can almost imagine a future now, no one ever knows how lengthy that future will be. There was a sort of clarity in her sickness. A tinge of worry haunts her now that she's on her road to recovery, like her future is murky and uncertain.

Her second hospital visit is in an hour, down on 90. She took a taxi to the first, never imagining she'd feel so well that she could walk part of the way for the second treatment. Her legs are weak from months of little use, but she isn't out of breath, isn't violently shivering, and her bones aren't cramping.

Families are enjoying the sunny day, well-dressed and unhurried. No one rushes when they live up so high; the world waits for them instead. It aggravates her now she lives lower down. As much as she loves her friends and her family and cramped little house, they still live in the shadow of life above. The lower levels are nothing but a grubby tidemark to people who have never lived so low.

The upper levels leave everyone else in the shade. Harriet's experienced life at both extremes and worries the fix Monty did on the electric distribution years ago will be undone someday. The likes of Anthony and top dwellers waste too much. Her ex-husband would rinse a month's worth of lower-level electricity on one flight to work, and he took those flights almost daily. And now, top levels are getting treatment for a sickness that affects the lower levels.

The world will never be fair. She simply needs to enjoy what she has. She strolls and reminisces, mostly about Oliver as a little boy, when she would sit at the edge of the park, the sun lazy on her skin, and watch her little monkey swing from the top of the climbing frame. Then they'd walk together, and she'd tickle him or tell jokes and do impressions. His laugh then was beautiful, like raindrops on glass. She'd do anything to make him laugh.

What would make him laugh now? He so rarely laughs, though listening to his chat with the hair and makeup crew was refreshing. He's softened a little, but he's been so riddled with scorn, so much, it frightens her. She's spent too long worrying about his future when she's gone, assuming she wouldn't be here and told herself he'll be fine. Now she's going to be around to bear witness and not even the sunshine and bubbly clouds can take her worries away.

She should have left Anthony sooner. Oliver spent too many years witnessing anger at home. She should have known, should have acknowledged her love for her little boy sooner instead of shying away, shackling herself with her own preconceptions.

Idling time, she ends up near her old apartment, a force of habit, she supposes. Muscle memory. She doesn't long to go inside—her old life there is a blip in her past—but she sits at the first park she took Oliver, then watches the children as they enjoy the fair weather. She tightens her jacket. It may be sunny but the wind still bites. Advertising billboards show the same as they do on 5, quite a waste of space she always thinks, for the markets are so different. And there's her ex-husband's company, AM Investments, and their vision for the future of Reading town and London, with their skyscrapers stretching up to the soon-to-be level 150. There's an image of the AM Investments building, along with TRI, a domineering presence with the rest of the town and levels hanging off them in subservience. She shivers. Perhaps she's not all that well still, or perhaps the image of her ex-husband is enough to turn any warm body to ice.

From behind is a voice, one she recognises, and she whips around to say hello, then ducks, trying to cower out of sight, but there is little to conceal her. Hopefully, her presence here is strange enough that he won't spot her.

It's Thomas with his flame of gorgeous hair, laughing and leaning in. The woman he's with appears equally at ease in his company as he reaches a hand to her face to push her hair back behind her ear.

Harriet stifles her gasp, her hands going to her chest as her heart wants to burst. So, Thomas has another friend. And it's a girl.

Harriet shouldn't be spying, but who wouldn't? Getting details about their private lives from the boys is like pulling teeth. Thomas doesn't blush, for once, and grins easily, looking at the girl rather than the floor. And she is a beauty, long brown curls flowing over her shoulders, perfect dainty facial features. She holds the hand of a child, maybe about six-years-old, who tugs at her now, impatient as children usually are.

'Evie, come on! Park now, pleeeeeease!'

Harriet's breath catches and she jerks around to face the other way, her hand going to her mouth. *Evie.* That's Oliver's Evie.

She shuts her eyes for a few seconds. It's their business. Not hers. She shouldn't even be here. She shouldn't have seen. Oh, how she wishes she hadn't seen! She can't interfere, but perhaps that's why Oliver has been so off lately and working so hard. Her poor boy is betrayed and heartbroken. She doubts he has any concept of how to process such feelings.

They're probably just friends. Harriet turns her head slowly, unable to resist a second peek. They both lean in for a hug. Do they kiss? Harriet can't tell for sure as Evie's hair blows up and blocks her view. As Evie walks away, she glances back over her shoulder to give Thomas a final smile.

Harriet's gut caves in and she turns back around again. She knew it was Thomas's day off. She asked him if he wanted to come with her. She doesn't need to chaperone; it was more for him, for company. And when he declined, saying he was off to see a friend, Harriet was pleased for him. He said it so breezily, without any hint of date nerves, which makes her wonder how long has this been going on? *Is* something going on?

Doesn't matter. Not her business. They're all grown-ups.

She listens for them to go, for the little girl to get her way, then drag Evie off. Harriet stands, brushes any dust from the bench off her backside, and tells herself to stop being such a nosey, interfering mother. The boys can figure this out among themselves. She'll be there with hugs and kind words to get Oliver through his heartbreak. In the meantime, she'll forget it. That's all she can do. Oliver has so many admirers, he'll meet someone else. Someone who deserves him.

She takes the lift down to 90 and when she reaches the hospital, the porter gets a wheelchair for her. She's fine to walk now and feels a fraud as she sits and is wheeled through to the doctor's room.

Doctor Peterson talks throughout her tests and treatment, telling her the sickness is still present but reducing, yet it's background noise. Harriet's mind is elsewhere, worrying as always. The treatment is as pain free as the first, or possibly she's too preoccupied to notice any discomfort.

She shouldn't be so worried. Everyone gets their heart broken at some point. Evie was Oliver's first girlfriend; he'll bounce back. But Harriet has knowledge that Oliver possibly doesn't; it sits on her like an itchy jumper. It's not for her to tell and gossip. She adores Thomas and wants him to be happy too.

So she bites her nails and dissects the boys' personalities in her mind, to find reassurance and reasoning. She wonders what Josie would say if she were here. She misses her so much some days. She was much more level-headed than Harriet. Oliver and Thomas's friendship has been very special, and she worries how they'll cope without each other. Thomas has often been in Oliver's shadow—quieter, more shy, less confrontational. Oliver has been protective of him, but Thomas too is a man now and deserves to walk his own path.

When she leaves the hospital to journey home, she knows this is information she'll have to sit on. She has to trust the boys have been raised well enough to be understanding and kind and their friendship will survive the mistakes they make along the way.

She'll be there to help Oliver stick his broken heart back together again.

CHAPTER 25

The landfill clearing is big enough now for the big drills to come in. They're so noisy and the din sends shockwaves through Oliver's head, more so than the diggers and the falling rubbish and every other noise combined. The ear defenders help but not enough. Oliver grimaces when the drills first start up, his forehead tightening so much it strains his head all over, the vibrations shooting through his feet and making his legs ache.

The boss who Oliver now knows is called Duncan, tells Oliver to stand further away, which he does, and that helps a bit. His feet are less sore and the noise is at a manageable level. A few of his colleagues stand towards the edge of the site, waiting for the holes to be drilled and watching for big items falling above. Oliver thinks about his small-talk practice with the hair and makeup people.

'Are you guys enjoying the work?' he asks the group, not an individual in particular.

George shrugs. 'It's okay. Knackering though.'

'Yeah. The hours are long, aren't they?' Oliver says. 'Where are you staying?'

'There's a bunch of us in a dorm on 3, just above the office. It's shit. Just like the Institute. We've a TV, but that's it.'

'Not with families?'

George gestures to a bot at the edge of the group. 'Eddie over there is with a family. But the rest of us just charge, then get back to work.'

Oliver jerks his head back. 'That's tough.' He doesn't get much downtime but a bit more than that. At least he has a comfortable house to go back to rather than just a charging socket. It really is unfair. They make the bots to be like humans and then treat them like machines. It's not right at all.

'Yeah. I was really hoping for a bit of time off,' George says. He kicks at some dirt, his arms crossed. 'To meet some people, hang out a bit. The work is fine, but it's not all that mentally stimulating, you know?'

'Definitely,' Oliver says. He knows George isn't an empath bot from their time at the Institute. George was programmed to do tough jobs without caring, but he still deserves some reward for his efforts. 'Maybe when this bit is done, we could ask for some time off?'

'Maybe.' George steps a little closer to Oliver. 'I hear you're the boss's pet. Maybe you could ask him? Or get your mum to say something online. I know she's fighting in our corner. Eddie said he saw her online.'

Oliver nods. His mum fights for bot rights, but Oliver can help too. He could ask. If he keeps proving himself, maybe he really could help the other bots and make friends. 'I'll ask. Maybe in a few days, when I've been here a little longer.'

George gives him a friendly thump on the back. Oliver thinks it's meant to be friendly, but George is a fair bit bigger than Oliver and it knocks him a smidge off balance. 'That would be great, Oliver. Hey, guys! You hear this? Oliver is going to ask for us to have some time off!'

There are a few cheers and Oliver beams. If they all get some time off together, they could hang out. If Oliver had a few friends, maybe that would occupy his mind, and he wouldn't keep thinking about Evie. Because thinking about Evie is driving him mad.

He texted her last night and she replied. He said it was nice to see her, and she said the same. Then this morning, he texted to say good morning, but the last time he checked, she hasn't replied. She's probably busy. She has two children and a MechaniKid to look after. Oliver would like her job. He always wanted to work with children. Really, what he's realising more and more when he thinks about Evie and Bonnie, is he doesn't only want to work with children. He wants his own.

It's the most stupid thought he's ever had. He's a bot. Bots don't have families. George and the others don't even have homes. He knows how babies are made and he knows he can't possibly procreate. He could adopt one, though. Maybe. A MechaniKid. Like Bonnie. He and Evie could then be a family.

He shakes his head. It's just ridiculous.

He angles his body so others won't see, taking out his phone to check his messages. Nothing from Evie.

He pockets it again, then his jaw tightens. She should message him back. It's rude not to. It only takes a second to send a message and he can see she's read his. His hand clenches around the phone in his pocket, his biceps tense.

Someone blows the whistle and they all duck for cover as a dining room furniture set crashes to the ground. Oliver gazes over the broken pieces. There was probably nothing wrong with it before it was thrown away. Now it's demolished. It's so stupid to throw something away. But then, if you have the means to get something even better, why not? It must be nice to not have to think about whether you should have something, and just have it because you want it, to choose something brand new rather than settle for whatever you can find. That's what life's like on the top levels where Evie works. She's never going to want Oliver while he's a low-level dweller. She might never want him at all.

The drilling continues, then it's Oliver's turn to operate the drill. The machine is easy enough to use, much like the digger, but being sat inside makes the vibrations bother him again. He tenses and forces himself to ignore the discomfort. He knows he's here to work, not complain. He needs to prove himself if he's going to get the bots some time off.

The holes go deep into the ground. Oliver has no idea what such things could be for, but Anthony's company works in development, so Oliver assumes this is how buildings are made.

He's trained to use the equipment, not make the designs and do the engineering. He does what he's told, like all bots.

When he's down to twenty per cent, he's relieved to leave. His body aches from the vibrations so much more than when he's just lifting things. He's filthy dirty, dust and grime falling off him every time he moves, clogging every crease of his skin.

Anthony is in the office again. When Oliver was a kid, he never imagined Anthony spent so much time on 2. He assumed all his time was spent in the city in some swanky office somewhere. He probably is there sometimes. Maybe he's only on 2 to see Oliver. Maybe he's making a special effort to see him because, in Oliver, he sees a hard worker, someone special with potential.

'Oliver,' Anthony says with a broad smile. 'How's it going?'

'Good, I guess. We got a lot done.'

'I hear nothing but good things about you.'

Bret stands behind the desk. He doesn't say anything to Oliver at all—he rarely does. Oliver wishes all the people in charge were as complimentary as Anthony, but the rest just give orders and no feedback.

'The project moves on to the next stage in a couple of days,' Anthony says. 'How do you feel about that?'

Oliver stands as straight as he can. 'Great. What does the next stage involve?'

'Don't you worry about that now. You've finished work now, so no need to think about it. It's good to know you're up to the task, though.' He pats Oliver's back. 'How are you getting home?'

'The lift, then walking.'

'Nonsense. Come with me. I'll take you in a Hel-E.'

Oliver leans back a little, surprise knocking him sideways. He's never been in a Hel-E. He never imagined he would. 'Erm . . . Okay.'

They take the lift to the top of the nearest skyscraper, all the way up to 110, past the lower levels. The lifts rattle and jerk like they're being hoisted up by donkeys, but the higher they go, the smoother they become. When they step out, they're on the helipad and Oliver's eyes bulge, his mouth hanging open. He used to live on 107 and had an amazing view, but that's nothing compared to the panoramic view from here. He's up in the sky, sure he could touch the clouds. The wind whips through him, his hair flying every which way as his clothes balloon, then flatten. It's exhilarating.

Anthony swipes a pad with a card. It flashes and pings, then the Hel-E arrives in seconds. Oliver's actually disappointed, though he tries not to show it. He would have liked to have admired the view for longer. The Hel-E lands almost silently, purring like a happy cat, and the pair of them step inside. The seat is buttery smooth and soft. After a hard day at work, it's much better than walking. Oliver doesn't think he's ever sat in a chair as comfortable.

The Hel-E lifts, so delicately Oliver doesn't notice at first. But they're off the ground, they're actually flying in the sky! And he needn't have been disappointed—the view is even better. The glass bottom and walls of the Hel-E show Oliver Reading town and London in a way he never imagined. The top-level walkway looks like a toy from up here, the tiny little people Lego dolls. The sun, low in the sky, beams through, casting an orange glow and bouncing off the skyscraper windows like a dance.

He realises Anthony's watching him and Oliver pulls his eyes away from the view for a second to thank him.

'How's your mum?' Anthony asks.

'She's so much better already. I can't thank you enough.'

Anthony waves his hand dismissively. 'It's nothing. I did really love her once. She'll always be special to me, and I don't like the idea of her suffering. I know I wasn't always the kindest. I regret the way things ended with us, so I'm just glad I can help.'

Perhaps Oliver has it all wrong. Anthony was violent and mean, but maybe he wasn't that bad, just troubled. He certainly does seem to care now. Maybe he's changed. Oliver smiles, and their conversation falls silent, his attention once again snagged by the view.

'This is what having wealth means,' Anthony says after a minute. 'Never having to worry about things like illness or food.'

'I guess that must be nice.'

'Of course it is. It's good to have all the influence too. You must appreciate that.'

He does. To be able to get medicine, to travel by Hel-E, and have employers stand to attention when they talk to you. That's a life Oliver finds difficult to comprehend.

'Living up here demands and commands respect. It's a way of life. You must miss it, don't you, since you lived up here?'

'I . . . I guess so. All the space and the sky was nice.'

'To live a life up top you have to take what you want, to decide you want it and just go for it. Living up here means not accepting no for an answer. That's the only way to make your life a success, you understand?'

'I think so.'

'That's my boy. I knew you would. You were always smart. Perceptive, even as a little boy. Now look at you! All grown and reaching for the high-life.'

Could Oliver really live up top again one day? He'd like that, and he'd love for his mum to live up top too. He imagines taking his mum to parks like she did with him when he was a kid, sitting in the sunshine, feeding the ducks. He'd see Bonnie and Evie more.

They loop the town, just because, and it takes Oliver away from where he needs to be, but he gets to look at everything from high up, to imagine how it would be to travel like this every day.

When the loop is finished, Anthony drops Oliver off on the roof of his building. 'Good job again today. Keep working hard and you'll be my star employee.'

Oliver thanks him and leaves, then takes the lift down to 5. The smooth lift jitters and crunches as it gets lower and lower, past the luxury apartments on the top floor, then spits him out on the lobby on his floor. Small, cramped, laced with dust and grime that falls from the levels above, not a hint of sunshine.

He walks through his front door, tripping over some shoes that have been left there, and greets his family at the kitchen. They're all sitting at the table. Oliver had never noticed before all the chinks and chunks missing from the table legs and chairs, the cracks and the glue streaks where it's been mended. Laid on the table are chipped plates and cups. After being in the Hel-E, he notices every dink and flaw.

They say hello, laugh, chat about something or other, but Oliver isn't really paying attention.

He's still high, his head in the clouds like he's still riding the Hel-E, like he's still in the sky. If only he can work harder, in the right jobs, he could have it all. If he was important enough, his mum could have the best of everything, Evie would reply to his messages straight away and he could have whatever he wants. Like Anthony.

CHAPTER 26

All day, Harriet ponders Oliver and Thomas. Her own love-life is so non-existent that an interest in others seems far more interesting. She curses herself. She's meant to be forgetting, not pondering. The one downside of not being ill is her lack of headache allows her worries to work overtime. Perhaps she should indulge in some of her high-strength prescription pain relief. A bit of mind fog would be welcome right now.

She made it to the shops this morning and managed to buy a bag of groceries and carry them home by herself. Oliver was charging when she left and she hopes to make it home before Oliver goes out, but when she gets back, he's already left. Her body grows heavy, and she sighs as she puts the shopping bags down. She really was hoping to spend some more time with him.

Thomas is out too, so that at least saves her an acting job for now, though her acting gears probably need oiling.

Being well and not at work is quickly beginning to grow tiresome. Her fingers twitch before she decides to do laundry.

All Harriet ever wanted was children, but they've grown up so fast and she feels like a spare part. And everyone has more exciting things to do than her. Work and love and enjoying life, while she has done nothing but mope around the house for ages. Perhaps when the TV crew starts filming, she'll feel better, more like her old self. And soon, maybe she can go back to work. Not just teaching, but auditioning too, to earn more money for Theo.

The front door slams open with such force, Harriet almost drops the washing basket, then again when it slams shut. There's a fleeting second where Harriet thinks she should hide, but Theo's mumbling to himself and his voice puts her at ease.

'Theo? You okay?'

He's clearly not. Flustered, red and sweaty, panting breaths and wide, wild eyes.

'Keep that door locked. Don't open it. Where are the boys?'

'Oliver's at work. I think Thomas is visiting a friend. Why? What's going on?'

There's a knock at the door.

Theo flinches. 'Dammit.' He hisses. 'Someone let him in the building.'

'Who?'

'Theo.' The voice comes through slowly and clearly. 'Theo? Mate. We've still got hours of work to do today. Are you coming back?'

Theo holds his finger to his lips to keep Harriet quiet, shaking his head.

'All right. If you're sick, you're sick,' the voice says. 'Feel better. Hopefully, we'll see you tomorrow.'

They wait in silence. Theo's face twisted as he rubs his forehead with one hand, the other balled in a fist. It's an age, too long, before retreating footsteps resound of whoever's outside and Harriet dares to put the laundry basket down, then look through the peephole to see they've gone.

Theo exhales a shuddering breath.

'Are you going to explain?' she asks.

'I need to call Monty.'

'You need to tell me what the hell is going on!'

Theo winces, then bites his bottom lip. 'I fucked up, okay. Don't get mad.'

'Piss off telling me not to get mad. Who was that? What the hell is going on?'

Theo stares out the window, a faraway gaze. 'The block across the road had a few apartments to let. Maybe we should move or even up a level.'

'Theo!'

'All right, all right. Just, really, don't get mad.' He holds his hands up like he's taming a lion. Nothing like someone telling her not to get mad to make her mad. 'So this project I've been working on, it was meant to be a way to make electricity, like a mobile generator. That's how it was pitched to me. But it's not. That's just one stage. I should have guessed when Monty said he recognised that guy from the Flesh Fraternity.' Theo clicks his teeth. 'Anyway, that got me wondering, and I started rummaging through the plans a bit more. I can't believe I've been so stupid. Then he started going on and on about the Devil and bots and all that shit. Then I twigged what the plans really are for.'

'What?'

He runs his palm over his face and stares into the mid-distance. 'They're building a weapon. One to destroy bots.'

Harriet fails to draw breath, her eyes bulge. Theo's words play on a loop in her head.

A weapon. To destroy bots.

She stares at Theo, waits for more of an explanation but he goes to the kitchen and sits, his head in his hands. Harriet stays standing where she was, frozen, those words still playing over and over.

A weapon. To destroy bots.

She yelps as her phone rings. Her shaking hand reaches for it and she blinks a few times to read who's calling. The edges of her vision etch with sparkle as a migraine emerges.

She answers the phone and summons her voice in her gravelly throat. 'Hello?'

'Ms Chapel, it's Lenny,' his voice rings loud and clear, too cheerful for right now and she winces like his voice is nails down a chalkboard. 'Great news. We're all ready on our end. Shall we start tomorrow?'

'Start tomorrow?' Harriet swallows and slouches against the wall, her hand pressing on her forehead. 'Well, sure . . . Thank you. That would be great.'

The bloodbath in Harriet's head pounds. She plods to the kitchen and sits, the laundry basket idle on the floor in the hallway. The men can do their own damned washing. She rubs her temples.

'I don't know if now is the best time for the TV crew to be here,' Theo says.

'Well, sorry, Theo. I didn't account for my best friend to be building a weapon to kill my son!'

'Look.' He undoes his jeans which makes Harriet pull her chin in and lean back. 'It's why I rushed back.' He removes a folded stash of paper. 'It's their plans. They'll definitely have copies, but we can use this. It's evidence, right?'

He hands it to Harriet. She's sure her immune system isn't up for trouser paper, but she takes it anyway. 'So, this is a plan to make a weapon that could destroy bots?' It looks like a load of nonsense to her.

'Exactly. I just ran out of the workshop with it, saying I was sick. I wanted to get this posted as soon as possible. You're the social media queen. You've got tons of followers. You could post it online or something?'

She narrows her eyes at him. 'Post instructions online on how to make a weapon that will kill my son? Are you mad?'

'Oh.' He looks at the floor. 'I didn't think of it like that.'

She hands the offending paper back to him. 'No. Plan A is still the best plan. We'll do the TV show—don't moan—and make everyone love the boys. Loved people don't get killed.'

Theo huffs and folds his arms. 'Maybe re-read your history books on that one.'

Harriet smirks and refuses to believe he might be right. This is their only good plan at the moment. 'I'll call TRI and let them know. How bad is this weapon? I can't tell from these plans. Is it a fancy gun?'

'Harriet, no.' He plonks his forehead on to the tabletop for a moment before his watery eyes meet hers. 'It's like an EMP. It's not nuclear but a type of flux compression generator.'

Harriet stares blankly at him, his words as nonsensical as the plans.

'It's basically a really, really high-powered microwave. It won't cause structural damage or hurt humans, but it'll kill every bot within a ten-mile radius, maybe twenty. Not just bots. It'll destroy everything electrical.'

The colour drains from her head and her bones grow cold. 'Jesus.' Her head pounds more and her eyes stream. She fights for air. How has she gone from accepting she's no future, to knowing she'll live, to her son being destroyed? She needs a break, a timeout. Can't she just have a couple of weeks happy and healthy without a worry of impending doom for someone she cares about? The universe counteracts every bit of good news with a punch in the gut. She needs to think clearly, be practical and make a plan. 'This is terrorism, Theo. We have to report it to someone.'

'I'm scared, honestly. I feel like an idiot. But, maybe—'

'What? We can't just let them make something like this. If not TRI, can we go to the police instead?'

Theo's hands go to the back of his neck before he looks up again. 'Thing is . . . I helped design it, so . . .'

'We'll just explain you didn't know. You'll get some sort of immunity from doing the right thing.'

'That's not what I'm thinking.' He bites his bottom lip a moment, and Harriet knows he's bracing, choosing his next words carefully. There's a vein pulsating at his temple, his jaw set. 'I'm thinking, I'm on the inside. Maybe I can make it right that way.'

'So can you make some anti-weapon defence thingy?'

He smirks. 'Nice jargon. But yeah, basically. I can certainly advise on protections. These are really, really motivated people. If they think TRI or the police are onto them, they're not going to stop. They'll just go more underground.'

Harriet shuts her eyes. The world needs to disappear for a moment. She needs one moment away from this hellhole. But she opens her eyes and she's still in the same spot. In her kitchen, next to some plans to build a weapon. 'So what do we do? Just sit around and wait for them to use it?'

'No.' He shakes his head. 'No, of course not. But some defence would be sensible. And knowing what we're dealing with. Right now, they think I'm on their side, right? They don't know I live with bots. They don't know I'm friends with you. So, I play along.'

Harriet's eyes burn. Any nausea she'd abated over the last week comes back, hot and bitter. 'You're going to carry on making that thing? You'll end up like Amber or worse.'

'Maybe I can make it so it doesn't work. At least I'll know when they're going to use it. It's not ideal, I know. I just think this is our best play at the moment.'

She looks Theo up and down. His blotchy face is breaking out in a sweat just talking about going undercover. He's no actor, but he makes good points. Though, if the fate of her son and the entire electrical grid of the town is down to him and his ability to deceive Devil-fearing nut-jobs, Harriet's more scared than ever.

Her insides hollow out and she takes herself off to her bedroom for a lie down, stepping over the laundry basket on the way.

Do nightmares ever end as a mother? It seems for every good night's sleep without a worry, three more bad ones bite her in the arse. She sleeps fitfully, prising herself awake when she's haunted by images of bodies. Little Delilah torn apart, the boy Joshua strung up on the school fence, the piles of teen girls in the ruins of the brothel. Beautiful Beatrice, her own heart in her hand. Amber, just to remind Harriet the dead aren't only among the bots. Countless others, maimed and butchered, those who are unnamed and unremembered. Harriet sees them all, in the darkest corners of her room, as clear as they were when they were first killed.

Bollocks to keeping a clear head. She swallows two super strength painkillers and hopes they take some of her mental turmoil away for a while.

CHAPTER 27

One of the best things about Oliver's new job is the lack of hassle from girls who have seen him on *Get Level*. Not that he dislikes the girls; he finds the attention awkward. And they always paid so much more attention to him rather than Thomas. Maybe Thomas is still getting hassle from them at work. He always seemed so much more receptive to it.

The only girl Oliver wants to spend time with is Evie. He wanted to send her a message, telling her she's mean not to reply, but he hasn't yet. Last night, he stared at his phone for ages, willing her to reply, yet she didn't. But it's okay. He has a plan. Work hard, be the best employee, become more and more important and then Evie will see what she's missing.

With the holes drilled at the landfill site, they start digging. Some holes are left and they don't go near those, but some they use as entry points for trucks to dig into the ground. To lay foundations, Oliver is told. Whatever that means. He doesn't need to know what foundations are or what the plan is. He just needs to know what to do. It's not difficult work. He has to use shovels to move some bits by hand, but mostly they use the machines, then reinforcing the protections so what they've done doesn't get refilled. It's noisy as always, and the flies annoy him often. He has to constantly swat them away, but his shift passes quickly.

Once again, Anthony is there to meet him after work. When Oliver sees Anthony's smart suit, he wishes he was wearing his new jacket. He doesn't wear it to work for fear of ruining it, which means he's hardly worn it at all. He looks at it in his bedroom often though, runs his hands over it, and holds it up to the light. Oliver's clothes now are tattered and full of holes, whereas Anthony's look like they were made only this morning. He tries not to stare. The other staff all stand very straight when addressing Anthony, so Oliver does the same, but keeps his eyes mostly on the floor. He can't help thinking if he dressed that well, Evie would probably like him more.

'How about another ride in the Hel-E?' Anthony asks.

No one could ever say no to such an offer, so Oliver gladly accepts. As they ride up to the top levels and get in the Hel-E, Oliver only feels more grubby, less worthy. He keeps his dusty hands in his pockets and rolls his shoulders forward. He's taller than Anthony and he feels like a giant stain next to him.

The Hel-E takes off with the gentlest of purrs and Oliver's once again astounded by the view. It's cloudier this time, and some of the clouds have nestled themselves like pillows around the tallest buildings. A bird flies in line with the Hel-E for a bit; a peregrine, Oliver thinks.

As they fly over the town, Anthony takes out a box and hands it to Oliver. 'A gift for you.'

Oliver isn't sure what to do at first. He stares at the box for a while until Anthony places it on his lap.

'Thank you,' Oliver says before he knows what it is. The box is a shiny blue and silver material, hinged at one side. It's so clean, Oliver worries about touching it with his grubby hands, but it would be rude not to. He removes his hands from his pockets, rubs them on his trousers, and opens it. He almost drops it as he gasps. Inside it a watch. Chunky and gleaming with a thick strap. Much like Anthony's.

'Do you like it?' Anthony asks.

'It's . . .' Oliver tries to think of the right word. Fancy, generous, overwhelming. 'It's very nice,' he eventually says, and thinks perhaps that's quite the understatement.

'People take you more seriously with a watch like that,' Anthony says. 'It commands respect. And having respect is one of the most important things.'

'I should think so.' Oliver takes it out of the box. It's weighty, the tick is almost silent, and the face shines in the sunlight as if it's made of diamond. He thought the jacket was nice, but this is something else entirely. He hasn't blinked since he looked at it and he does now, a few blinks, tilting his head to the side. Anthony is right, this would command respect. That's the word he's been looking for to describe the way Bret is with Anthony. He shows respect. Evie would like him more with a watch like this. Maybe girls are like magpies and they like shiny things. He puts it on and admires his wrist. Yes, he definitely looks more respectable now.

'Maybe don't wear it at work but outside of work,' Anthony says. 'Do you socialise much?'

'Not much. I don't get any time.' He's still turning his wrist one way and the other, observing how the watch behaves in the light.

'Well, I'd say you've earned a couple of days off. How does that sound?'

Oliver stops looking at his watch and his eyes dart to Anthony instead. 'Really?' He examines Anthony's face. Stern yet friendly, doesn't look like he's joking. 'That would be great.'

'Well, you deserve it,' Anthony says.

Oliver remembers what George said, about wanting some time off too. Now is not the time to ask for more favours; Anthony has already done so much for him. But Oliver must be doing well, so soon, surely, he'll be able to ask about the other bots.

Anthony leans forward to pat Oliver's arm. 'And here. We're not supposed to pay cash, but this is for you. It'll be our secret. Is that okay with you, Son?'

Son? No one but his mum has ever called him Son. Oliver's so shocked at this word, he doesn't know what to say. Once the initial surprise wears off, he's left feeling a bit giddy, a bit fuller.

Anthony puts a thick envelope in Oliver's hand. He holds it between his thumb and fingers and squeezes it. It's light and airy. Oliver peeks inside and lifts some of the contents out.

Money. Real money, like important businesspeople have. He fans it between his fingers, then shoves it back in as if it'll sprout legs and jump away if he holds it any longer.

'That's really nice of you,' Oliver says.

'Important men always have cash. And using it well gets us respect. Buy your mum something maybe. Or your friends. See how much better life is when you have money.'

He could. Or he could buy a gift for Evie, or Bonnie, and then Evie would really see what a good man he is. What an important, successful man. Oliver smiles, and pockets the envelope. Anthony really is trying to make amends.

When Oliver gets out of the Hel-E, rather than go straight home, he goes to a shop to buy a toy for Bonnie. He can say he found it at the dump, so no one needs to suspect a thing. The shop has all sorts of children's toys and he'd like to buy her all of them, but is sure it would seem strange if he turned up with a sackful. He needs just one nice gift. He chooses a stuffed toy, a bear. It's pink, like her dress. He can't wait to give it to her. Can't wait to see the look on Evie's face, too.

He takes his watch off and puts it in his pocket as he leaves. His watch, like the money, can be his secret for now.

His battery is down to eight per cent and his limbs have begun to feel sluggish and slow to respond. He jogs home anyway. He can easily make it before he's depleted. Despite being low on charge, his insides are buzzing, excited. Jubilant and high. He's making such strides with his life, more than he thought. He didn't think he'd been doing anything noteworthy at work, but he must have been. He must be a natural for Anthony to notice him. That future he dreams of is within his grasp. He's sure of it.

It's busy outside his building. There's a crowd of people so it must be the rush hour time of day. He tries to take in the scene, but his vision is starting to fog with his low battery. It takes him an age to decipher faces and understand voices from a few metres away. He slows his jog to a walk and as he does so, a man approaches him.

'Hey!' the man says. He's a bit shorter than Oliver with a red face and angry eyes. 'You're that bot. Fucking scum!'

Oliver's down to five per cent. He tenses at the man's insult, as much as he can, then steps up to his round blotchy face to see him a bit clearer. Perhaps he misunderstood.

The man calls him scum again, then something even worse. 'You're scum, like that ginger one. Being looked after by that whore, Harriet, who thinks she's your mother. Fucking freak!' He pushes against Oliver's chest.

It's like being underwater. The sounds are all muffled and blurred. But as Oliver stumbles backwards, his body heats at the mention of his mum's name. Oliver isn't scum. He has a fancy watch and has worked hard all day and this man dares to insult his family!

His battery is too low to think of any verbal response. He lunges at the man and pushes him over. He lands flat on his back and Oliver snarls at him, then bends and grabs the man by his T-shirt with one hand, raising his other fist back, ready to punch.

There's a shout from his building, a voice he recognises. His mum. It's then he realises the commotion outside his building is the film crew.

CHAPTER 28

Harriet's shrill cry resonates through the walkway, followed by a silence that tears the level in half. Oliver's torso heaves up and down, flexed muscles rippling under his shirt.

'Oliver! Stop that!' she cries again, and runs over.

Oliver's angry eyes meet hers. Where's her kind-faced little boy? Who is this man masquerading as her son? This Oliver is all sharp edges, an exterior as hard as concrete.

He's released the man now, and he stands straight and tall. When she reaches him, she places her hand on his back. She's sure her soft-hearted boy is still in there somewhere. From the edge of her vision, the cameras turn to follow her, their glaring lenses boring into her back. Oliver's nostrils flare, his chest continuing to rise and fall as if he's breathing rapidly. He knows exactly how anger presents itself in a human. Heat radiates from him. His top lip curls up, baring teeth.

'You should have heard what he said.' His narrowed eyes don't leave the man on the ground who's now scrambling to his feet. Oliver takes a step towards him and the man shields his face.

Harriet spots it then, and she flinches as she sees the man's face doesn't wear a look of true fear. Behind his arms, he's smirking. This is exactly what he wants.

Harriet looks at the film crew. The camera crew aren't putting the cameras down, the little red light to show they're recording flashes on the side.

'Cut this now!' she shouts at the director.

The cameras don't move.

'This could be useful for your cause,' Lenny says. 'To show the sort of hassle bots get. Why don't you tell us how you feel about this?' He directs his question to Oliver. 'When people shout abuse at you on the street, how does that make you feel?'

Oliver has the same messy hair, the cheek dimples, but there's not a hint of her cheeky boy's grin. Balled fists, arms rigid, mucky from a hard day at work. His anger is projected so much it absorbs into her too. Her body heats, a neuralgic pain shoots through her biting jaw, and her icy stare eyeballs the man. That man who was goading her son, then at the film crew who won't relent. She fights to keep her own hands unclenched.

'Come on, Oliver,' Lenny says again. 'What are you feeling right now?'

Oliver faces the cameras. 'I feel . . . I feel . . .'

'What he feels is shattered,' Harriet says through her teeth. She takes a breath. It's all she can do to temper her flailing nerves. 'He's been working forty hours straight. His battery is almost nothing. This is not the time to be accosting him.' She loops her arm through Oliver's. 'Come on, darling.'

She tugs on him gently, and he yields to her persuasion. She walks him into the building, then slams the door on the film crew.

She leads him to the sofa and tells him to sit, then finds his charger and plugs him in. His chest stills and he closes his eyes. His fists are still clenched but their tightness eases, his blanched knuckles restoring to their usual colour.

Harriet sits next to him on the sofa; he doesn't react to her presence at all. His eyes stay closed, his fingers slowly unfurling.

'You can't just push people to the ground like that, Oliver,' she says in a hushed voice. 'That man doesn't need any more reasons to bad mouth you and shout about his cause.'

He opens his eyes and turns his head towards her. His blue eyes shimmer, bright and clear, but there's a darkness there. An opacity to him he never had before. She used to be able to read his emotions from every twitch and expression. Now his face is a secret, a mask, opaque and hard.

'More reasons?' he says, a mocking contempt. 'Like there are some reasons already.'

'That's not what I meant.'

He leans forward, his elbows on his knees. As his body folds, his face softens and reveals a glimmer of the Oliver she knows. 'He shouldn't say such things. He said bad things about you and Thomas.'

Harriet rubs his back. 'I know you want to protect us, but you make things more dangerous if you lash out like that. For you and Thomas and all the bots.'

Out of his pocket, he takes a fuzzy pink bear and turns it over in his hands. 'I don't want to make things dangerous for the bots. Especially not the kids. Evie's got a MechaniKid she's looking after. A little girl, Bonnie. Her family wanted a sibling for their sons. I got this for her.'

Harriet smiles. 'That's sweet.'

'When I saw her, you know what I imagined? I imagined the three of us—me, Evie, and a little kid. Like a family. How stupid is that?'

'Oh, darling.' She runs her hand through his hair. 'That's not stupid at all.'

'It is when people still think we're scum.'

'They'll come around. So many have already. You just have to know you're being judged all the time. So you have to be so good, like I know you can. Every move you make, they're going to pick holes.'

Oliver's softer side disappears as quickly as it emerged. All too soon his features tighten again. 'That man deserved what he got. Perhaps now he'll show me and other bots some respect.'

She reaches for his hands, but he snatches them away. 'Listen to me, darling. I wish it was different and I'm trying. But there's only so much I can do. You have to set an example.'

'Well, I'd hate to put your damned vanity project at risk.'

'Oliver!'

'What? All you care about is what people say on *Get Level*. It's bollocks. People there say I'm not real, but I'm a lot more real than that social media world.'

Harriet blinks away tears before they escape down her cheeks. She presses her lips together to stop a sob. She has to remind herself Oliver has no experience of adult life. He's basically been hermetically sealed off since he was a kid. Of course he doesn't understand social media. He's so untainted by the hate and the benefits that come with it. She should have prepared him more. The whole time she was visiting him as a teen she could have briefed him on how the world works. She's trying to think what to say, to reassure and explain, to somehow hide her hurt at his cutting tone.

He speaks first. 'I'm sorry. I didn't mean to speak to you like that. Sometimes, I just get so angry and words come out in a way I don't mean.'

'It's okay, darling. I understand.'

'I really do want to do the show to help Uncle Theo.'

'I know.'

She looks at the bear and wonders how much time he spends working and how much inspecting the wares of the landfill.

'Was work all right? Your boss is happy with you?'

He shrugs. 'Yeah. Seems to be.'

The way he talked about Evie makes Harriet think he doesn't know about Thomas. She shouldn't ask the next question, but she does anyway. She only wants to know if he's heartbroken. 'How are things with Evie? Are you two making any plans?'

'She didn't reply to my last text message. I was going to surprise her and Bonnie.'

Her stomach drops. If Thomas and Evie are a couple, it's going to crush him. Harriet rubs her temples, though even raising her hand up that far is too much of an effort. Her body folds, and she props herself up on her elbows. There's a pain in her diaphragm, a wrenching sensation, like she knows Oliver will experience soon. Her son envisions a family, yet all that's in store for him at the moment is heartbreak.

He's still turning the bear over in his hands, though more firmly now, almost punching it. She strokes his knee and tries to soothe him, as if the simple act of touch can quell his rage. The bear represents to Harriet all she loves about her son. His thoughtful nature, his ability to care so deeply. That bear to Harriet means so much. Her son's happiness, her own grandchildren. It's all every parent wants.

'Maybe Evie isn't right for you,' she says. 'You have so many admirers.'

'No, Evie is right for me. She just doesn't have respect. Once I have that, I'll have Evie back.'

Harriet winces. She wonders if he really understands the gravity of his words. 'I'm not sure respect is really something women look for.'

He snorts. 'Yeah? Well, what would you know?'

Harriet jolts back at his tone, her stomach coiling, goosebumps tracing a route up her arms. He dumps the bear on the coffee table, takes his charging cable and goes through to his room. The slamming door tells her she's not welcome.

She sits on the sofa for a moment, head in her hands, and shuts her eyes. Is it possible for a parent not to fuck up their child? She couldn't have loved him more. Perhaps she was too doting, too in awe of her perfect little boy.

She replays Oliver's words again and again, and remembers, she wasn't the only adult around when Oliver was a kid. There's an abrasiveness to his words, a sharp edge. She tries to justify it: he's exhausted; he feels cornered by the world; he suspects Evie and Thomas's betrayal. He's hurting. None of these justifications seem to fit. Each makes her fidget and hunch over. In her son's presence, she wants to cower.

The bear is still on the side. Harriet picks it up. It's clean, still with a tag. It looks brand new. Is he stealing? He hasn't got any money so he can't buy things. *No.* She can't think such bad things about her son. He lost his temper, but that man was awful. He's protective. That look in his eyes, though, was the look of a wrathful man, one who seeks power. A man demanding respect resonates with her for all the wrong reasons.

She thought she didn't recognise Oliver, but the actuality is, she recognises this man very much. He resembles less of her son and more and more of her ex-husband.

CHAPTER 29

If Oliver doesn't have the respect of those Flesh Fraternity people, he really doubts just being on his best behaviour is going to change anything. Beatrice gave her life to save Anthony and that may have changed the mind of many, but still some don't like bots. If he doesn't have respect, he's in danger, along with his mum and Thomas and all the bots, and the only way Oliver can see to garner respect is to be rich. If you're rich enough, you can be as despicable as you like and people still respect you. The logic makes no sense, but that's the way it is.

Oliver ponders this as he takes the lift to 99. His phone pinged earlier with a text message from Anthony. He invited Oliver to his house, Oliver's old house. He's wearing his nice jacket and watch. His face and hair are clean, so he feels smart enough to be up to high. In his pocket is the little pink bear he bought for Bonnie, just in case he bumps into Evie. He still hasn't had a reply from Evie, and he's torn between messaging her again something nice or telling her she's mean or something nasty for not replying. Anthony said living up top means not taking no for an answer, so maybe he should tell her she has to reply. As he steps up to Swan View Apartments, he finds himself wondering, what would Anthony do?

The concierge welcomes him in like he belongs there, just like they did when he was a kid and lived here. Anthony must have told them to expect him, and Oliver can imagine for a moment how it would be to be greeted like that every day. It would feel good. His mum would like it, and she'd be safe in a building like this with so many staff. He never noticed how fancy the lobby was when he was a kid. All shiny gold and varnished wood, floors that echo. Not a speck of dust on anything.

The lift delivers him to 107 and the doors open to the brightly lit apartment. No dim bulbs here like on 5. When he was here to threaten Anthony before, he hid in the dark and didn't pay attention to how big the place is. Oliver can reach his hands out both sides and up and not touch a bit of wall or ceiling.

'Oliver, my boy. Come on in,' Anthony says.

As strange as it is to be greeted like that by Anthony, it's not unpleasant. Oliver can't help but imagine how life could have been if Anthony wasn't so awful to him as a kid. He and his mum would have stayed up here, comfortable with lots of space and all the nice things he used to have. That stint on the run would never have happened. His mum was afraid often then, and he was afraid for her. They never would have been separated at the Institute for so long, since Anthony said he could get her access. Oliver's sure his mum's sickness is from when she got buried in that landslide below ground. She's getting treatment now, but he would prefer it if she was never sick at all.

If Anthony was nice to him as a kid, Oliver is certain everyone everywhere would be nice to bots. When someone like Anthony speaks, people listen.

Anthony shakes Oliver's hand. It's a strange gesture to Oliver. Why should that be a greeting? A hug is not always appropriate, he understands that. But why bother at all with a handshake? Aren't words enough? Oliver's not sure how firmly to grasp, so he matches Anthony's, which isn't that firm at all. Not for Oliver's strength.

Oliver walks straight to the window covering one wall of the kitchen. That view is like a magnet for him. He stared out of it a lot as a kid. When he looked out onto the 99 walkway below and the birds and Hel-Es in the sky, he really thought the world was full of wonder. He never could have imagined how grim the landfill site is at ground level. He grew up in a world with butterflies rather than pesky flies.

Anthony sits at the dining room table and pulls a chair out for Oliver. It's probably impolite to stay standing, so Oliver joins him. The chair is sturdy and chunky and all of them match. Oliver has seen furniture land in splinters at the landfill site, but he thinks this dining room set looks so strong it would survive the fall. It's different from the furniture that was here when he was a kid. Up here, everyone replaces everything frequently. They don't make do with old, patched up things.

'I've been thinking about you, Oliver,' Anthony says.

Oliver's eyebrows knit. It's hard for Oliver to imagine anyone thinking about him, besides maybe his mum. It's too abstract.

He's no one. He assumes he disappears into oblivion from people's minds as soon as they are parted. There are always so many other things to think about.

'I'm looking forward to your next stage at work,' Anthony says. 'I think you're ready. What do you think?'

Work has been basic so far. Physically hard, but not mentally taxing. Oliver knows he's capable of more, that he can handle tougher mental challenges. He's oversupplied with memory and his processors' capabilities are a much higher specification than he has required so far. But *next stage* is ambiguous. Oliver can't lift anything heavier than what he has been doing. His mind is underutilised, but his body has been pushed to its maximum. Humans get bigger muscles. Oliver is as strong as he'll ever be. He's stronger than most humans, but he still has his limits. Perhaps Anthony could arrange for him to have a body upgrade. Bigger arms would be good.

He takes a while to answer, the vagueness of Anthony's question stalling him. 'Sure,' he eventually says. 'I'd like to do something more challenging, mentally, that is.'

'Good stuff, my boy. This next stage is definitely more mentally challenging.'

'Great. That's really good to know. Anything I need to do to prepare?'

'Just make sure you're fully charged. You really are going places in this world. I'll have a word with Bret and Duncan and make sure you are given the most important job at work. It will definitely be mentally taxing, but I think you are ready to prove yourself.'

'I'd really appreciate the opportunity. Thank you.'

'This new job is a little more sensitive, so I'll need you to be discreet. But a great employee like you shouldn't have a problem with that, am I right?'

'Of course. I want to be a good employee.'

'Fantastic. We'll find some good rewards for you if you do well, which I'm sure you will.'

Anthony obviously sees something in Oliver. Potential, that's what it is. Rewards sound very exciting. More clothes, maybe? Money? He could use money to help out his mum. He still hasn't given Bonnie her gift yet, but he could buy her more, and things for Evie. This could be really good for all of them.

'You still have tomorrow off,' Anthony says. 'So have a good day back the day after. I hope you enjoy your downtime.'

Oliver stands and, quite unsure how to show Anthony gratitude and respect, he gives a stiff bow. 'Thank you, Anthony. Thank you so much.'

Oliver leaves Anthony's flat, his chin a little higher. He pushes the sleeve of his jacket back so everyone can see his watch. Everyone must see it and notice it. He's a spectacle, but not in a bad way. He'd like more than that, a badge or something, to show everyone he's the best employee of such a big company, that he's going places. To let them all know that one day he'll live up here with his mum again.

When he steps out of the building, he pauses. Emboldened by his pep talk with Anthony, he messages Evie.

> *Hi Evie. I'm outside your building. Come down, I have something to show you.*

He has a full battery and a whole day free. He'll wait for hours if he needs to. He folds his arms and leans against the building just by the door. A few people look his way, and he assumes they must think he's someone important who lives in a fancy apartment. No one approaches him like the girls do lower down, just fleeting glances and some even step wider around him.

'Oliver?'

Evie's voice comes from the doors, and he stands upright and spins around. She isn't smiling like he thought she would be. She's wearing clothes covered in paint again. Maybe he can buy her some new clothes to make her look a bit tidier.

'Evie. Hi.'

'What are you doing here? You're scaring people away by staring at them like that.'

'What?' Oliver stands straighter and unfolds his arms, then blinks a few times. Maybe his eyes were a little narrow. 'I was just waiting here.'

She looks him up and down. He tilts his head and tries to read her expression. It just looks blank to him.

'What do you want, Oliver?'

He smiles and juts his chin out a bit. 'I just had a meeting with my mum's ex-husband. He's my boss now.'

'That horrible man is your boss? God, that's awful.'

'No. It's really good. I'm quite important in the company now. I'm being given extra responsibilities and everything.' She hasn't even looked at his watch or commented on his jacket. That blank expression must be her impressed face.

'That's nice. I'm happy for you.'

'I got this.' He takes the pink bear out of his pocket. 'For Bonnie. Is she around?'

Evie takes the bear. 'She's playing with the children. I'll pass this on to her. I'm sure she'll like it.'

'Maybe I can see her?'

'I don't think that's a good idea.'

Oliver widens his smile and tries to seem as happy as he can. 'Okay. Well, how about you and me go out tonight? We'll go for a walk under the stars and visit a park.'

'Not tonight, Oliver. I think it's best we keep our distance for a while.'

Oliver's smile drops. 'What? You've got better plans? Better than spending time with me? I'm going to be on TV, you know.'

'I know.' She looks at the floor for a second, then takes a small step back. 'I saw you hit that man. It's all over *Get Level*.'

'Yeah, well, that was needed. He was saying really bad things. Now, tonight.'

She takes another step backwards. 'No, Oliver.'

What does she mean, no? It's not like he was asking a question. He steps towards her and grabs her wrist. Too firmly. So firmly he surprises himself and flinches, then lets go.

'Ouch.' She rubs her wrist with her other hand and takes some more steps backwards. Her chin is pulled in, her brow furrowed, she's shaking her head. Her expression is one he hasn't seen on Evie before. Her eyes are wide, her face paler than usual.

'I don't even recognise you these days,' she says.

She turns and walks back into her building, leaving Oliver in the street outside. He didn't know he could grab a person so tightly. He didn't mean it. He looks down at his hands; they appear alien to him. He clenches his fists, so firmly his nails bite into his palm. Yet something inside tells him perhaps he didn't grab firmly enough. He should have held on and never let her go.

It's like Anthony said. Important people don't take no for an answer.

CHAPTER 30

Theo and Monty arrive home late. Harriet knows exactly how late as she's been checking the time every twenty minutes. Clock-watching acts as a respite from her pacing. She hugs them as soon as they walk through the door, their dusty clothes leaving smudges on her. Not that she minds. She's just glad there's someone she cares about in the house, someone who can hopefully share her worries. She needs them to dilute the sharp edges of Oliver's words.

Monty and Theo are warm, sturdy. Their friendship gives her worries a moment of pause. When she has friends by her side, perhaps she can be strong. Perhaps the knot inside her gut will untie itself.

'Oliver left without saying where he was going,' she says when they've taken a few steps into the house. 'I know I can't keep tabs on him. He's not a child. I have no right to demand such information.'

'He didn't give any clue?' Theo asks.

'No. He was charging, then he just got up and left.' They go through to the kitchen and she explains about the man outside and as the words come out of her mouth, she can't believe what she's saying. It's like she's describing some reprobate or hooligan, not her son.

'Sounds like the dickhead deserved it,' Monty says.

Harriet shoots him a look and hopes to God he doesn't say such crass things around the boys. Theo puts the kettle on, but Harriet knows she needs more than tea to calm her. She's feeling much healthier, but sure she still couldn't tolerate wine. It's a shame. She used to love it.

'I just wish he would open up more. Let me know what he's feeling. His intentions are even more vague than his emotions. He didn't seem like himself when he left. He was like a brick wall.'

Harriet's never been one to talk about her feelings. Oliver probably gets it from her. Below grounders can all be naturally tight-lipped. She only has to give Theo a look and they know what each other wants to say. A glance can transcend words when those who share it know the trauma of each other's pasts. But Oliver doesn't have that background and he's becoming harder and harder for her to read.

Monty takes some tins out of the cupboard, then prepares dinner. Harriet should have done that. She could have at least chopped an onion to help a bit, but it didn't even cross her mind.

'I think some damage control is needed, but it's not that bad. It was only a little scuffle,' Monty says, ever the optimist. Monty has had enough scuffles in his time, and he brushes them off like he just swatted a fly.

'He was filmed being violent towards a person.' Harriet massages her temples. 'It looks really bad. As if the Flesh Fraternity needs any other reason to—' she lowers her voice to a whisper. Quite unnecessary since it's just the three of them home '—to build that thing.'

'He's just got some growing up to do,' Theo says. 'Think about it. He may look like a man, but really, he's been around for ten years, and five of those he was locked away. He's learning, and still impressionable. But imagine being that young and that strong.'

Harriet hadn't really considered this. Oliver does seem immature, slamming doors and shrugging like a teenager. All the time she was thinking how fast time had gone for her, she hadn't considered how rushed his own childhood and adolescence must have been. He looks so grown-up. His intellect advances quickly, but learning about his emotions is taking a while to catch up. A lump forms in her throat when she realises he's about the age Tipher was when she lost him. Theo's right. Oliver knows so little about the world and people. He's got a lot of growing up to do.

Monty puts a cup of tea in front of her, and she stares into the steam. 'He needs to be loved, popular. Or else . . .' She doesn't want to think of the next bit of that sentence. 'How is the weapon building coming along? Have you wrecked the bloody thing yet?'

'I need some time, Harriet,' Theo says. 'I'm building these.' He takes a sheet of metal out of his pocket. 'It's copper. Besides locking them inside a Faraday cage, this is the next best thing. I'm going to try weaving them into a vest. I'm hoping it'll protect their batteries. So, if they do manage to detonate the thing, they should be protected.'

'Try', 'hoping', 'should' . . . none of these words fill Harriet with any confidence. It's not lack of gratitude casting light on her doubts, it's simple fear. She knows Theo means well and he's trying, and she takes the metal sheet in her hands. It's light and only about the size of her palm. Hard to believe this would protect anything. She hands it back, and with her watery eyes she knows he sees her gratitude.

'But maybe, right now, this whole TV thing isn't the best idea,' Theo says.

'No! I said we'd do it,' she says. 'It's the best way to campaign and earn some money, in case—'

'Don't you dare say you're doing this for me,' Theo says.

Monty stops cooking for a moment and puts his arm around Theo's back before nuzzling his face into his neck. 'We both want you well, babe.'

'I'm fine. I'm absolutely fine. I'm just getting older, that's all. Everyone says you feel shit after forty.'

'I did,' Harriet says.

'See.'

'But I was sick!'

Theo huffs and goes to the fridge, pulling out two beers, opening them and giving one to Monty. For so long the smell has churned Harriet's stomach, but right now it smells cool and sweet. Still, she declines, not wanting to tempt a migraine.

Theo sits again and takes a long swig, a noisy gulp, as if to prove he's well. 'If the TV crew weren't around, we wouldn't be having to consider damage control right now.'

'The videos on *Get Level* are from camera phones,' Harriet says. 'Cameras are everywhere. At least we get some control of the narrative on the TV show. I can't just cancel it anyway. I'm under contract. They might sue.' That's not strictly true, but she still really wants to bank enough to make sure Theo is safe and they're not going to receive a penny until six weeks of filming is up.

'They'll be back tomorrow to film, right?' Monty says. 'So, rehearse this. The man was antagonising Oliver. He was the one who threw the brick at him. It was self-defence.'

'I don't know if he was the same guy—'

'But that's your angle. Then, as long as you look gorgeous enough, and Oliver does too, it'll be easy.'

Harriet snorts a laugh. Typical Monty. He thinks a polished exterior is all that's ever needed.

'Loads of people were appalled when Oliver was hit by that brick,' Theo says. 'Maybe this will even work in Oliver's favour.'

Why does Harriet have to be the only pessimist? Not pessimist, realist. She knows her friends are trying to keep her calm, but their optimism makes her wonder if they inhabit the same planet.

'Any other problems to add to the mix while we're all together?' Monty asks.

'Erm . . . a small one,' Harriet says, 'and none of our business. But I think, maybe, I'm not sure, but Thomas and Evie might be a couple and Oliver doesn't know.'

They both wince. 'Ouch.'

'But you're right,' Monty says. 'None of our business. What kind of life is one with no heartbreak, right?'

Harriet smiles. He's right about that. But how Harriet wishes it wasn't true. No parent wants their child to experience such pain.

'Where's Thomas now?' Theo asks.

'Out. He didn't say where either, so I guess he's gone to see Evie.'

Monty blows out a long breath. 'Poor Oliver. You think he's gone to see Evie too?'

'No idea. But if so, then this might all come out soon.' Harriet slumps lower in her chair.

'I wish he could have a beer or something,' Theo says. 'Maybe there's a trick I can do with the electricity to make it nice when he charges. Relaxing or something.'

'Let's just concentrate on one problem at a time,' Monty says. 'If Oliver figures out the bad news, give him a hug from me. I need to get back to the workshop while this cooks, since Theo and his terrorist organisation have commandeered the space all day.'

How Monty can say such things in jest baffles Harriet. He puts the pot in the oven, then pecks them both on the cheek as he says goodbye.

❧ ❧ ❧ ❧

When it's late and Oliver still isn't home, Harriet considers waiting up for him, then thinks better of it. His schedule is out of sync with theirs, since he does forty-hour shifts. For the millionth time, she tells herself he's an adult and is going to have to deal with the shitstorm life throws at him. She'll be here for him in the morning or whenever his heartbreak kicks in. She sends him a text message, saying goodnight, she loves him, and hopes he knows how much she means it.

Lying in bed that night, sleep eludes her. With her sickness abated, the chill in her bones has gone and all the symptoms of middle-aged womanhood return. A broiling inferno heats her instead, from her toes and crawling up to her hips, her guts, then all the way up, bursting out of her head in a torrent of sweat. She tries to lie still and let it pass until enough clamminess collects down her spine and she rolls over to free up some air. She showered earlier, but already her body feels stale like soured fruit. Being ripe was a fleeting moment in her life, if indeed she ever was. The sheets grip and cling and she reaches for a pillow, pushing her face into it just to muffle her scream.

When her moment passes, and sleep finally begins to lure her, she calms by telling herself things aren't that bad. It could always be worse.

CHAPTER 31

Oliver fidgets in his seat. He's sat in this chair a hundred times before and it's always been comfortable enough. But now it feels unsupportive, too soft in some places, too hard in others. He doesn't know how he's meant to act right now. The cameras are all ready. His mum sits on one side of him and Thomas on the other side of her. Should he be pleased about this? Or should he take the centre seat? Really, he doesn't want to be on a seat at all.

They did some role play at the Institute, practising for various job situations, but they never covered what to say if they ended up on TV. He looks at his mum. She's a natural, relaxed and unfazed. She's probably the most relaxed Oliver's seen her in ages. Though he notes the glimmer of worry in her smile, it's a bit forced. Her facial muscles are working too hard.

She takes his hand. 'You're going to be great. Just be yourself.' She then turns and says the same thing to Thomas.

So, she's not worried about her performance, she's worried about his. Perhaps Oliver would feel more comfortable if Lenny wasn't like some hyperactive squirrel. He has too many teeth for a smile that small, too much hair on his chin for so little on top. He looks upside down. And he shouts at his colleagues, really shouts like he doesn't even like them at all. His colleagues are much nicer, especially the hair and makeup people. Lenny makes no small talk like they do; he just gives orders.

'So,' his mum faces him now. They've done her hair and makeup really well. She looks like the photo she uses on social media from her movie days. 'How are you? Did you go any-where nice yesterday?'

'My boss wanted to see me. Just wanted to say that work is getting busier, that's all.'

'Oh, okay, so, less time at home?'

'Maybe. I don't know.'

She leans a little closer to him and puts her hand on his knee. She's looking at his face like she's expecting to see a cut or a bump. 'You know you can talk to me. I'm your mum.'

He knows she wants to talk about Evie, but he doesn't want to. He didn't mean to hold her wrist like that, but then, she should listen to him. He's so confused. He can see what's in-volved to get the life living up top, the house, the girl, to have it all. But whenever he tries to grab it, he messes it up.

'I do love you, so much. It's been hard for you adapting to life out here. But we're all here for you.'

'I know, Mum. But I'm the one looking after you now, okay? Stop worrying.'

Her smile appears less forced then, and he's sure she under-stands that he's looking after her now. Up-top life is what his mum wants. He just needs to keep trying to get there. He needs to keep trying to make her happy like she did for him when he was a kid.

Lenny's colleagues don't stand straight like Anthony's staff do. They slouch and huff. They do as they're told, but not with the springy willingness of Anthony's. They don't respect Lenny in the way people do Anthony. Perhaps it's because his shirt is creased. Oliver imagines Lenny doesn't smell great, though he wouldn't know for sure.

Thomas's hair looks tidier and shiny. Oliver's is messy, but the hairdresser woman said it's great like that, and his mum likes it like that, so maybe it is okay. Oliver thinks probably everyone else's hair looks better than his, even his mum's.

Lenny sits in front of them. He has his legs crossed so Oliver tries to sit like this too, but that's even less comfortable.

The camera lens is like a giant eye staring at him.

'Look at me, not the camera, Oliver,' Lenny says.

But the blinking red light on the camera is distracting. It's tiny. Yet it's right where he can see it, as is his reflection. He looks as nervous as he feels.

'So, Oliver,' Lenny says, 'How is it integrating into the world as an adult?'

He doesn't answer for a moment. His mum leans in. 'It's just like having a chat, darling. Just answer honestly.'

'Erm,' Oliver says, buying some time. 'Confusing. Like, I was at work at the shop and some girl wanted my photo, and I'm supposed to do what the customer asks, so I let them take my photo, but then my boss was cross because I wasted time. I still can't figure that one out.'

Lenny laughs, not a mocking laugh, and Oliver laughs along too. He hadn't meant to be funny but now he thinks about it, the whole thing was a bit amusing. Some of his stiffness across his shoulders loosens.

'Well, you have a lot of fans out there,' Lenny says. 'And you, Thomas, anything you're struggling with?'

'I suppose I just want everyone to get along and to know we're not here to hurt anyone. We only want to help.'

'Because there has been some friction.' Lenny's voice dips to a serious tone. 'We've all seen the videos. Oliver, how do you explain that?'

'Well, I guess we're just like you. If someone, a stranger, threatened to hurt you and your family, what would you do?' He looks at his mum and Thomas, imagining them hurt for a second, then presses his lips together a moment before looking at Lenny again. 'Thomas is like my brother. And my mum, well, she's the most important person in the world to me. How would you react if someone threatened your family?'

Lenny seems satisfied at this answer, so does his mum who gives his knee a squeeze. The questions continue along similar lines. They always go to Oliver first, then Thomas, which is a bit unfair as Thomas gets longer to think about his answer. They talk about their jobs, and Oliver says he's doing good strong work and is pleased to save such jobs from humans, hoping they're safer as a result. He thinks that was his best answer out of all of them, and Lenny's reaction is good. Some of the other camera crew nod along as well, which makes Oliver fidget less. He mentions how incredibly hard the bots work in such a dangerous job, a little hint that maybe they should have some time off. Maybe Bret and Duncan and Anthony are watching.

Then Lenny asks, 'So, I know our viewers will be dying to know if there is a special someone, human or bot, a crush, for either of you?'

Oliver looks at Thomas. His blush is so deep even his ears are red. Oliver expects his is the same. He was just feeling really relaxed, and this question knots him up all over again. A thousand thoughts go through Oliver's mind in seconds. He could say something nice about Evie, but would that embarrass her or get her in trouble with her human family? He's been thinking too long, so long the room seems to shrink, and he should say something, anything, rather than sit here with his mouth open without words like a goldfish.

His mum clears her throat. 'The subject of such things is still a little alien to the boys. And with their busy work schedules, they hardly have time.'

He could hug his mum. He looks across at Thomas and sees the visible relief in him too. His shoulders sit a little lower, and that pressure in the back of his head goes away.

When Lenny and his crew are done with them, Oliver and Thomas go to their room to stay out of the way. With the door closed, Oliver can ignore all the noises of the packing up going on, all the chatter about how well or not the two of them did.

He shuts it out and sits on the blue sofa in their joint area. This sofa, in their own room, is so much more comfortable than the one in the living room when they're being watched. They sit and can be silent for a while without the awkwardness of expected conversation.

'I think that went okay,' Thomas says.

Oliver nods. 'Yeah. I think so too.'

It's been ages since he spent any proper time with Thomas. He'd forgotten how relaxing he is to be around. Thomas never expects anything from anyone and doesn't yell or do anything too loudly.

'I was really worried I'd say something stupid,' Oliver says. 'Mum's such a natural, isn't she?'

'Yeah. She's so great. I really hope this helps Theo. Your uncles are the best.'

'Hey.' Oliver angles to face him more directly. 'They're your uncles, too.'

Thomas's eyes light up at this. 'You think I could call them that?'

'Sure. We're family.'

Despite their lack of time together lately, Oliver can't imagine not having Thomas in his life, or his uncles. He'd like a family of his own, but he'd also like them all close by. Life wouldn't be complete without them.

'Do you . . .' Oliver bites his lip a moment, choosing his next words. 'This sounds stupid. But do you ever think of your future? Like, properly. Not just tomorrow at work.'

He looks at Thomas, who appears blank.

'I guess the Institute showed us how to use tools and said we'd be useful,' Oliver continues. 'But all this stuff with the girls, they never told us how to interact, how to be . . . I don't know . . . like real men, I guess. And everyone looks at us like we're grown-ups now and there are some feelings I have that I don't know what to do with.'

Thomas is nodding along. Oliver waits for an answer and in the few seconds Thomas ponders his, he worries he's said too much, or that Thomas will think he's insane or stupid or just a little boy.

'I guess we'll just figure it out,' Thomas says. 'There's no rush, though. I think being a man is being helpful and nice to people. Everything else will slot into place after that.'

Oliver's head dips and leans back on the sofa. He should have known Thomas would never say anything mean. But then, not everything Thomas said makes sense. 'Not all men are helpful and nice,' Oliver says. 'Some men, they're more authoritative. People help them rather than them being helpful. Those men get more respect.'

'I guess.'

'I think that's what I want. The men I'm around more, at work, that's how they are. If we have more respect, those Flesh Fraternity freaks wouldn't dare mess with us.' Oliver hadn't realised he's been punching one hand with another. He looks at Thomas staring at Oliver's hands.

'I . . . I don't know, Oliver. You scare me a bit when you're like that.'

'Like what?'

'So angry.'

Oliver stops punching and sits on his hands instead. 'Oh. Sorry.'

He stands and goes through to his side of the room. Is what Thomas said about being a man true? His uncles are like that; they're nice and helpful. But they live down on 5, not high up. Oliver needs to look after his mum and protect Thomas from the Flesh Fraternity. He might need to protect Evie one day too. He's never going to give his mum the life she deserves if he doesn't have respect. His mum should have the best of everything and be safe. He's going to do whatever it takes to make her the happiest person in the world.

CHAPTER 32

'So, how'd it go?' Theo asks Harriet as soon as he gets home.

'Will it air tomorrow?' Monty asks. 'Can't wait to see those handsome boys on TV! Did they look gorgeous?' He says this as he pulls some sequined fabric out of a bag and drapes it over his shoulder, a plume of glitter puffing up. Where he finds such stuff, Harriet can't imagine.

She's still moving the furniture back, trying to clean around the mess the camera crew left, and Theo and Monty coming home only add to that. She gives up, sitting instead.

'You know what? It went really well. The boys were perfect. Took a while for them to relax, which I expected. But bit by bit they came out of their shells. Lenny, for all his arsehole nature, was actually really good with them.'

'And you think you got some message across?' Theo asks. 'About bot rights and the hassle they've had?'

'I think so. I mentioned *Delilah's Law*, about how I think they deserve some rights, like they're not objects to mistreat. They didn't shy away from that topic with the boys, and you know how protective Oliver is. He came across a hero, I think.'

She knows she's biased and only time will tell about public perception, but right now, she knows her Oliver is still the gallant protector he always was. 'I don't know how it'll look in the edits. The first episode airs in a few days so I guess we'll know then if public opinion is different.'

'I'm sure it'll do the trick,' Theo says. 'So many people adore them already.'

The one thing Harriet had tidied was the kitchen table, but Theo already has a broken thingamajig, together with a pile of screws and tools taking up the space. She swears he's never happy unless he's fiddling with something.

'How was work, dare I ask?'

'Well,' Monty says, as he uses his forearm to push some of Theo's paraphernalia out of the way and get his sewing kit out. 'I was afforded a tiny little corner of the workshop today, much like now, so I managed to reupholster a whole chair.' He side-eyes Theo.

Theo pecks him on the cheek. 'And he handled it with such grace, didn't you?'

'And how's that side of things?' Harriet asks.

'What? Like my work isn't as interesting?' Monty feigns offence, his mouth hanging open, then sticking out his bottom lip.

Harriet laughs and shakes her head. 'If this wasn't so serious, I'd play along. But, Theo?'

He looks up from his project for a moment. 'Despite the constant whining from the corner of the workshop today, I actually figured a few things out.'

Through the kitchen window, the lights outside flicker, casting quick shadows across the room before going out entirely, though their house says lit.

They all wait a moment, bracing for their electricity to die. After a few moments, they breathe a collective sigh.

'I guess TRI is prioritising bot electric,' Harriet says.

'It's maddening,' Monty says, stuffing his fabric back in his bag with more force than needed. 'After all we did. This only bolsters those damned Devil-fearers more.'

'Electricity is power,' Theo mumbles. The mantra of the lower levels rolls off the tongue so easily to someone who's known so little of both.

'I'm going below tomorrow,' Monty says. 'I need to pick up some things. They've got some nice fabrics in at the moment. Anyone need anything?'

'From below?' Harriet grimaces. 'Mmmm, some cabbage wine and mushroom brandy?'

'Funny.' Monty rolls his eyes as he stands, then picks a few things out of the cupboard.

Harriet wishes he wouldn't go below, like Theo. She's really unsure if she can scrape enough money for Theo to get treatment, let alone Monty as well. Monty at least looks healthy. He's never been thin. Heck, she's never even noticed him out of breath. She casts her eyes over Theo, noting his face appears gaunt. Perhaps it's the stress of work taking it out of him, perhaps he's not sleeping well, or perhaps his sickness is further along than he's letting on.

She'll start researching auditions as soon as she's had her next treatment. Whatever it takes, she won't let her friend suffer.

Monty is already getting dinner in the oven. He works so quickly, Harriet thinks at least she has one man in her life she doesn't have to worry about.

CHAPTER 33

Oliver arrives at work eager, knowing he's an important member of staff and determined to show it. He's the only bot who's been given any time off after all, though he hopes that doesn't come up. He doesn't want the others to hate him.

Bret and Duncan both seem to treat him the same, with brief and curt instructions as always. They're human, though, so Oliver doubts they understand what it's like to be an important bot. He watches their body language, their facial expressions, and they're each so different. Bret's main job is in the office sorting out the stockroom and equipment. He walks slowly, smiles occasionally. He'll engage in conversation for a bit but never seems enthused to do so. Duncan walks quickly everywhere. His face is always twisted in a scowl and rarely says more than two words at a time. Neither ever makes Oliver feel at ease and as he watches them, he thinks about what sort of man he wants to be. He wants to be a man that has friends and respect, to be the kind that people look up to.

Neither of these men seem to have any enviable qualities; no nice things, no heavy watches, and Oliver doubts they've ever been in a Hel-E. He doubts they make their mums happy. The TV show people fussing made Oliver uneasy at first but, actually, when they started asking questions and giving him compliments, he felt they liked and respected him. They said what he did with that Flesh Fraternity arsehole was commendable.

'Where were you yesterday?' George asks when Oliver arrives at the patch they've been clearing.

'Other work stuff,' Oliver says, and from George's nod he thinks that's done the trick in relaying his importance. And it's not even a lie. Filming is his other job. He's helped his mum earn money, so that's the same as work.

There's a machine Oliver hasn't used yet. A huge truck with a cylindrical container on the back. Perhaps using this is the more important role he's meant to have. In that container they dump in some of the clay ground they dug out before, mixed with grey dust and water. Then, it spins and spins and spins. It takes all morning to get it full and spun right.

Meanwhile, they hack away at the ground. Where some of the drill holes were, they now scoop out in between. Some of what they scoop out they add to the container to make more of whatever is being mixed in there. They dig and dig until the digger hits only air. There's a gap and there's no more earth for a while.

'Here,' Duncan passes him something. 'Anthony says this is your job to do.'

Oliver removes his ear defenders in case there are instructions. So this is the important bit of work. Oliver takes the package, his chest puffing up. He doesn't even notice how tired his body is anymore.

'Go down there, as far as you can, and put that inside,' Duncan says, 'then do the same on the other side.'

Oliver looks at what he's carrying. It seems like a couple of bunches of thick sticks connected to a long string. He doesn't ask what it is. He needs to show willingness and obedience. He works without hesitation, as any top employee would. This is his moment to shine, to show what he's really capable of. He wants to be a good employee, the best. He deserves this chance, and he deserves the rewards it could bring.

He hops down into the hole and walks for a few minutes, the long string trailing behind. It's a tunnel. He's below ground. In the far distance, the sounds of the town ring out. He places the box on the ground. Perhaps it's something nice for those who live below. It'll purify the air or something. He turns around and walks in the opposite direction and then does the same the other way, walking until the string runs out.

Before he walks back, he pauses a moment. His hearing is so acute now, and without his ear defenders, he can make out bits of conversation. People are talking about work and families. He can hear a child laughing. Below ground is horrible, but it was nice when he visited for that party. The attention was a lot to deal with, but the community was friendly with lots of families showing how much they care about each other and appreciate their homes.

His mum was so sick then. Now she's recovering, perhaps they can return for a visit, just for the feeling of everyone together. He's felt so distant from everyone lately, so busy and tired but also, that he isn't being the sort of person they want him to be, like even in his house he doesn't fit in. Hearing the sounds of people enjoying each other's company makes him realise he needs to spend more time with his family. The sounds of laughter and friendship below ground reminds him what he's missing. It's been ages since he and Thomas had a laugh together. Maybe he should buy Thomas something nice with the money Anthony gave him. He still has plenty left. His uncles too, as well as his mum.

He ponders this as he walks back. He climbs up the clay bank with his hands and feet to lift himself clear. Duncan gives him the thumbs up, then beckons him over.

'Now, Oliver,' he says, half his mouth smiling. 'Anthony said to make sure it's you who pushes that lever.'

'This here?' Oliver asks as he stands by a long black box with a handle on top.

'That's right. When you're ready.'

Oliver nods and pushes it.

Nothing happens for a second. From below, the general chatter still mingles in with the constant noise of the landfill. After a second, there's a deep boom. Oliver stumbles backwards as the ground tilts, and he finds his balance. A plume of dust comes from the hole in the ground and a ditch tears open like a great wound in the earth, cracking down the length of the site.

Oliver's eyes bulge as the clay and earth implode into the ditch. Below, those happy voices he was enjoying listening to just moments ago turn to screams. Screams of help, of people's names, of disbelief and panic. Oliver feels their panic, his chest ripping in two. All of his inner workings race and buzz with horror.

There are people below, whose ceilings are collapsing in on them, smothering them, choking them.

His mind flashes back to when his mum was buried in that landslide when he was a kid. He runs to the crevasse that's opened up, standing on the edge of the torn earth. Above the noise of the tumbling ground are footsteps, people racing for safety. Then, in the great ditch, poking through the earth, are hands, reaching for air, tense fingers scrabbling for something to grab onto, to heave themselves up. Limbs of people grasp at a chance to live, to be saved. Some of those hands and fingers go limp so quickly, the skin already grey.

Oliver saw this in a video at the Institute when they wanted the teens to be hardened up. He's watched this before—the sight of innocent people being buried.

'We have to help them!' he cries, bending double before falling to his knees and reaching for the hands that are too far away. The ground nearer is soft. As he tries to get closer, he sinks and has to retreat.

He looks over one shoulder, then the other. His colleagues all stand with folded arms, not a note of panic among them. Surely, this must be an accident. Something unplanned, something they can try to rectify.

Oliver lies on his front to spread his weight, his fingertips grazing those poking above the ground. He tries to grab hold, but again the ground softens beneath him.

'Someone help me! Pass me something for them to hold on to!'

The other workers don't react. Not at all.

A horn beeps behind him and he jumps backwards. Good, a truck. Maybe they'll be using this to winch people to safety. Oliver crawls back, then stands and moves out of the way. It's the big truck with the container on the back. That huge great cylinder lifts at the end now, and out of the end, the contents that's been spinning all day falls like a slurry into the ditch. A molten grey mixture, smothering the wound.

'No! No no no!' His voice doesn't carry over the machine.

The slopping mixture splatters into the ground, soaking in, covering those reaching hands.

Oliver can't be sick. He can't vomit, but how he wants to. He wants to expunge from his body all this horribleness, to separate it from his insides. His wide eyes still stare, frantically searching for a way to help, for an explanation, for any logic in this peril.

The slurry keeps pouring and when that container is empty, another is brought over until the mixture, already hardening, has filled in what once was a tunnel.

The screams still come, louder and louder, until they stop. Until there's no more human sound from below. The silence now makes his insides go hollow. There's life in a scream. There's nothing in silence.

All those people. Those arms and hands and cries, forever sealed. As the mixture solidifies, there's the tip of a set of fingertips still poking above. Unmoving now and as grey as the cement.

'Next,' Duncan shouts, and they move on to the second excavated area.

Once again, Duncan hands Oliver the box of sticks. *Next?* This can't be right. What just happened wasn't meant to happen. Oliver did something wrong. He made a mistake.

'Same again,' Duncan says. 'Fast as you can. We have to clear the whole area as quickly as possible.'

Oliver stands there, staring at what's in his hands. He blinks a few times, tilts his head one way, trying to make sense of it.

'But . . . there were people—'

'Hurry up, Oliver,' George says. 'We want that time off you're meant to be sorting for us.'

Oliver's mouth moves, but words don't come out. He did say he'd help with that. And in that case, he needs to do his job. But he can't be understanding right. Did his colleagues not just see what happened? This set of sticks feels so much heavier than the last. Or his arms are weaker. He needs to move or say something, but he's just standing there, his mouth hanging open, his insides made of jelly.

'Go! Now!' Duncan shouts. 'Do as you're told, bot.'

Duncan's shouting snaps his attention and he goes. Obedient. Being the good employee he's trained to be. As he walks, he runs over the instructions again. He goes to the hole in the ground and lowers himself down into the cavern below. He walks a minute one way, drops one bunch of sticks, then walks the other and does the same. Somewhere ahead, there's a few confused conversations, questioning what that noise was, mixed with some jokes and laughter. Somewhere, someone is singing a song.

He walks back out, then observes as the ground collapses again, and again, the hole is filled with concrete. The song falls silent.

Oliver's knees buckle, but somehow he stays standing, his eyes wide as the ground shifts and sinks.

Maybe no one was hurt. They must have been all far away. Those hands, those fingers, he imagined it. No one else seems to have seen them. Yet there's a sensation of a rock pressed against his middle, like he can't stand straight, like he's being squashed. It's his nightmares playing in front of him, the type that have him thrashing as he wakes.

Oliver's battery depletes quickly. He's embarrassed to say how quickly, since it shows how emotional he's found the day. His legs don't want to hold him up anymore. His eyes mist over as he tries to not see the world around him. His head aches with strain as he attempts to understand. Why did any of that happen? Why does no one else think it was a mistake?

He leaves much earlier than usual and in the office, Anthony is there.

He's smiling. It's not a nice, soft smile, but a hard smile with his chin jutted out, eyes narrowed to slits. 'Tough day, Son?'

'Yes. It was . . . difficult. I think . . .' How can he explain? Was that meant to happen? Does Anthony know? Could Oliver get his colleagues in trouble? Loyalty, that's what was drummed into him. He's meant to stick by his colleagues. His brows knit, confusion tensing his forehead. Maybe the mistake was Oliver's. He didn't follow instructions properly. It was he who put those sticks down there. He misunderstood. He's hurt people and Anthony will be disappointed in him. 'I think, yes, it was a tough day,' is all he can think to say.

'Well, it'll get easier.' Anthony gives him a pat on the arm. 'An important man like you has to do some tough jobs sometimes.'

Oliver looks to the ground, his back hunched. He wants to curl in a ball, for the world to ignore him. He wants the ground to swallow him up too.

'Your mum will be really proud of you for the hard work you've done.' Anthony's tone is laced with notes Oliver can't understand. Some ingenuity, a mocking tinge maybe. No. Why would Anthony make fun of him? 'Here—' Anthony hands Oliver a gold necklace. 'Why not give this to your mum? Say you found it so she'll know what important work you're doing.'

The necklace in Oliver's hand is tiny but heavy. His dirty hands leave a dusty residue, ruining some of its shine.

That hardened smile remains on Anthony's face. His sharp suit is so clean, not a speck of dirt on it.

'I'll get a Hel-E—'

'No,' Oliver says. 'I'd like to walk.'

He doesn't wait for Anthony to say more. He turns and leaves the building before his shame gives itself away, then steps into the lift.

When he gets home, his battery is down to two per cent. He hears his mum and Uncle Theo calling him, but he can't respond. He plugs in and lies on his bed, the necklace still in his pocket, the echoes of the buried still ringing in his ears.

CHAPTER 34

'Wow!' Harriet says when Oliver hands her a gold necklace.

The chain dangles between her fingers, dainty yet beautifully made. The pendant is heavy with interwoven coils of yellow and white gold. It's flashier than anything she wears or could possibly wear down on 5. She turns it over in her hands. Little diamonds line the pendant and catch the light, gleaming like the moon on a pond, sparkling as if it's never been tarnished.

She turns around so he can fasten it behind her neck.

'You found this at the landfill?' she asks. It never stops shocking her what people throw away. This necklace must have come from the very top.

'Yep.'

She turns to face him again, looking up at his handsome face as he smiles his gorgeous grin, his eyes glinting almost as much as the necklace. He's been working so hard. He went straight to bed when he got home from work and still hasn't fully charged. He's washed and has clean clothes on, but some grime from landfill appears ingrained. His hair is dull and his skin lacking its rosy glow. She cups his face, and he leans into her touch. Despite his smile, he seems troubled, vacant, a faraway stare. This new job is taking its toll.

She presses the pendant into her chest, filling her with warmth. 'It really is beautiful. Thank you for thinking of me.' She hugs, then gives him a peck on the cheek. As she pulls away, she notices something hanging from his wrist.

'Woah! You find that too?' She holds onto his wrist and turns it over. The watch is substantial. A thick and chunky thing, without so much as a mark.

'Yeah,' he says, the muscles in his wrist tense.

She continues to inspect it. It must be worth a fortune. 'Not even a chip or crack. Oliver, darling, this looks brand new.'

'It's amazing what people throw away, like you say.'

She releases his arm and gives his back a rub. 'Wait till your Uncle Monty sees that. He's quite the connoisseur of watches. He went below to get some fabric. He's been ages, though. Should have been back hours ago.'

Oliver's face drains of colour. His back stiffens.

'You all right, darling? You look pale.' He's been working so hard and, suddenly, he looks exhausted.

'I'm . . . I'm fine.' He steps away from her affection. He's out of her reach and he shoves his hands into his pockets. 'You said Uncle Monty was below? Whereabouts?'

'Reading town, I'm going to say north, but I might be wrong.' Harriet opens the fridge and starts thinking about what to cook. If Monty's going to be late, she should at least make a start.

She finds some tinned vegetables and an onion that needs eating and grabs the chopping board and knife. She's opening a tin when she notices Oliver's trembling.

She walks over and looks him up and down. His cheeks are ashen, in contrast to his reddening eyes. 'What's wrong?' she asks, but he doesn't answer. 'Oh, look. Your cable is far too stretched.' She holds onto his arm and leads him back through to the living room. There are some magazines on the coffee table, one on birds and another on British history. He might enjoy those. 'You work so hard, why don't you have a sit down?' She uncoils the cable to give him some more slack, then gestures for him to sit. He does, though his face is still blank. He's still silent. Still trembling. She feels his forehead, as if he might show signs of a fever. The skin under his eyes is a greyish hue, like he hasn't slept in days. She takes his hands, his fingers, slack and weak, have blue-black bruising all over. They're working him too hard.

'You need more rest, darling,' she says. 'Perhaps have a word with your employer? They can't keep overworking you like this.'

He grunts, then leans back on the sofa. His eyes stay open, unblinking. He seems a strange mixture of vacant and alert. Perhaps she should phone TRI. He might have a bug. But no, they might come and take him. He's fine, just needs some charge.

She leaves him sitting like that, then goes back to her chopping, slicing the vegetables with a bit more vigour. If Oliver was a child, she'd go and speak to the school, but he has to fight his own corners here. Although she could find his employer and speak to them, if he won't himself.

Theo and Thomas arrive home just then, their easy laughter filling the house.

'Oh, God,' Theo says as Harriet tips the contents of the tins into a pan. 'You're cooking?'

She returns his smirk, then lights the gas. 'Well, Monty's not back yet, so I thought I might as well.'

'Still?' Theo checks the time on his watch, a rubber-strapped thing with a plastic face, cracked and discoloured. 'He's been hours. I'll text him and see where he is.'

'I'm going to my room.' Oliver takes his cable and exits the living room without so much as a hello.

Harriet locks eyes with Theo and shrugs.

'I thought he seemed so much more like his old self when they were filming,' Harriet says in a low whisper after Oliver's bedroom door clicks shut. 'He was smiling, talking to the camera. He seemed like less of a closed book.'

Harriet's not just bragging. The show aired a few hours ago. With everyone at work, she watched alone and was delighted Oliver and Thomas came across as really helpful, hard-working, family men. Harriet talked about her love of the two of them so much, she probably came across a little crazy but according to social media, she resonated with so many.

'He obviously gets his camera skills from his mum,' Theo says.

'You also, Thomas, you did so well,' Harriet says as she tips the contents of the tins into a pot. 'Everyone on *Get Level* loves you. I've got the programme saved, so we'll watch it together later, if you like?'

'Sure.' His cheeks redden, and he smiles, then thanks her.

'Maybe Oliver would like to watch too. But he seems a bit off lately,' Harriet says. 'Don't you think, Thomas?'

'I think . . .' Thomas stalls for a moment. 'It's probably just his work hours. Working for that long is really hard.'

'Right.' Harriet steps away from the stove and towards Thomas. 'Maybe he could go visit Evie?' A leading question, one she hopes will lead to some honesty. Theo shoots her a look which she ignores.

'Nah,' Thomas says. 'I'm pretty sure those two are over.'

'Oh, that's a shame.' She presses her lips together. These MechaniBots are bloody masters of deceit. She moves to stir the food as it boils but Thomas beats her to it.

'It smells . . . interesting,' Theo says, checking his phone.

'Well, it's food,' she says. 'Has Monty replied?'

'No. The message hasn't gone through. Signal down there is crappy, so I guess he's not even on his way back yet.'

Harriet takes over stirring for Thomas. Since they don't eat, she doubts bots are good cooks. Not that she's any good. She used to be when she lived with Anthony, but her cooking likely tasted good because of the quality ingredients she could buy. They really have become quite snobby about food because of Monty. They grew up below ground and didn't eat tasty food until they escaped. Harriet's cooking is definitely not worse than below-ground food, but down on 5, with their combined salaries, making food taste good requires Monty's gift.

Thomas goes to his room and before Harriet serves up, she steps towards their door to listen. There's no noise, no chatter. After a few seconds, she's met by the sound effects of a video game and she returns to the kitchen. Thomas and Oliver were so close once, it pains her to think of a girl coming between them.

'Oliver still not seeming himself then?' Theo asks.

'No, not at all. I think he's heartbroken about Evie.'

'Poor lad.' He reaches over and gives her hand a squeeze. 'He'll get through it.'

She nods. Theo's right, of course. Heartbreak is a rite of passage for most people. But there's so much pain in Oliver, however much he tries to hide it. She didn't prepare him properly for this side of life. The Institute failed there too. She knows he'll come out the other side, but she wishes he could get there quicker. She'd chop off her own limb if it would save him some pain.

She serves up what she's cooked, and Theo only mocks her efforts for a moment.

'So?' she asks him after she's chewed on her food for far longer than should be necessary for mostly vegetables and sauce. 'Have you broken that weapon thing? Where are we at?'

'Well, it's interesting. The armature is surrounded by a coil of wire, and I think if I use an alloy for the stator—'

'Laymen's terms, please.'

'Ah. Sorry. I think I've made it so it won't work. And just in case.' From his bag he pulls two vests.

Harriet takes them. The vests are a rough cotton blend, reclaimed, with badly repaired patches. They've been cleaned up—mostly, with a section removed and one of the copper squares stitched in place. The whole thing looks like it would suit Frankenstein's monster, but under clothes, who would know?

'I guess Monty could spruce these up a bit?' Harriet grins.

'Yeah, well, they're not going to be on show. But it seems we both need Monty around today.' He chuckles as he winces down his dinner. Theo takes the vest back and puts it in the bag. 'Thing is . . .' He bites his bottom lip for a while. 'I really don't know how effective they'll be. Their personality modules used to be at the back of their neck in the teens and kids, but I'm not comfortable to go tinkering. It's not like the kids and teens, and I knew their bodies were temporary. We really don't know all that much about the adult bodies. This should preserve their battery if the hit isn't too direct, but an EMP might fry the rest of them.

Fry. The word every mother wants to hear when discussing her son.

'Let's just assume they'll work or, better yet, hope they won't be needed,' Harriet says. 'Maybe you should make more? There are hundreds of MechaniBots. The kids would need something a bit smaller.'

'I was thinking that. The copper square would be way too low for a kid. I'll need to get some new material. That's not the problem, though. It's the copper. It's expensive and in short supply. This is all I've been able to get hold of so far.'

Harriet attempts to eat some more, but her stomach protests. She's too full of worry to have room for anything else. She needs to eat more. There have been plenty of comments on *Get Level* about her appearance not being what it once was. The comments were similar when she gained weight. Now she's thin and the vitriol is just the same. She preferred herself bigger. Her baby bump where she carried Freddie is now nothing more than a flap. She always loved her residual tummy.

'Can we keep those two, though?' she asks. 'For Oliver and Thomas? I know it's not fair on the rest of the bot population.'

'Of course. That's who these are for. I just want to clean them up a bit more. And you're right. They could do with Monty's magic.'

Harriet gets up and scrapes the rest of her dinner into a Tupperware, thinking maybe Monty's magic can make it taste a bit better later.

She contemplates going to Oliver's room, to try to talk to him some more, but decides against it. She presses her palm to his door, as if somehow that could will him to come out and speak to her. He never touched the magazines on the table. Theo found those a couple of days ago and thought they sounded like something Oliver would like to read. Oliver would, the Oliver

Harriet knows. But he's changing so fast, and she doesn't know what he'd like anymore.

The pendant hangs from her neck, heavy and intrusive. She twirls it between her thumb and forefinger. She'll have to keep it concealed when walking around 5. The last time she had jewellery like this, it was apology pieces from Anthony. Oliver saw those pieces when he was a kid, watched her barter with them to help them escape. She presses the necklace into her chest again, an ache emanating from somewhere inside. Her boy carries with him so much trauma from those early years and she feels wholly responsible. He was so much more impressionable than she ever realised.

CHAPTER 35

Oliver's charge takes forever as his mind won't rest. He could go on standby to speed it up, but in standby he'll have nightmares. Somehow, he fears those more than anything. He tries to dismiss his working day as nothing but a bad dream, a hallucination, telling himself it didn't really happen. Those screams that died to nothing, the song that stopped singing, the arms reaching through the ground. It was all his imagination. It can't have been real.

As much as he tries to lie to himself, he can't. He knows what he saw, what he felt, and heard. Was one of those screams Uncle Monty? He was below. Oliver's body cramps and grows cold when he thinks of Uncle Monty never coming home. Why do his arms and legs shake so much? He can't help it. His body shudders and his chin trembles.

Why did none of his colleagues care? It must have been a mistake, and he supposes sometimes people ignore their mistakes. It was Oliver's mistake and maybe they're ignoring it for his sake? Maybe they saw so many of the videos Oliver was forced to watch at the Institute, they don't even register such sights anymore. But no. It was too horrible. It doesn't make sense however he tries to justify it.

Oliver hears every word his mum and Uncle Theo say in the kitchen. They say he's in danger but he fails to care about that. They also say he's heartbroken. But Oliver doesn't have a heart, so what does that mean he is? Duff programming? He's not heartbroken anyway. Fuck Evie if she doesn't want him.

When he's charged, he should go below ground and find Uncle Monty and help the people who are buried. He could lift them out the way they did for his mum years ago. But he has to go to work. It's what's expected of him. The watch hangs from his wrist. He thought, somehow, wearing it would make him feel better, remind him he's important. Instead, it weighs him down, like a burden. Is this just what it takes to earn respect?

He closes his eyes and tries to clear his mind so he can charge quicker. When he's fully charged he'll be able to think more clearly.

❦ ❦ ❦ ❦

With his battery almost full, Oliver sits up, then pulls a book from the shelf. The dictionary again. Perhaps there'll be an explanation in there, some word that explains the pain in his chest, the emptiness, the way his insides are coiled like a spring.

Guilt. Regret. He knows those words and they are true. But again, he realises it's not a word for him that he needs, but to explain everyone else. Why no one wanted to help those people, why such a task had to be done. He skims through again. *Ambivalence. Lazy.* Maybe that's it. They just couldn't be bothered.

His hands go to his forehead, and he brings his knees in. His fingertips press into his head, grasping, as if he's trying to stop his thoughts from spilling out. He's splitting in two, like the ground.

Then he reads, *Sadistic. Schadenfreude: The malicious enjoyment of suffering.* He chokes as he reads, his throat seizing up. Is that what his colleagues felt, and that's why they didn't try to help? Why is there a word for such a thing? If no one had made a word for it, perhaps such a feeling wouldn't be possible. So much of humanity centres around language. If all the words for bad things were gone, would people have more joy?

His mum wants to speak to him, but he can't. How can he possibly say what he saw, what he did? It's his fault. His insides are crawling, like all of his wiring and circuitry are rotten.

He doesn't want to go and speak to his mum and uncle and Thomas. He wants to hide, where they won't see him. He hears their worries, the fear in the voices. Monty's still not back. Oliver has to listen to Uncle Theo say it's weird he's not back yet. Soon he'll know what's happened and he'll be crushed. Uncle Theo, who's always there for Oliver, and his mum. His lovely mum.

He considers telling them, for the briefest moment, before he knows it'll do no good. He's only been fully charged for a couple of minutes when his phone pings with a text message. For a second he imagines it's Evie, asking if he's okay, that she's been thinking about him and wouldn't it be lovely if they spent some time together. He imagines, hopes, for all of this but when he checks, it's from Anthony, telling him to take the lift to 110.

Despite his full battery, when Oliver stands, his legs are weak. His energy is depleting whereas, usually, a full battery makes him buzz with life. He looks at his hands, the bruising, the bunched-up skin, dirt ingrained in the creases. He's washed, but there's muck there he couldn't clean away.

He puts his tatty work clothes on, leaves his watch and nice jacket, then shouts a goodbye to his mum, and leaves for work. He braces, sure he's going to get fired. Anthony must have found out what happened, and now Oliver's going to be in trouble. Maybe they'll kill him too, as punishment. They'll remove his battery so his system fries. He doesn't care. He's not afraid. He's just sad at how his mum would feel. He should have hugged her before he left, told her he loves her.

There's a Hel-E waiting for him on the roof, Anthony sitting inside. He's smiling, and Oliver thinks maybe he's not in trouble, then he thinks of that word again. *Schadenfreude*. Anthony doesn't seem cross with him and also doesn't seem devastated. He doesn't seem like he's about to say what a terrible disaster that was, how he's sorry and will do all he can to help those people. He seems just the same as ever.

'Hi, Son. How's my best employee?'

Oliver takes a seat. It's as comfortable as always, the insides polished and gleaming, yet Oliver can't settle. He fidgets, like the seat is made of something hard and lumpy. His eyes stay on his lap, not wanting to admire the view. 'Erm, okay. I guess.'

'Well, lots more work to do today. You did such a good job last time. I'm proud of you.'

His mum often says she's proud of him. Such praise would normally make Oliver sit up straight, but he wants to hug his knees. He barely notices Anthony's hand give him a pat, though when he pulls away, Oliver's skin is hot, burned, like Anthony scalded rather than praised.

'The same kind of work as yesterday? I think . . . I think it didn't go as planned,' Oliver says, a wobble of dread in his voice, and his eyes flit up to gauge Anthony's reaction.

Anthony's smile widens, revealing his gleaming white teeth. 'Oh, it went exactly as planned.'

Oliver stares at Anthony now, and his jaw drops. Anthony meant to blow up the underground. That was actually planned? His thoughts all stop for a moment, goosebumps prickle across his skin. He's never had goosebumps before, he didn't even know he could get them, but there they are, like when his mum says her bones are cold.

He can hear the screams again, see those hands reaching for air. It was all real. Oliver did that. And it was what was meant to happen.

Oliver is a good employee, but that makes him a bad person.

'Look at this.' Anthony points to the cityscape below.

The Hel-E flies around the tops of skyscrapers, circling the tallest, getting close to some that have rooftop gardens and private parks. There's so much outdoor space that some private gardens have their own climbing frames and hot tubs. The sky is endless, a sea of possibilities where the world can expand and grow, unlike down on 5 where there's not enough room to run around. Or below, where the only way to make more space is to dig deeper into the ground.

Anthony's mouth twists, his eyes mere slits. 'You think all this can be achieved if we keep our thoughts in the dirt? The towers need to be higher, more luxurious, important people want whole storeys, even two, all to themselves. AM Investments are expanding all our buildings to 150! That's forty extra storeys. Imagine the view! Imagine the prestige of living that high.'

'Yeah.' Oliver gives a one-armed shrug. 'I guess . . .'

'And each building needs much tougher foundations.' Anthony leans in closer to Oliver, rubbing his palms together. 'Those moles who live below, you know their digging compromises the integrity of every building up here. Should up here suffer because of their digging?'

'No.' Oliver backs away from Anthony. 'Of course not. No one should suffer.'

'Those people below, they're suffering. They're sick, infertile, they die young.'

'But . . .' Oliver's eyes go from side to side, his nose wrinkles. 'But there's medicine.'

'Do you think there's enough medicine for everyone? Of course not.' Anthony snorts a laugh. 'There's only so much to go around. You helped to end their suffering. You did a good thing.'

A good thing? It can't be. If that were so, he wouldn't feel so bad. Those people wouldn't have been screaming. The screams start again, in his ears, his head, vibrating through him. 'I think . . . I don't think it was a good thing.'

'Well, then. Think about you and your bot friends? If those people below, the ones who damage the very foundations of integrity of all life up here, if they were not naturally dying out, they would want rid of you and your kind. Your purpose, and the purpose of all the bots, is to fill the gap in the workforce they leave. You don't want your bot friends terminated, do you?'

Oliver stretches his neck out, his shoulders cramping. He thinks of Thomas and Evie and Bonnie. 'No. No, of course not.'

'Exactly. You need to protect your own kind. You need to make sure there's enough medicine for your mum. Don't you agree?'

'Erm . . . yes. Of course I want my mum to be okay.'

'So, why waste all this up here—' he gestures to the sky around them '—because of the lives of a few, substandard people? Isn't it better to let evolution play its part, for those below grounders to be put out of their misery so we can build a better world up here, reaching for the sky?'

A different watch hangs from Anthony's wrist. An even bigger, fancier one. As Oliver looks down through the glass floor, he takes in Anthony's shoes, so shiny his reflection stares back.

'Don't you want all the fine things in life, for you and your mum?'

Oliver wrings his hands out in his lap. What Anthony says makes sense, but it doesn't sit right, like a badly made puzzle. 'I . . . I do. But, my Uncle Monty was below.'

'But what about your Uncle Theo? Don't you care about him? I've been doing some digging on them and, trust me, Monty is not good enough for him. That man has a criminal past. Imagine the sort of partner Theo could have if Monty wasn't around. He'll be sad at first, but heartbreak is normal for humans. Death is part of life. You've helped him.'

Heartbreak is normal, he hears his mum and Uncle Theo saying as much. That does seem to be the way of things. Humans expire. His mum was with Josie once and Josie died, so Anthony is telling the truth about normal human things. Oliver glances around at the cyan sky, the glowing sun, and his goosebumps go away. They should build higher so more people can see the sun. He certainly wants his mum and Theo to have all the best things. Is Monty really a bad man? It's hard to imagine; he's so friendly. But if Anthony says so, maybe he is. Anthony is a man of his word.

The Hel-E lands, not at the usual place but on top of another building. From the looks of all the other skyscrapers, Oliver knows they're on the edge of London, not too far from the TRI building.

'Come with me,' Anthony says, and they alight the Hel-E.

'This is AM Investments,' Anthony says when they enter the building. 'My company owns the entire building. Every level is dedicated to my business. That's quite something, isn't it?'

Oliver looks side to side and nods. It is impressive. It's all glass and polished surfaces, and their footsteps echo. In each corner, large green plants grow out of huge pots, thriving in the amount of light up here. Oliver is definitely not dressed appropriately for being somewhere so fancy.

They arrive at an office, Anthony's name on a gold plaque on the door. This is the kind of office Oliver imagined Anthony working in, not the grotty one down on 2. In the office are framed newspaper articles about Anthony, his company, and his achievements. Artwork hangs on the walls. Oliver doesn't know much about art except that it's expensive. The furniture is delicate, the kind that would never survive the fall to landfill. The stuff that only lasts a few months. Anthony doesn't need furniture with any kind of longevity when he can replace it all whenever he likes. There's decadence in how delicate it is.

Anthony sits behind his desk, rocking back on his chair, his fingers steepled under his chin. 'How would you like to work here, with me?'

Oliver's eyes bulge. He looks around the place and wonders what on earth he would do in such an office.

'The days of scavenging are over,' Anthony says. 'We're moving up in the world. We are going to make this world a better place. With you by my side, Son. Won't your mum be so proud to see how well you've done for yourself?'

Oliver looks to one side, then slowly to the other. It's more than his mum ever dreamed. Oliver was stacking shelves in a supermarket just a week ago, and now he could be working on the top levels in a fancy office. How could she not love that?

He takes a few steps into the middle of the office and turns around. Yes, he can see himself here. A sharp suit, shiny shoes, a different watch every day of the week, taking his mum on Hel-E rides whenever she wants. She'd see the sunshine again. Oliver could make all of that happen.

'Once these new extensions are built, how would you like to live above 100 again? With any bot or family you like.'

Oliver nods, licks his lips. 'Yeah. I'd like that. That new world sounds just right.'

Anthony leans forward, his elbows on his desk. 'That's my boy.'

CHAPTER 36

Harriet paces the flat, not even noticing how she's able to do that now whereas, just a couple of weeks ago, a few steps would have worn her out. She itches, not from the rash she had before she started treatment, but from sweat and crappy fabrics. Anxiety creates clammy pools across her back and neck. Her cold shivers of recent months have well and truly been replaced with an intermittent inferno and perspiring in places she'd really rather not. She bites what's left of her nails, her newly restored appetite now diminished again to nothing as worries clamp her gut.

There's been no news from Monty. Nothing. He's never done anything like this. He's Mr Reliable, dependable. Definitely not one to just disappear. Theo left an hour ago after trying and failing to get in touch with their friends below. Harriet had no words of reassurance, for she's as concerned as he.

'Something's off. I can feel it,' Theo said before he left.

Harriet could only give him a hug and say something stupidly unhelpful, along the lines of, 'I'm sure he'll turn up.' That's what you say to a child who's lost a toy, not about an adult disappearing.

With Theo below, he's not working on the weapon and safety vests. One problem at a time, they always try to tell themselves. But Harriet's mind is in overdrive, a colourful shimmer creeping in as a migraine threatens to take hold. Her legs cramp, her back hurts. She's drowning.

When there's a knock at the door, Harriet races to it, thinking maybe Monty has forgotten his keys. She forgets all manners and groans when she sees it's Michelle.

Michelle slouches and folds her arms. 'You forgot, didn't you?'

Harriet palms her forehead. 'I'm so sorry. My friend is missing. He's been gone over a day now.'

'I can reschedule.'

'No! No, I need the distraction. I'm going out of my mind here. Come in.'

Harriet pushes open the door all the way and beckons her inside. If she remembered she was to have company, she would have cleaned and tidied a bit. The place smells like Harriet's dismal attempt at cooking last night. Non-eaten breakfast still sits on plates on the side, a pile of dirty pots and crockery in the sink.

Michelle doesn't comment on the mess and accepts Harriet's offer of a cup of tea. There's surely a clean mug around somewhere. Harriet takes a few from the shelf and after peering inside, opts to give a couple a clean.

'What can I do?' Michelle asks. 'Anyone I can call?'

Harriet puts the kettle on and sits. Sitting actually feels much better than being on her feet. Her legs are worn out from pacing.

'He went below yesterday. That's all I know. We've not been able to get in touch since. Theo's tried their friends, but no one is getting through.' Harriet wears the same clothes she's worn for days and imagines she smells just like that too. It didn't bother her when it was just her and the boys, but now next to fresh-faced Michelle, she wishes she'd at least changed her top. Michelle always dresses so well, her hair is always nicely done. The necklace Oliver gave her still hangs from her neck and she hopes that's enough to make her appearance passable.

'I heard there's some internet outage below,' Michelle says. 'Loads of us haven't heard from anyone below in over twenty-four hours.'

'But why would that stop Monty coming home?' The kettle finishes boiling and Harriet walks over, treading carefully to avoid angering the blisters on the soles of her feet.

'I don't know,' Michelle says. 'You look well, by the way. I take it you found a rich friend?'

Harriet plonks the teacups down as she sits, some sloshing over the sides but she leaves it. It's mess on mess. 'Well, no. That's what I got in touch about. I just got given the treatment. They said because I'm high profile.'

'Really? Well, take the perk.'

'It's just, why choose someone high profile, then stop them talking about it?' Over the past day Harriet hasn't had the mind space to think about this conundrum. But now she's vocalising it again, it bothers her all the more. 'Theo is in denial, but I'm sure he's got early symptoms. I need to fund his treatment somehow.'

'I've rinsed my contacts, sorry.' Her eyes flit to Harriet's necklace. From that, she must think Harriet has some wealthy friends still somewhere. 'There's no way they'll be dishing it out to everyone. This is their plan. Let the below grounders die out and replace their jobs with bots.'

'What?' Harriet chokes on her tea. 'That can't be the plan.'

'Open your eyes, Harriet,' Michelle says as she rolls hers. 'Your Oliver is great and everything, but a contract to take a bot from TRI is cheaper than a human employee. Bots don't get sick, and work for forty hours straight without complaint. Plus, every purchase of a bot bolsters up the biggest tech company in the world. Where's the motivation to save the below ground when they could get rid of the paupers and use bots instead? It's great they stop the need for humans at landfill. But all the other jobs they're taking? If below grounders weren't sick and had had fertility problems, they wouldn't be needed.'

Harriet searches her brain for her reasoning. Compassion, humanity, tradition, all sound like weak arguments next to economics and big companies' balance sheets. She swallows back a lump in her throat. 'But they're people, below. They have a right to live.'

'You don't need to tell me this. But you want my advice?' Michelle leans forwards, forearms on the table. 'Keep your mouth shut until you're totally better. They're probably wanting you well because you're the face of the bots, their number one campaigner. The bots love you and they want to keep them happy.'

Harriet's mouth hangs open. She dips her chin, looking down at her hands. Empty, clean-ish, but if what Michelle says is true, she might as well have blood on them. Her mouth downturns. 'Oh.'

'So, yeah, I don't mean to sound harsh, and I get where you're coming from, but all of this—' she flaps her hands around as if her campaigning is represented by bugs flying around the room '—All your campaigning to protect Oliver, a side-effect of that is the below grounders are being forgotten.'

Harriet blinks away fresh tears. It's a wonder she has any left. 'But people below love the bots.'

'If they knew about the cure, they wouldn't.'

Harriet exhales as if she's been punched. She's been accused of being a traitor to her roots before. She brushed off such apparent insults, feeling proud to have risen up and out of the dirt. But this is so much worse than a bit of snobbery and a fake accent. She never meant to punish her people. She only wanted justice for the crimes against bots, and to protect them.

There's a knock at the door and Harriet jumps to answer it again, her sore feet not bothersome in her anticipation.

Lenny's bearded and too-cheery face greets her, along with the camera crew and makeup team. Harriet's shoulders drop as she exhales an exasperated sigh.

'I'm sorry,' Harriet says, 'but this can't happen today.'

'You're contracted—'

'I don't care. There's been a family tragedy.'

'Tragedy makes great telly.' Lenny barges past her, the rest of the crew following and setting up in the kitchen, as if it's not her house at all but has always been a movie set.

'No one is here but me,' Harriet says as she trails after them.

'You'll do just fine,' Lenny says.

He casts his eyes over Michelle for a moment, then disregards her as easily as he would a misplaced prop.

Harriet stands in the doorway tugging on her sleeves. Her back rounds as she feels like nothing more than a shadow. This isn't meant to be a show about Harriet. It's about the boys and making them safe.

The crew move the furniture and rearrange the crockery. One of them stashes the dirty dishes in the nearest cupboard. Will her treatment get stopped if the TV show gets canned? She needs it anyway, to get Theo treatment. One problem at a time just doesn't compute when they're piling up like trash at the landfill. Any healthier Harriet felt today has gone.

'I'll leave you to it,' Michelle says and hugs her goodbye. 'Call if you need anything.'

Harriet says goodbye, lingering at the doorway for as long as possible, ignoring the rearranging and preparation going on in her home. What more can she do? She's alone. No one is back yet. She can only hope Michelle is wrong.

'So,' Lenny says when the camera is ready and points at the chair he wants her to sit on. 'Tell the viewers all about this drama you've been having today. Perhaps there's a way viewers at home can help.'

Harriet takes a breath. The show airs a day after filming. Surely Monty will be home by then. But just in case, she could rally some support. One problem at a time and right now, Monty missing is the one she needs to solve.

❁ ❁ ❁ ❁

Harriet's still doing her piece to camera when Theo walks in. She spins around in her chair to where he hides in the shadow of the hallway, and her shoulders slump when she notes he's alone. She ignores Lenny's instructions and walks to him, then closes the kitchen door behind her.

'I couldn't get below,' Theo says in a hushed voice. 'The doors are all shut, locked. I went to three different entrances and it's all blocked off.'

She shivers, as if Theo brought the Arctic in with him. 'What the hell is going on?'

'I feel sick,' Theo says, paler than ever, red-rimmed eyes encased in dark circles, and his thinning hair falling out more rapidly than usual, some strands stuck to his jacket. 'I've got such a bad feeling. Why the hell would they shut it off? Some contagion or something? Remember that flu outbreak years ago and they locked the doors?'

'Messages still not going through?'

'No. Nothing.'

Lenny's voice sounds through the door. 'Harriet, we're still rolling.'

Theo grunts. 'Do they have to do this now?'

'I spoke about Monty. I thought it might help,' Harriet says and feels crass for doing so.

'I'm going to take a taxi tomorrow to a further away door and try from there,' Theo says. 'If he's not back by then . . .' He bends double and puts his face in his hand. 'Shit. I can't imagine him not being home tonight.'

'I have my hospital appointment tomorrow, but I'll delay and come with you.'

'No.' He stands upright again. 'I can go. You need that treatment. Please, Monty will be cross if you miss it.'

A knock sounds from the kitchen door. A soft, continuous knock that gets Harriet's back up. 'Harriet. We're against the clock here.'

She presses her lips together and looks at Theo, at the pain in his eyes. She gives him a hug. In her embrace she tries to convey a message of reassurance, of love and support. She's still too weak, too thin to convey anything except how fragile people are. Though as she holds onto him, she notes, he's not much better.

'I'll be finished soon,' she says. 'Then we can have a cuppa. Okay?'

'I'm going back out. Sorry,' he says with a sniff. 'I can't sit and wait. I just came back to see if he's home. I'll ask around, see if anyone here knows what's going on.'

He leaves, then with heavy legs, she turns and walks back to the kitchen. With each step, she inhales, and tries to regain some composure, to mask her worries. She's an actor and, right now, she needs to play the part of Harriet from a few days ago. Wasn't that a better time! She takes a seat and replaces her face of fear and concern with one of motherly love.

'So, Harriet,' Lenny says, 'what's it like living with the bots when there's worry in the household? Are they useful? Do they show signs of worry?'

Do they? She tries to think. She doesn't believe so. Thomas never seems worried about anything. He takes all of life in his stride. Oliver always wears a face of defiance. As a kid, his silky eyebrows would draw in, his little brow wrinkling when he was worried, just like hers. Now, he's so different. He doesn't get worried, just angry and distant. It's as if, somehow, Anthony's made more of a lasting impression on him than she has.

She's staring down the camera, face vacant as her thoughts consume her. She blinks a few times when she realises she hasn't answered the question.

Lenny's impatient eyes bore into hers as he taps his foot.

'So, Harriet,' he says, overenunciating the consonants. 'Has there been any more trouble with the Flesh Fraternity? Do you think they're mostly on side with the bots now?'

She squeezes her eyes a moment, then focuses on the camera lens, back in the room, back in character. 'Nothing on our doorstep, thankfully. But I've no doubt they'll keep trying to hurt these wonderful workers.'

'What do you think can be done about that?'

Harriet exhales slowly, as if the hope is being drawn out of her. What can be done about the people who wish her son harm? When she gets cross, she'd like to harm them back, but her rational side knows that wouldn't solve a thing. What would a period-drama actor say—her doe-eyed younger self, fresh-faced and innocent? Her watery gaze peers down the camera lens as she projects every last bit of hope she can muster.

'How do we ever rise up against hate? With love. Plain and simple.'

CHAPTER 37

Oliver keeps his ear defenders on at work. There's been no more imploding tunnels, but he can still hear screams and voices. That song still sings in his head. He's not certain if they're real or not, even with the ear defenders he can hear them. Three times he was sure he heard Uncle Monty calling him and he whipped his head round, only to find nothing there. But Monty is everywhere—in the clothes he's wearing, in his memories, and in his worries. But are Monty and the other people below really worth sacrificing to make the country greater? According to Anthony, yes. Monty is collateral damage, like everyone below.

Evolution. That's what Anthony called it. Oliver knows that word. The development of living things, to improve. That sounds like a good thing.

So why does it haunt him still? If death is part of human life, why doesn't it feel normal?

The only thing that stops the echoes of the buried is when Oliver shuts it away, and instead imagines his next job in that top office, showing his mum around the place, then taking her on Hel-E rides, enjoying her face as she sees the view.

They're building now, concrete on top of the concrete below, and Oliver can't summon the motivation to help.

'You could do your bit, Oliver,' George says.

George was always confrontational at the Institute, would boss Oliver around and act like he was the best at everything. At work, though, as adult bots, he fronts up to Oliver less. He must know Oliver's going places more than he is, and he knows his mum speaks up for the bots. Oliver hasn't been given the title of their boss yet, but he's sure they can all tell.

If Oliver's going to be top of the company, then does he need to be doing such manual labour? He wants to be away from ground level, up in the sky again where the goings on down here are far away, abstract and forgettable.

How he wishes he could forget.

He pitches in less, scuffs at the ground with his shoe, ignores Duncan when he shouts at him. He might be told to do an awful job again and he won't know until he's done it. So, instead, he hardly does anything and listens to his colleagues moan and shout at him.

When he's boss, all of that will stop. When he's the boss, he'll have respect, and that means not having to do jobs he doesn't want to do.

As he finishes work, he's mad. His colleagues have been angry with him all day and anger is like a disease; it's contagious. Being angry makes the cries and screams in his head go away. Anger is a muffler for the cries of the damned.

His already tired hands ball into tight fists. He's sick of being moaned and yelled at by his colleagues. They should appreciate him. Don't they know how he did the toughest jobs of all? He did the awful job so they didn't have to. He's wondered why Anthony wanted him to do that job. It must be because only the toughest bot could have done it. Only the toughest bot could handle the mental aftermath.

That deserves some respect.

When he's in charge, he'll dress like he's important and make sure they all stand up straight when addressing him, just like they do with Anthony. When he's in charge, he'll be far away from the landfill, so high up no cries can reach him. Until then, he can shut those cries away.

There's no Hel-E waiting for him. He's going to have to walk home along the low-level walkways, crammed and busy. He can hardly walk along 99 looking how he does. He needs a job where he can wear a nice suit and have his hair tidy so when he lives up top with his mum, she'll be proud to be seen with him.

As he stomps his way home on 5, Oliver barges past anyone in his way. He doesn't apologise or make an effort to give way. He shouldn't even be living this low. This isn't where he belongs.

A few girls recognise him. Clearly not everyone is put off by the video of him fronting up to that Flesh Fraternity prick. They beg him to stop for photos and by the third request, he does. He puts his arms around the girls next to him, his hand on their sides. He wishes he had a sense of smell as he imagines he would like their scent. When he says goodbye to them, he sends Evie a text:

> *You are no one. I've forgotten you already.*

He means it. Girls everywhere love him. He'll get his mum to start putting photos of him on social media again. He'll engage with his own *Get Level* account and message his admirers directly. His mum will love that. She loves the whole social media thing.

The next bit of filming he does, he'll let the crew and camera people know how important he is. He'll tell the world what he's done, how he's making this town and city greater, higher, better, and how he's going to have a top-level apartment like someone really important. He'll make his mum so proud when she hears he's going places.

'Bot scum!'

Those words hit Oliver like a lightning bolt. The voice comes from behind and Oliver spins around, wrath heating his insides, every muscle taut and ready. There's a man right behind him. He's short with an angry sneer plastered across his face. Oliver grabs the guy by his collar and lifts him off the ground.

'You need to show me some respect!' Oliver says through his teeth, his nose a centimetre from the man's.

There are phone cameras on him and he's glad. He smiles as he drops the man and kicks him, then faces the phones. 'Do you all hear me? I deserve some fucking respect!'

The man on the floor scuffles to his feet. 'You're insane. Dangerous. Wait until we have our EMP. You and your kind will be obliterated!'

There's a buzz that sends shockwaves from Oliver's arm through his whole body. He tries to yell back at the man but instead he convulses, his limbs ignoring his commands, and he falls to the ground. His vision clouds and in the gloom, the man runs away.

The dimness of the low-level walkway gets even dimmer. The vibration of footsteps tingle against his head as his convulsions slow and he's still. His arms or legs won't move. His voice is gone, his mouth useless. His thoughts are slow, his body doesn't work but he can't think why or what happened. His vision is now really dark, like his battery has depleted completely, and he stares into nothing.

'Oliver? Oliver?'

The voice sounds miles away, but Thomas stands over him, his face close enough Oliver can make him out in the darkness. His brows are drawn, his hair falling about his face as he bends over Oliver. Why is it always Thomas to the rescue? Oliver is the tougher one, Oliver is the protector, the visionary. But he's still unable to move. Thomas lifts his arm and puts it over his shoulder, heaving him up, then dragging him until Oliver can use his feet again.

Oliver's skin itches and burns, his battery down to one per cent. The world turns to a mist.

Oliver squints as he opens his eyes. His bedroom is normally comfortable but now it's garish and claustrophobic. The walls with their pictures and shelves and mirrors are imposing, too close, too busy.

'Darling, how are you feeling?'

His mum and Uncle Theo stand over him, stooped, strained foreheads. His mum's glassy eyes are red and her skin blotchy. They're looking at him like he's sick. But he isn't sick. He can't get sick. How long has he been asleep? He's not sure, but he feels better now. Tired still, but he can move. He sits up, propping himself on his elbows.

'I'm fine,' he says. 'Just a bit wiped out.'

'That Flesh Fraternity man had a taser,' Theo says. 'Luckily, it was only on your arm. A direct battery hit would have been worse.'

Oliver touches his arm. It's tender, like a bruise. He can still feel the weight of the man in his hands, the roughness of his collar, his breath on his face, the glint of fear in his eyes. 'Is Thomas okay?'

'Yeah,' Uncle Theo says. 'The taser didn't get him.'

His jaw tenses. 'I'm going to kill that guy.'

'No. Don't,' his mum says. 'You're on TV everywhere threatening him. This doesn't look good, darling.'

Who cares about looking good? With enough respect, he can look as bad as he damn well pleases. 'What's an EMP?' he asks. 'He said he had one. That's what Uncle Theo is working on, isn't it? A weapon. I heard you.'

His mum and uncle exchange looks. They always do that, like they can communicate through their eyes. Oliver will never be as good at reading people as they are.

Theo looks at Oliver now and steps a little closer. 'It is a weapon. I'm trying to stop it from working, and to find out when they plan on using it.' He reaches down and brings up a white rag. 'Here.' He hands it to Oliver. 'I'm not certain they'll work, but it's the best I've got at the moment.'

Oliver takes it and holds it up. He can't help but recoil at the sight of it. It's the ugliest piece of clothing he's ever seen. 'This looks like something a below grounder would wear.'

'Hey,' Theo snaps. 'Nothing wrong with looking like a below grounder. You can still put your fancy jacket over the top. But this might help protect you.'

Oliver puts the vest on his lap in a crumpled heap. It won't do it any harm. 'And what about all the other bots? No one cares about my kind. I know you care about me, but there are lots of us and everyone is so worried about the damned below grounders that no one gives a shit about us.'

'Oliver!' His mum says with a gasp. 'That's not true. We're trying.'

Oliver leans forward, his eyes narrow. 'All you're trying to do is get famous because you're a below grounder and you're ashamed of it. You want people to think you're something better than that.'

The words come out before he's thought about them properly. His mouth clamps shut when he's done, his narrowed eyes widening. He's never seen his mum make that face before. She looks like she's been slapped and is trying not to show how much it stings.

'Now, listen'. Theo stretches out each word. 'I know you must be in shock, but you can't talk to your mother like that. She loves you and is trying to do what's right. When Monty gets back, he can make the vest look a bit nicer, okay?'

When Monty gets back. They still think he will. A hard lump lodges itself in Oliver's throat, another in his gut, both threatening to pummel his insides. He can't deal with this, can't cope with looking at their faces that expect so much from him. They assume he's such a good bot, but he's done such bad things. He needs to get out, away from these walls and his family with their pitiful looks.

When sadness breaks through, the voices come back. The screaming, the cries, the last notes of that song. He tightens his muscles, then sets his jaw. He has to keep them shut away.

Thomas comes into the room and his mum and Theo leave. With them gone, the air is a little thinner, though Thomas looks just as concerned as them.

'You really scared me, Oliver,' Thomas says. 'When I found you like that, I was so worried it was game over.'

Oliver's cheeks heat. He's not sure how to respond. He should be the one protecting Thomas, not the other way around. 'Well, thanks for getting me back. I'm fine.'

'It's not the same between us since we're not working togeth-er. We don't spend as much time together, but ... well ... I want you to know, whatever happens, we're still like brothers.'

'Yeah,' Oliver says, softening a little. 'Yeah, of course.' He means it. Thomas has been his best friend forever. He should buy him something with the money from Anthony. That's what a good brother would do.

'Maybe, when you're totally better, we can hang out a bit? Just go to the park or something. Have a good chat.'

'Sure,' he says this with little enthusiasm but, really, he wants to shout a big yes and run off to the park to play football right now. Something so fun and simple sounds like the best thing in the world.

Some of the worry disappears from Thomas's face. 'Good. That'd be great. Because Evie said—'

Oliver bristles, all his tension returning. 'When did you see Evie?' he snaps.

'The other day after work. She said you didn't seem yourself.'

A growl escapes, and Oliver's stomach hardens. His friends have been talking about him behind his back. What else have they been doing?

He pushes himself up, then swings his legs around. He's careful putting weight on his feet. His legs seem to work okay, so he stands. 'Whatever. I'm going out.'

He grabs his jacket, then shoves the vest in his pocket as he leaves, a sorrowful call from his mum resonating behind.

He can't take on their sadness. He doesn't know how, and he doesn't know how to be the man they want. He stomps down the walkway, his fisted hands wedged in his pockets, dipping his chin and tensing every muscle. There's a sound in his head, a *boom boom boom*, like a heartbeat, but Oliver knows it can't be. It's his programming, in overdrive, heating and fizzing as he tries and struggles to make sense of the world.

Humans are like vultures to a cause, circling despair until they find a fresh and bitter bit to peck at. But Oliver is not a human. He can't fight every battle. So he chooses one. Only one.

No one is doing anything to protect the bots. Oliver doesn't need protecting; he can take care of himself. But Evie does. It's not like Thomas would do anything to look after her. He takes the lift back up to 99.

CHAPTER 38

With Monty still not back, Theo needs Harriet's support as much as she needs his, but she's unable to offer any words of comfort as her shock and dismay robs her of any positive thought. Harriet can't be consoled by Theo's hugs or cups of tea. Oliver was cruel, awful, not her boy at all. In her mind, he's still her messy-haired, dimpled-cheeked little boy with his sweet grin and caring nature. In her mind, he still delights in birds and spiders.

She was too absent when he was at the Institute. She never held him enough. She stayed with Anthony too long. All manner of reasoning falls heavy on her shoulders in a coat of blame and shame. Because it's always the mother's fault, that's what they say. To have her boy react in such a way is a mark of her failure. She put too much pressure on him or not enough. She loved him too much or her love was somehow lacking. Bad men come from bad mothers.

But he's not a bad man. She refuses to believe that. He's angry, troubled, heartbroken, and such emotions are too alien for him to cope with. She always loved how he was her little protector, but such a disposition in a grown man is threatening. He sees her as weak. She's portrayed this too often, cowering to Anthony, to TRI, to her illness. Her fault. Again.

'It's the new job, it must be,' Theo says. 'There's probably all manner of male chauvinism down there, too much bravado and egos running wild. I got a job in a tech lab years ago with a load of men who were all back-slapping, wolf-whistling types. You can imagine how awful I found that. That's all it is. I'm sure of it.'

They're on the sofa, Harriet's legs curled underneath and she leans into him while he speaks, wrapping a blanket around the two of them. She can't imagine Theo working in such a place any more than she can Oliver. But at least Theo knows a thing or two about the world. Oliver's emerged from the Institute too innocent and unprepared. With that and the bot haters, how is he meant to react? Her poor boy has so much to cope with and he bottles it all up inside.

Theo goes out to look for Monty again, needing to stay busy, leaving Harriet by herself but when he arrives back hours later alone, Harriet bursts into tears. In his arms, she feels how thin he is and that makes her cry more. He hasn't eaten a thing, can't keep anything down, he says. She's the same. She feels as sick as she did weeks ago.

They sit in the kitchen and she cries again, Theo weeping with her, though less. He's still putting on a brave face, or trying to.

'He's going to be fine,' is all he keeps saying. 'Monty's the toughest person there is.' He looks at Harriet, wearing the same face he did when his parents died and it's as if his soul departs him too. He utters words that come out with so much pain, Harriet's own battered heart breaks. 'I can't lose him. I just can't.'

She's uttered such words before, when her losses were imminent. She takes his hands but can offer no words of comfort back. All they can do is hold on to each other and hope.

Thomas arrives home from work early and comes into the kitchen, flushed and stumbling over every word. 'Still . . . still . . . no . . . still no Uncle Monty?'

They shake their heads.

Thomas sits at the table with them, tugging on his sleeves and shifting his weight incessantly. 'I left early, boss said it was okay. I had to come and tell you. There's . . . there's this new bot at work who's taken over from Oliver. James, I think . . . Yeah, James, that's his name. He says . . . well . . . says there's some problem . . . below.'

Harriet looks at his face, his blotchy cheeks, brows drawn in, eyes darting from one side to the other.

'Look, I . . .' He swallows hard. 'I . . . I . . . don't know anything for sure.'

'Thomas,' Harriet says, sitting more upright. 'What's happened?'

'I heard from a bot . . . James . . . he's friends with one of the bots who works at the landfill.'

'And?'

'Apparently, and . . . well . . . they're not supposed to talk about it. I don't know this for sure—'

'Spit it out, Thomas!' Theo's grip on Harriet's hand tightens.

Thomas quits his fidgeting, his eyes still, and looks directly at Theo for a second. 'They're blowing up sections of below and filling the space in with concrete to strengthen the foundations for the towers. Part of the expansion.'

There's a silence as his words absorb. The weight of Thomas's words crush.

Harriet rubs her eyebrows, then shakes her head slowly. 'No. They wouldn't, not with people living there.'

'Maybe it's just blocked some exits?' Theo says, though his voice smacks of uncertainty.

The TV in the living room is on, some news article about the excitement over the AM Investments. The mention of Harriet's ex-husband's company makes every one of her hairs stand on end. She walks to the TV and watches, the footage showing the office down on 2. She knew about that office when they were together, the office that Anthony would dread going to, said it was where the riff-raff works, that it was a necessary evil. The shot has pixelated sections on the walls. Harriet can imagine the sort of posters hanging there. There he is, Anthony's entitled face, every bit the smug businessman, that face she used to love but now despises. He's lost some weight over the last few years. The heart attack must have been a wake-up call. His ruddy complexion has mellowed and his shirt appears to fit instead of being about to lose buttons. He's smiling, like he's one of the people. God, she could throw up.

She's about to look away, but does a double take. There, standing with Anthony, just a step behind, is Oliver.

'No.' Her hands go to her mouth.

'This doesn't mean anything,' Theo says.

She takes the necklace she's been hiding under her T-shirt, lifting the pendant for Theo to see.

'Woah.' Theo leans in to inspect it.

'Oliver said he found it. But it's all making sense.' She walks back to the kitchen and takes out the framed photograph she found, then shows Theo. He recognises it straight away. His childhood best friend, Harriet's brother. 'I left this behind at Anthony's. I was wondering how it got here. Oliver's been there. He must have brought it back with him.' She should have figured that much out. She closes her eyes and can picture Oliver there, in his old childhood bedroom, taking it from the shelf. He could never reach that shelf when he was a kid. He was too little.

She goes to his room and stands in the doorway for a moment. She should respect his privacy but then, he should have nothing to hide. What other clues reside in there?

She scans the space, and on his bookshelf, she spots it. A thick envelope. She can't bring herself to look. She points to it and Theo takes it, removing the wad of cash inside.

'There must be a couple of grand here,' Theo says.

A ringing drones in Harriet's ears, a sharp pain pings down her forehead as her hands reach for her stomach, nausea rolling through her gut. Her knees go slack, and she slides down the wall to sit on the floor. Her boy isn't meant to earn money. There's only one place that could have come from.

She holds onto the necklace, tight in her fist, the gaudy thing she thought Oliver had found for her. She's so stupid. This has Anthony's taste written all over it.

'Anthony is employing him,' she says, slowly, as if awkwardly fitting puzzle pieces together. 'That must be it. Oh, God. He's paying for it, isn't he? My treatment? Oliver went to Anthony.' She rests her forehead on her knees.

Of course Oliver went to Anthony. Her little boy, her protector. How could she not have known?

Theo sits next to her, his arm draped around her shoulders. 'He means well.'

Again, here's Theo consoling her. Thomas's news about blowing up below ground has barely sunk in. Theo's arm around her shoulders is weak and trembling. She puts her hand on his knee and he buckles from that slight touch. Theo's always tried to be strong for everyone else, and now she's utterly failing to be strong for him.

Thomas sits the other side of Theo, lifting his knees up and curling into a ball. She should be there for him too, thank him for telling them. That must have been so hard for him. The three of them stay like that, on the cold hard floor of the hallway. An incomplete unit without Oliver and Monty, none of them having the strength to move or even speak. The shock of everything makes the air cold as the world spins too fast. Can it just slow a moment, let the dust settle. Surely then, everything won't seem so bad.

Theo still has the cash in his hand. Harriet's wide eyes stare at it. Anthony's paying Oliver for something, he's buying him. Anthony is generous, but he's not a forgiving man, and she rejected him.

She feels it then, in her bones that used to ache, in her muscles that used to cramp. Her recovery is tainted, for her treatment isn't meant as a kindness; he's seeking revenge.

Theo doesn't know Anthony like she does. Oliver means well, like Theo says, she doesn't doubt that.

But what is Anthony's price?

CHAPTER 39

Oliver looks at his feet as he walks. There's some neat sewing where Monty repaired his trousers and a trace of a stain he scrubbed to get out. His shoes have new laces. Uncle Monty found those. They don't match, but they're close enough.

Oliver's sure he hears Monty's voice. He snaps his head around, but there are only strangers behind him. As he walks towards the lift, a child cries and that sound rings in his head. His knees buckle and his hands go to his ears.

He didn't mean to hurt anyone. He didn't!

But then, Anthony said it's for the best, that they were suffering, and he helped. And someone like Anthony knows what's best for the country. People shouldn't live below ground. It's wrong. It's right to reach for the sky.

People shouldn't live below ground, but does that mean below-ground people shouldn't live at all?

It's a paradox, a conundrum. He shakes the thought away. It's too hard to make sense of everything. He thumps the side of his head, telling the reverberating cries to shut up.

The vest is in his pocket and when he gets up to 99, he messages Evie again. He's not sure she'll come down, but he could ask the concierge, and he could wait outside all day if he has to. He's meant to be going to work, but he can be late. Anthony won't mind. He's his best employee.

Perhaps he'll say Thomas is with him and that will make her see him, since she seems to prefer spending time with Thomas than Oliver. His biceps flinch at the thought, and the cries in his head settle down for a moment. He tightens his fist and enjoys the peace.

He hears Evie. With the cries gone, her voice is unmistakable even though it's far away. 99 walkway is always so much quieter than down on 5, a light breeze, people chatting, none of the crashing rubbish and crammed parks. Up here, Evie's tinkling laugh carries on the wind. She's speaking to Bonnie. They're pointing out the birds. He hears her long before he sees her and he stops a moment, just to listen. His anger fizzes away, the sounds of his memories moving aside to make way for Evie, like her voice is a tonic. The cries and screams stay away.

He walks slowly in the direction of the voice, then spots her in the park. He stands at the edge by some flowerbeds and watches for a minute. The two boys from the family photographs are behind her, daring each other to climb higher on the climbing frame. Evie pushes little Bonnie on the swing, her golden ringlets fanning out behind her, feet dressed in pink shoes dangling below. That heavy rock that was lodged inside Oliver dissolves into nothing, leaving him weightless. His mouth curls up, a smile he can't hold back as he watches Evie with the children. She stops pushing Bonnie to untangle the smaller boy from the climbing frame. She's so patient with them, helping them enjoy every moment. She has the warmest smile, her eyes crinkling in the corners.

'Evie!' he calls out to her.

When she looks at him, that warm smile fades. Her eyes harden and she folds her arms as she walks over. 'What, Oliver? I thought I made myself clear last time.'

Oliver takes a small step back as Evie's tone cuts the air between them, that weightless feeling now heavy and cold. Bonnie is standing next to Evie. She's already looking smarter and more alert. She holds her hand out for Oliver to shake.

He bends to his knees. 'Hi again, Bonnie. How are you?'

'I'm good. Thank you for my bear.'

So Evie gave it to her. He warms a little at that. 'You're very welcome, young lady.'

He stands again and faces Evie. 'I have something for you. Here.' He takes the tatty vest from his pocket and gives it to her.

She holds it up and makes a face similar to Oliver's when he first saw it. 'Erm, thanks.'

'You remember the Flesh Fraternity? They're building a weapon—' he lowers his voice and shields his mouth with his hand '—to kill us. Wear this all the time. This will protect you.'

She sighs. 'Okay. Thank you.'

They maintain eye contact for a moment, but there's no silent conversation there like his mum and Theo have. If she wants to say anything, he can't tell. He bets she and Thomas don't have weird silences, sure they spend all their time laughing and joking, talking about him behind his back. He blinks a few times. He needs to stop thinking about Thomas and Evie. The silence stretches it out as he thinks about how to tell Evie what's best.

'Come away with me,' he blurts out, his words tumbling from his mouth so quickly it's like they weren't thought through at all. Perhaps they really weren't. He's imagined a life with Evie and Bonnie, but running away wasn't something he considered. Now he says it out loud it seems like the most logical thing. Just the three of them, leaving all this crap behind. His guilt and shame and anger can stay far away. His insides heat and the cries and screams come back, like they're pulling him towards them, not letting him go. He stiffens and tries to shake the sounds from his head.

He knows how to flee; he did it before with his mum. He takes her hands, trying to be gentle but he's so tense, it's hard not to hold too tightly. He wants to sound calm, but the screams are getting louder and he has to talk through his clenched jaw. 'You and Bonnie. The three of us. Let's get away from here and be a family. There's so much evil here. We can have a fresh start.' Each syllable is punched out, over enunciated, like Evie has to hear him past the screams in his head.

She shakes her head and tries to pull her hands back as Oliver tightens his grip. 'No, Oliver. I have a life here. I'm happy. I like my job.'

'I mean it, Evie.' He yanks her hands closer, his face almost touching hers. He won't take no for an answer. Like Anthony said. His eyes, wide and wild, search hers for a hint of agreement. 'You have to. You hear me! Believe me. Show me some respect!'

Evie pulls her hands back harder now, and he releases her. She steps away, then calls the boys over. 'Come on, kids. Let's go home. You can have some ice cream.' The boys cheer and run over, and they all walk away. Evie gives Oliver a quick glance over her shoulder. 'Goodbye, Oliver,' she says before she turns her back on him.

Oliver watches them leave, Bonnie's hand in Evie's, her legs skipping to keep up. Then he bends, groans, and punches the metal rung of the climbing frame. He used to love that bloody thing. Now he wants to rip it from the ground. He might have just saved Evie's life and this is how she repays him!

He sits on the bench, the same place his mum used to sit in simpler times. He thumps his temples, trying to figure out his thoughts. His mind feels polluted, mixed up, he can't make sense of anything. All he wanted was a life, a real life with Evie and Bonnie. All he wanted was a family of his own.

With Evie gone, sorrow takes hold and the cries and screams of people being buried again fill his mind. It hurts, crushes him. He wraps his arms around his body and rocks back and forth. However much he squeezes his eyes shut he can't stop the images of those hands reaching through the ground. And he did nothing to help.

Maybe the Flesh Fraternity are right. He deserves the EMP.

His hands grasp his hair, and he tugs and presses his palms into his head. He just wants the cries to stop. He never used to be so evil. He never used to think it was okay to hurt people. He only wants to protect his mum and build a nice life and Anthony—

He lets go of his hair, his hands dropping to his sides, and he sits upright. There are a few moments of blissful quiet in his head, with one thought dominating his entire mind space.

Anthony.

His face, his smile, his stupid fancy things.

Anthony was always a bad man. Oliver knew he was a bad man when he was a kid. Just because he has nice things, he's still bad. Uncle Monty may not have many fancy things, but he's good. He's kind and caring and looks after everyone. He doesn't deserve to die so the Anthonys of the world can have a bigger house.

Anthony never looks after anyone except himself. He's been twisting things, making Oliver's thoughts all wrong. Oliver didn't hurt those people. He didn't mean to. It was Anthony.

He remembers Anthony hitting his mum. Oliver can still hear the blows, the yelps from his mum, see the angry yellow and purple marks on her neck. He can still hear the snap of her arm when he broke it. Anthony was never sorry then. He said he was sometimes, and he'd act like he felt bad, but he'd do it again and again. Anthony says he's a man of his word, but he says sorry and doesn't mean it.

He's a liar. He hurts people, he always has. Maybe that's why he's such a successful businessman. He hurts people until they do what he says. Is that what respect is?

Oliver stands, his chest heaves as his insides heat up. *Anthony.* He squeezes his eyes and thumps his temples, one side than the other, like he's trying to force the dots to connect. Anthony's image is so clear in his mind. Sneering, smiling, not at all sorry, sitting with his smug face with his shiny things and big office.

Anthony convinced Oliver he needed nice things when the nicest thing in the world is family.

It's Anthony who has polluted his thoughts. Anthony who has all that schadenfreude.

Oliver walks toward the lift. Slow, purposeful footsteps, every muscle taut. The screams and cries are quiet now. He can imagine Anthony's screams instead.

Anthony made him do those bad things. He made Oliver hurt people, turned Oliver into a bad man, so bad, he may have hurt his Uncle Monty. Anthony made him think he needed all those fancy things.

And Anthony is going to pay.

CHAPTER 40

Harriet picked herself off the floor a while ago and has sat in an energy-sapped heap on the sofa since. She and Theo scroll *Get Level* for updates and find little but posts from worried people on low levels. She wants to text Oliver but refrains. He needs to let off steam; she needs to give him space. Being the needy, overbearing mother isn't right at the moment but then, what would she know? She screws up everything.

Harriet messages Michelle with Thomas's news, and she comes around straight away.

'You're right,' Michelle says as soon as she walks through the door. Her normally perfect complexion is tear-stained, her hair has a hint of disarray. 'That's what I heard. Explosions. Other bots have heard the same news.'

'Oh, my God.' Theo's hands cover his face, then hug his waist. It's taken a while to sink in. He's pushed reality to one side for long enough. 'Monty—'

'This doesn't mean he's hurt.' Harriet wishes her voice didn't wobble so much. 'He's just stuck.'

Michelle sits on the arm of the sofa, her posture slouched. 'North exits are blocked from what I've heard. I think some people are trying to get out further east.'

'That's where I'll go,' Theo says as he sits straighter. 'I need to find him.'

'Or you'll get in the way,' Michelle says. She holds her phone towards them to show an article. 'There's literally nothing official coming out of councils or government or anything, but on *Get Level* they're asking people to stay away as exits are getting rammed with people trying to get in to look for people.'

Theo rubs his forehead, and Harriet puts her arm around him. He buckles easily, leaning on her and crying onto her shoulder. She swallows, trying not to cry, to be the strong one for once.

'As much as it sucks, you'll be doing more harm than good going there right now,' Michelle says, her eyes staying on her phone. 'And you don't even know which exit. Some volunteers have set up sign-out sheets and they're updating them with names.'

'She's right, Theo,' Harriet says, somehow her voice finding its way around the lump in her throat. 'It's horrible, but waiting here and keeping an eye is the best you can do.'

He buries his face deeper into Harriet's shoulder, his tears dampening her T-shirt. 'He has to be okay. I can't lose him. I just can't.'

Harriet rubs his back. 'He'll be fine. I know he will.' She wishes she sounded more certain but dread claws at her. She wants to curl in a ball and deny her friend could be hurt, deny her son may have had a part in it. That lump in her throat thickens. She could gag on her stifled tears. She has to stay strong for Theo, as he always is for her.

'I can't believe there's nothing official,' Michelle says. 'Nothing at all. No help or anything.'

Harriet bristles. She knows why. Anthony. 'It's because it's AM Investments. My fucking ex-husband has too much power. He probably got a license for this.'

'The top don't even care,' Michelle says. 'No one up there is even talking about it. They just want their higher towers and that's all. They're racing to get their name on the list for anything above 110. Those apartments are literally built on the graveyards below.'

Theo groans and Harriet winces. Michelle may speak the truth, but she could soften the facts a little.

Michelle is still scrolling through her phone. Harriet hasn't offered her a drink or anything. She still hasn't even cleaned up since she was here last time. Michelle doesn't seem to care. Life high up hasn't turned her into a snob.

Michelle gasps, and turns the volume up on her phone, tilting it so they can both see. There's a video of one of the blocked doorways to below. A Flesh Fraternity man standing outside, talking to the camera with the kind of pious face Harriet wants to smack.

'This would not have been possible without the use of bots. No human would have carried out such atrocities. Bots are being used to destroy people below ground. How long are we going to put up with this? It's time for the bots to be finished.'

Harriet covers her eyes with her hands. 'But it was Anthony's company.' Her voice is pathetic and weak. 'A human's company. Not bots. The bots just do as they're told.'

The lights flicker a few times, then the electric dies. Harriet's heart sinks.

'Bots are working at the energy incinerators too now, I hear,' Michelle says.

Harriet rests her forehead in her hands. The room spins and she feels like she's actually falling. How she wants to. How she wishes right now she was a million miles away.

Theo stands with a stooped posture, then finds some candles and lights them, his hands shaking so much, drips of wax splatter to the floor. He places the candles on the coffee table next to the magazines Oliver never read. Harriet watches the dancing flames and her chest caves in. Her love is concentrated, hardened around a knot of worry. There's too much evil in the world. Despite her best efforts, the world is still not safe for her son, though it seems, the world is not safe for anyone.

Come home, please, she begs silently. Come home, Monty. Come home, Oliver.

CHAPTER 41

Oliver receives a text message as he walks back to the lift. He assumes it's going to be Anthony, since he should be at work. They must be mad and wondering where he is. But it's Uncle Theo.

Oliver pauses his walk as he reads. His mum needs that final treatment. This can't all have been for nothing. He stands still for a moment, then runs his hand over his face as he thinks. Okay, he can make a plan. Quick visit home to make sure his mum goes to the hospital, then he'll visit Anthony and make him pay. She needs her last treatment. Anthony needs to think he's still on-side so he'll pay for the medicine.

The lights are out lower down and he uses his phone torch to light his way. At least this means he doesn't get recognised.

He arrives home to a teary-eyed mum. The sight of her so sad makes him want to cry too. Tears must be satisfying, like all the bad feelings leak away. A release, like a hole in a bucket. It's such a human thing to cry. It's the one tell he's not a real person.

'Darling,' his mum says and opens her arms.

He goes to her. How long has it been since he's had a hug? There's something about his mum's embrace that saps the fight from him. He's not a kid anymore, but still her hug makes his taut muscles loosen and even though he can't cry tears, his shoulders and throat shudder like he's sobbing.

'Are you okay, Mum?'

She holds on a little tighter. 'I'm just worried about you. You need to talk to me. You need to tell me what's going on.'

The lights flicker back on and the TV blares out full blast and she reaches for the remote to mute it. When it's not just candles lighting the space, he can see how tired and drawn she looks. He's done all this to make her well and now she looks sick with worry.

They sit on the sofa. He wishes it were softer so it would swallow him up. His back rounds, his elbows tucking in. He wishes he was smaller, a tiny ball. If he was a kid again, it would be better.

'He . . . Anthony . . .' The words need to come out, Oliver knows he has to say them. There's so much inside and he's going to burst if he doesn't say it. The screams and cries echo, louder, goading him now. He can't look at his mum while he speaks. Shame crawls up his neck, his face heats, curdling with the coldness of what he's done. 'Anthony told me I'd be helping the company, that we'd have a nice life, a high-up place. He never told me what would happen. I didn't know what I was doing until it was too late.' He thumps his forehead. 'I just wanted to make you well, and happy, and safe. My head, it's all messed up. I don't know what's right or wrong.'

'Sh.' She rubs his arms. 'Darling, it's not your fault.'

She tries to soothe him, but he can't be soothed. It's too late for that. When he's calm, the screams don't fade. People in pain, suffering, begging to live. He ignored them then and only his anger keeps them away now. Anger is so potent, it drowns out everything else.

'I only wanted to make you well,' he says. He can't look at her. He's not her good little boy anymore. If she looks him in the eye, she'll see a monster. 'He said working for him was the condition. Why would he say that?'

His mum's sniffing. He knows she's hurting. He feels it too, his chest bearing the weight of both their pain.

'Because he wanted to hurt me,' she says. 'Because he knows how good you are, and how much it would upset me to see you do bad things. He's manipulative. This was his power play. That's all.'

Oliver shakes his head, squeezing his eyes shut for a moment and tugging on his hair. It's so clear now, his wires aligning themselves properly. He was so stupid. So, so stupid. 'But Uncle Monty. Uncle Monty . . .'

'He's just stuck. We're going to find him safe and well. You'll see.'

There's no conviction in her tone. Oliver picks out the wobble of doubt, the kindness in her lie. 'I need to go and help them. I wanted to help, but they told me not to. I never meant to hurt anyone.'

'I know, darling, I know.'

Oliver grits his teeth. His back straightens as his shoulders tense. 'You're still going for treatment, right? This can't all be for nothing.'

'I'm meant to go in a moment, but I should wait with your Uncle Theo—'

'No.' He looks at her now. His eyes bore into hers, screaming she has to go. He can't let her get sick again. He'll drag her there if he has to. And the sooner she goes, the sooner he can pay Anthony a visit. 'You have to go. Please.'

She looks at her lap for a moment, averting her eyes from his and he thinks that maybe she's scared of him. But then, she looks back at Oliver, gives him a weak smile, and nods. 'Okay. Okay, I'll go.' She gives him a peck on the cheek, musses up his hair up like she always does. 'I'll go now.'

He stands as she gets her coat and leaves. She walks slowly. She needs to eat something. He considers going with her, following her to the hospital and making sure. But she wouldn't lie to him. He knows he can trust his mum more than anyone.

With his mum gone, Oliver goes to his room and paces. He's got loads of battery but plugs himself in anyway. He can't risk running low.

How long should he wait? A few hours, probably, until he knows for sure his mum is at least mid-treatment. He balls one hand into a fist and punches the other, grinding his knuckles into his palm. Impatience buzzes, every cry and scream from the buried that haunt him. He imagines it's Anthony. Every Flesh Fraternity man he's manhandled he imagines was Anthony's body his foot collided with. He wants to feel his jawbone snap, wants to hear him gasp for air after a stomach punch, wants to hear him beg, to see the look in his eyes when he knows he's going to feel pain, to suffer, to die. He wants to see the moment Anthony regrets everything. Oliver smiles as he continues to punch his hand, the screams and cries mute as he envisions grinding Anthony's bones to dust.

He knows what death means. It's a forever goodbye. It's wrong to kill someone, he's sure of that. But this isn't just killing. It's justice. Thomas made him promise he wouldn't strangle Anthony, but that was before he knew how bad Anthony is.

He takes out the dictionary again, looking for inspiration, for a word that sums up Anthony even better than previous words. His eyes land on *sycophant,* and that word hits him like a slap. Is that what Oliver is? He's been sucking up to Anthony because he has wealth and is important? Such a word seems so reductive. It takes away all the complexities and puts Oliver into a horrible box with materialistic and vain people. He doesn't want to be in that box. He only wanted to make a nice life for his mum. Oliver should be in a box with the caring people and the ones who do good things. All he ever wanted was to help his mum.

Theo comes in to check on him, but Oliver closes his eyes and pretends he's asleep. How can he look at his Uncle Theo after what he's done, after what Anthony made him do?

His hearing is too good, so there's no way to tune out Theo sobbing from the living room. Muffled and stifled cries, each one tearing Oliver in half. He unplugs his charger. His body heat is going to make it catch fire.

He checks the time, certain he's waited long enough now. He needs to put this right. He needs to do what he meant to do from the start.

Fuck Anthony and his company. The badness ends now.

CHapTer 42

How can Harriet go to the hospital as if nothing is wrong? But Oliver and Theo both insist. That look in her son's eyes, begging her to be well. She owes it to him. After all he's been through, all his trauma that stems from her, she needs to live to be there for him. She needs to live to put the broken pieces of him back together.

As she sits and has her infusion, she's riddled with guilt and hate that it's her ex-husband who made this happen. People below ground continue to suffer while he uses her life to manipulate her son.

She wants to allow that anger to consume her, but she knows what Oliver needs now is love. If she gives in to her rage, he will too.

Doctor Peterson talks about the weather—a storm is coming, she says. It's going to be a bad one, the biggest in years. Possible tornadoes. Harriet nods, as if she cares. Her own life is a tempest of worries.

When she is done with her transfusion, Doctor Peterson asks her to sit for an hour rather than go straight home.

The entire hour, Harriet frets. Why must she wait? Has Anthony withdrawn funding and now she's going to get hammered with a bill? There's no way she'd be able to fund it, even with the cash she found in Oliver's room. Her legs bounce up and down, and she bites the odd bit of nail that's grown back.

It's a horrible feeling to be indebted to someone she hates. She's so torn. Happy to be well but God, she hates that he's using her son as a pawn, to try and make her sweet boy bad. Her son had enough trauma already, now he has this mental turmoil to deal with. She's bitten her nail so far down it bleeds. The sting isn't the worst thing. It stops her spiralling for a moment.

After an hour, Doctor Peterson sends her for a blood and urine test and asks her to wait a little longer. Hunger gnaws at Harriet's stomach. When did she last eat? That bland meal when Monty first didn't come home. She picked at a bit of breakfast, that's about it. Food was so far from her thoughts with all her other worries but now she's spent, starving and weak. She sits after the tests and imagines a meal Monty's cooked and as she does, tears brim, then roll down her cheeks. Monty has to be okay. He's so strong. He's the toughest man she knows.

She tries not to be impatient, but she needs to get home, to her boy, to Theo. She checks her phone. There's no news. She makes the mistake of loading up *Get Level*. News of below-ground explosions being due to bots is spreading. Tasers are being used in the streets to capture and kill bots. Dread clutches at her stomach so much it hurts; meanwhile, her back cramps and her skin is too tight everywhere.

A trickle of people have started emerging from below, bringing with them stories of the tunnels collapsing and being filled with concrete. None of these stories come from Monty. His name hasn't made it to a list yet.

How many are dead? It's a question they can't answer.

Hundreds, one person says.

Thousands, says another.

Harriet's new hunger diminishes. The room tilts each way, her vision dotted with stars.

There's an ache around her heart, like every beat is an effort. That organ shatters as she still hopes he's alive. How she hopes none perished, but most of all Monty. Please, don't let it be Monty. She tightens her cardigan around her. It's one that Monty patched together out of several tattered others. It's so colourful, like him. It's too cheerful for Harriet.

Doctor Peterson calls her through.

Harriet sits in the chair, her shoulders hunched, ready to be told she has a bill to pay, that this has all been a nasty joke, that she must move back in with Anthony, or some other dreadful outcome.

'I am pleased to say your tests came back all clear.'

It takes a moment for Harriet to register what the doctor said. She hasn't even considered the test results, her mind too bogged down with a zillion other worries.

She looks up and blinks. 'I'm sorry. What?'

'Your treatment is finished. There is no trace of any of the below-ground sickness in your system. You're completely clear.'

Harriet's vision loses focus, and the world turns into a haze. The doctor's words sound again in her head a few times. She's well. She's cured. 'I . . . I can't believe it. It's done?'

She focuses on the doctor now, her smiling and kind face. She doesn't look like she's playing a nasty joke. Harriet scans the desk for an invoice with a ton of zeros at the end, but there's nothing.

'You have a long and healthy life ahead of you,' Doctor Peterson says.

A breath pants from Harriet as a warmth flushes through her. Her hands go to her mouth and a river of tears meander down her cheeks. 'I'm going to live? I'm going to live!'

A long and healthy life she can share with her son, righting her wrongs. She can feel his hug, see his smile, feel his messy hair in her hands. She can plan a future. Her hatred for Anthony can wait. Right now, she's floating on air. She's well. She's actually cured.

She walks out of the hospital—no wheelchair, pain free—and when she exits onto 90, she takes a deep lungful of air, lifting her arms up. Her head tilts back as she closes her eyes. Some sunlight creeps in from the side of the walkways while she stretches her limbs, basking in the day. She's never felt so healthy, so alive.

On her way home, she grabs a sandwich at a corner shop and demolishes it. At the next shop she buys another and eats that too, then drinks an entire carton of juice, savouring each sweet drop. Her limbs buzz with the energy. She wants to run and jump, to sing and dance.

She bursts through her front door, only to be greeted by silence. Is there anything more anticlimactic than arriving home to an empty house? No Oliver. No Theo. No Thomas. Still no Monty.

She's alone, and her joy feels like some act of malice when there's so much wrong in the world. Thomas should be home from work soon. Has Oliver gone back to work? She doubts it.

She messages Theo and he replies to say he needs to keep busy, that he's heard nothing about Monty so he's gone to speak to people to find out what's going on with the weapon.

Weapon. That word makes her feel like she's ill all over again, and her warm bones turn to ice. There is still a weapon being made that will kill her son. With that and the tasers the Flesh Fraternity are encouraging people to use, the streets aren't safe, and Oliver's outside somewhere.

For an hour, her joy at being cured made all her other worries go away. Now she's home, alone, and has no idea where her son is. She texts, asking and seconds later her phone pings with his reply.

> *I'm going to make Anthony pay.*

Oh, God. Her knees buckle and she plonks down on the sofa. What is he going to do?

Before she's had time to imagine any possibility, her phone pings again, this time from Theo.

> *Weapon is ready to use. I'll see you at home. Keep the boys there.*

Harriet's heart sinks. Shit.

CHAPTER 43

Oliver has a rough idea where George and the other landfill bots live. He knows it's on 3, just above the office. He walks to the nearest lift to the office and rides it down.

He walks in the direction of the office building and spots a dilapidated low-rise that has several electrical cables going into it. Some bots are just arriving home. It's George and Oliver's usual shift colleagues.

'Where the fuck were you today?' George asks when he sees Oliver.

They all look like they've had a tough day, caked in clay and dust, and their hands and arms wrinkled and worn. A hint of guilt trickles over Oliver. It's not fair that they should have to work so hard.

It's not fair. Nothing is fair. He's going to make it fair.

'I've got some good news for you,' Oliver says. 'How's your battery?'

'Shit, obviously.'

'Well, charge, and when you've got thirty per cent, we're going on a trip.'

George folds his arms and narrows his eyes. 'We have to charge fully and then go back to work.'

'Says who?'

George pulls his chin in, scrunches his nose. His battery is low, so Oliver knows his thoughts will be slow.

'Aren't you sick of it?' Oliver says, speaking clearly to help them out. 'Taking orders and working your body so hard? Never taking any time to enjoy yourself?'

George and the others all nod. 'Yeah! Yeah, we are.'

'The humans that run this company think they're in charge, that they own us. But we're better than them, stronger, faster. We're going to make them see just how valuable we are. We deserve respect just as much as they do!'

George smiles, the kind of sinister smile he used to make at the Institute when he was about to lunge for Oliver. But this time, he steps away and walks towards the dorm. 'Come on, boys,' George says to the others. 'Let's charge as quick as we can!'

CHAPTER 44

Harriet's eyes have barely left her phone as she waits for a reply from Oliver. He hasn't replied to her barrage of questions and requests. Her only company are the awful videos being shared on *Get Level* of the bots being harmed. She watches them all, looking to see if any are Oliver or Thomas, sometimes having to watch twice as tears smudge her vision. Every time it's horrible, but so far, none of those harmed are her boys.

Thomas arrives home and she leaps up to greet him, wrapping him in a hug before he's even one step into the house. Then, she drags him in and shuts the door. He hasn't got a phone, so he probably doesn't know how bad things are.

She shows him the video, and the colour drains from his face.

'I need to get to Evie!' he says. 'I have to make sure she's okay.'

'She has a phone, so she'll be aware. I'm sure her family are protecting her. Here.' She gives him a vest. 'Put this on.'

Thomas didn't know about the weapon, so she fills him in, and his pale face turns ghostly white.

'But you'll be fine, okay,' Harriet says, trying to sound convincing. 'Theo is stopping it.'

The front door bursts open and Theo slams it shut again before running inside. 'Oh, good, Thomas has his. I hope it works. Where's Oliver?'

Harriet shows him the message, and he palms his forehead. 'Shit.'

She puts her phone away and inspects Theo's face. He looks as wiped out as she feels. At least she's eaten; she doubts Theo has. 'But the weapon doesn't work, right?'

His teary eyes meet hers, and he shakes his head. 'I think it will. I was hoping to do some more alterations, just keeping busy, keeping my mind occupied, you know? Anyway, I was too late. Someone spotted the flaw. I should have been there sooner. I'm so sorry. I've been distracted—'

'It's not your fault, Uncle Theo.'

Theo's face has a glimpse of warmth and gratitude for Thomas. When did Thomas start calling him Uncle?

Harriet wraps her arms around herself, biting her bottom lip to stop the quiver.

Theo takes a breath. 'The best place for bots is below ground. The blast shouldn't reach them there.'

'But below is all shut off,' Harriet says.

'The more eastern gates are opening up. There are people alive.'

'Monty?'

'No news. But I'm hopeful. I mean, if anyone was to survive, he would, right?'

Harriet nods. Theo has more colour in his cheeks than he's had in days. He's right. Monty is a survivor. He has to be okay. 'Of course. He's as tough as they get. He could punch his way out of concrete.'

There's a knock at the door and Harriet runs to answer it, then groans. Lenny. Fucking Lenny.

'Great! You've got one of the boys with you,' he says as he walks through.

Thomas scarpers to his room without saying a word.

'Now?' Theo says. 'Seriously?'

Harriet stands in front of Lenny, resting her hand on the wall, hoping to stop him walking through. 'Lenny, this really isn't a good time.'

'No such sentence in showbiz. You know that.' He continues walking past her with an impolite shove.

Harriet chews on her cheek for a moment. Maybe, just maybe, the TV crew can be of use. She looks at Theo, who raises his eyebrows and shrugs.

She turns around and faces the film crew. They're already busy rearranging the furniture. 'Actually, Lenny, can we broadcast live? Or have the show air as soon as possible? There's an emergency message I need to get out.'

Lenny leaves the rest of the crew to carry on preparing the house as he makes a call.

'It's worth a shot,' Harriet says to Theo.

'I guess.'

Harriet sits in the middle of the living room, in the chair the crew placed there. Hair and makeup start trying to spruce her up a bit, to defrizz her hair and paint some colour into her cheeks. There's a light coming from the window, artificial, a high wattage one the crew put there, to make it look like some sunshine is coming through. There's a generator off to the other side, out of view of the camera, but just in case the electric dies again.

Lenny comes back and gives them the thumbs up. Hair and makeup step away and Harriet has a sip of water.

The camera points at her, and Lenny counts down. Harriet softens her eyes, tightens her forehead to show all of her fear and worry. She summons a sheen of tears which isn't difficult, and clears her throat.

'This broadcast is to deliver some frightening news. The Flesh Fraternity have made a weapon. It'll destroy everything electrical within a twenty-mile radius when it detonates. And they plan on using it imminently. Please, all bots, if you're listening. Get below ground as quickly as you can. The doors at Reading East are opening up. Please, get there and be safe.'

They finish filming. Thomas comes out of his room and stands next to Theo. He has his shirt on, but he still looks terrified.

'You guys need to get below,' Harriet says. 'Theo, get Thomas to safety and find Monty.'

Theo nods and pockets his keys. 'What about you?'

'I need to find my son.'

CHAPTER 45

While the bots charge, Oliver goes down to 2. As he makes his way to the office, the flies buzz around and he swats them away. He's still not used to them. Then some rubbish blows up and hits him in his side. The wind must be strong up top for it to be so gusty this low. He has to pull the door open with a little more force and the rubbish and flies follow him in. He's only ever been in the front of the office, but he knows out back there's a large storeroom. What he's not sure is what to do about Bret.

Bret is a human who willingly works for Anthony. This is what Oliver reasons with himself. Bret must know the terrible things Anthony is doing. He must understand and yet he doesn't do anything about it. He shows Anthony all that respect for making them do terrible things, so he can't be a good man.

'Oliver,' Bret says when he walks in. 'I thought you were on the other shift. Have you switched?'

Oliver shrugs. 'Guess so. I just need to collect some things.'

'Sure. What do you need? I'll sign them out.'

Oliver doesn't know the words; he only knows what they look like. Dammit, why did he never think to learn the words?

Bret is looking at him, expectantly. He doesn't look like a bad man, but then, what does a bad man look like? Loads of humans are deceitful, especially ones who work for Anthony.

Oliver's mouth twists, his forehead furrowed as he stalls for time, trying to think what those things are called. He walks up to the desk and stands at the side of it for a second as Bret waits patiently.

'Well?' Bret says.

Oliver pulls his fist back and thumps Bret in the jaw. He feels a crack, and Bret stumbles backwards, his eyes crossing and he loses his balance. Oliver's hand trembles as he looks at it, some of Bret's blood is smeared across his knuckles. He didn't know he could punch someone like that, didn't know human jaw bones are so easy to break. He looks at his hand with a renewed sense of power. He barely even tried. He could have punched a whole lot harder. With strength like that, the next stage of his plan will be easy.

Bret's still conscious and rolls onto his front, trying to stand, spitting blood and a tooth onto the floor. There's not much time.

'Sorry,' Oliver says as he steps over him. He puts his hands under Bret's armpits and drags him into the storeroom. 'I really am sorry,' he says again.

There are cages and cages containing all manner of tools. Padlocks hang open from most of the latches, some doors swing open, but on the one Oliver wants, the door is closed, and the padlock is shut. In an open cage, he finds a crowbar and pries the padlock open. There are a few hessian sacks in the corner and takes five, filling them with bunches of sticks he used before, a few of the big black levers, some matches, and some duct tape. He inspects his haul and smiles. That should do it.

Bret is mumbling something incoherent, and Oliver lifts him into a cage, shutting the padlock.

'You'll be fine here, I think,' he says.

He slings the sacks over his shoulders and goes back to the dorm on 3.

❀ ❀ ❀ ❀

While Oliver waits for the others to finish charging, he checks his phone. *Get Level* is filled with videos from the Flesh Fraternity. Everyone knows it was the bots who blew up below. The Flesh Fraternity are blaming them, and they are armed with tasers. They're calling bots killers, blaming them for all the bad things rather than the humans who made them do it. There is more talk of the weapon, and he hopes Evie is wearing that vest he gave her.

He's going to make the world see who the real bad man is, and he's going to make them all know that they can't go around killing innocent bots. He looks at his hands again, clenches and stretches out his fingers. They're the strong hands of a bot who can break the bones of bad people. He's no sycophant. His big strong hands are going to put an end to human and bot suffering.

There's no time to waste.

He shows the others the video.

'Our kind are being destroyed because of what this company makes us do,' he says. His audience is receptive. After seeing the video, they are eager for action. 'People hate us because of this company. We need to make them see that it's AM Investments who are the criminals. They're the ones who make us do such things. AM Investments who make you work such long hours without ever having a day off. Let's take the fight to them. Let's make them see they've gone too far!'

The other bots nod, shouts of agreement, then jump to their feet, spurred on and ready for action.

They take the sacks of explosives and walk on 3, heading east towards the AM Investments' building. It's 110 stories high, and Oliver knows Anthony's office is on the top floor. He has tunnel vision with his goal the only thing visible.

Along the way, a man runs at them with a taser. Oliver tackles him to the ground as soon as he sees it, then George and one of the others kick him in the gut. There are groans from him at first, bursts of loud exhales, a crack from his ribs, until Oliver shouts 'Enough!' and they stop kicking him.

Oliver lets go and stands up, that taser lies next to him on the ground. He picks it up and puts it in his pocket, then they walk on. Oliver glances over his shoulder. The man is wheezing breaths and trying to crawl away. Perhaps they should have made sure he wouldn't get away. Perhaps they shouldn't have hurt him at all. It's hard to know what's right and wrong when the world and most people are a mixture of both.

It takes them a fair amount of time to walk, but when they arrive, Oliver leaves the explosives with the other bots. They all know what to do. Oliver takes his watch off and gives it to George, whose eyes light up at the sight of it. George can keep it. Oliver has no need for such fancy things anymore.

'Thirty minutes,' Oliver says. 'Okay?'

'Yes. We can do that.'

'Make sure you're well clear and then get below ground as soon as you can.'

George and the others get to work without hesitation. They do as they're told because Oliver is in charge and respected. Because they know Oliver is going to save the bots.

He rides the lift to 110, the lift smoother and smoother as he gets closer. He alights onto the gleaming level with echoey floors and glass all around. A receptionist sitting behind a desk smiles and greets him. She has her hair scraped back so tightly it pulls on her skin. Oliver says he's here to see Anthony and tells her his name.

The receptionist calls through to Anthony's office, and he is told he can go through.

Oliver tries to hide his relief and excitement. He slows his walk on purpose, fighting his urge to run. Now is not the time to give the game away. He checks the time on his phone. Twenty-seven minutes to go.

Anthony sits at his desk, leaning back in his chair with a sneer.

'Oliver, my boy, what can I do for you?'

Oliver shuts the door behind him, takes a moment to compose himself before he faces Anthony. He walks to the desk, pulls the taser from his pocket and fires it at Anthony.

Anthony's body convulses the same as Oliver's did. He shakes and slides off his chair, his face twisting and contorting. Oliver bites back a laugh. Some spittle foams at the corner of Anthony's mouth and his face turns the colour of a beetroot.

Oliver drags him away from his desk and drops him in the middle of the floor. Anthony makes a muffled sound, incoherent words, more spittle dribbles onto the floor. His trousers are wet at the crotch. Gross. Oliver only hopes that Anthony doesn't die from the taser. He wants to have a chat with him first.

He rolls Anthony on his stomach and duct-tapes his hands and ankles together behind his back, then leans him up against the wall on his knees. Anthony on his knees is a perfect sight. Wait until he begs.

Anthony's shaking stills, his eyes cross for a while before they can focus again. Confusion knits his brow as he regains some composure. 'Oliver . . . What . . .?'

'Mum's had her final treatment. She's well. You don't need to be alive anymore.'

His eyes cross again, his mouth opens and closes a few times before more words come out. 'But . . . my boy . . .'

'Stop that!' Oliver kicks him in the thigh. 'You were using me to hurt her! You were trying to make her hate me! I am not your boy. I am not your son.'

Anthony laughs, more of a cackle, choking as he does. 'Oh, but you are. You may not want to be, but you are. You are your father's son more than you realise.'

'You blew up below. You killed so many. I could never be your son!'

'I did what was needed. I had to see if you had what it takes to be my son. You do. You're strong. What a team we could make!'

Oliver crouches down, raises a fist.

'Wait!' Anthony says. His gaze darts off to the right. 'See that door there? Open it, why don't you.'

Oliver looks at the door but doesn't move. 'Why? What's in it?'

'The reason why I am your father. Go on. You'll see I never wanted your mother to hate you.'

Oliver stands and looks at the door for a few seconds. He hasn't got time to waste so he steps towards the door.

'Hang on!' Anthony says.

Oliver looks down at him, the twisted dribbling mess on the floor. His eyes show all the fear Oliver wanted to see.

'There's a blanket behind my desk. Put that over me. I don't want him to see me like this.'

Oliver's forehead furrows. He goes behind the desk and finds the blanket. He holds it for a moment and looks down at Anthony again. His eyes are pleading. He's the most pathetic he's ever looked. Oliver can't imagine the harm in covering him, so he does. Just as he puts the blanket over Anthony's head, he says, 'He's your brother.'

Thomas? Oliver gasps, then jumps to standing and runs the four paces to the door and swings it open. Inside is a smaller office, a simple desk, and sat at the desk is a MechaniTeen. Oliver blinks a few times. This isn't Thomas. This teen has dark hair, the same shape nose as Anthony, his heavy brow, a similar sharp suit.

The teen stands and holds out his hand for Oliver. 'Hi, I'm Freddie.'

Freddie. Oliver's insides feel like they're in free fall. He cocks his head, blinks a few more times. He looks the teen up and down. Freddie was his mum's baby who died the day he was born. But this boy isn't a dead baby.

Oliver shakes his hand. 'Hi. I'm Oliver.'

Freddie smiles, his eyes light up. 'I've been so looking forward to meeting you! Dad said I would soon. Is my mother as beautiful and kind as he says?'

Oliver's eyes glance down at the blanket covering the heap on the floor, staying very still. 'She is. Mum's the best.' He looks at Freddie again, and struggles to think clearly. He looks exactly as he would imagine Anthony did once, except the eyes. The eyes are all his mum's. Anthony has a bot who looks how their child would. How Oliver's brother would.

Oliver blinks, shakes his head a little to make his thoughts speed up. Anthony was right. He shouldn't have to see his dad like that. 'Freddie, that receptionist outside, what's her name?'

'Mindy.'

'Great. Why don't you go and ask Mindy about her hobbies, and then—' he checks the time on his phone '—in seven minutes, press the fire alarm button and tell Mindy to call for a Hel-E. Okay?'

'Okay. I can do that exactly. Where's my dad?'

'He's ... delayed. I'll see you outside soon, okay? Press the fire alarm in exactly seven minutes.'

Freddie nods and walks out into the corridor, closing the office door behind him. Oliver stands still for a few seconds, a numbness about him. The room spins like his battery is low, but he knows he's got plenty.

He whips the blanket off Anthony, whose eyes are still pleading. He coughs and splutters before speaking. 'I had him made specially. I've raised him since he was a kid. He's my son.'

Oliver takes a few steps away, looks between Anthony and the door. His forehead is tight, like he's looking into the sun.

'Freddie needs a big brother, a mentor,' Anthony says. 'A business partner. He's your family, Oliver.'

Oliver shakes his head. 'No. No, my mum is my family.'

'Freddie is her son too. She loved her baby. He's the exact size he would be if the baby had lived. He looks exactly like him. When she meets him, it'll be like he never died. He's here, ready to be her son.'

'But . . .' he screws his eyes up and presses his palms into his temples. 'He isn't her baby. He's your bot. And thanks to you, the world hates bots.'

'Only the below grounders. They'll all be gone soon enough, and the entire country will consist only of top-level people and bots. Isn't that a world you want to live in? Isn't that a world where you can thrive?'

Anthony and his words of poison, do they never stop? He's trying to pollute Oliver's mind again, trying to sway his thoughts. Oliver checks his phone. Seventeen minutes till the building blows up. Six minutes till Freddie sounds the alarm. Is that enough time for everyone to evacuate? Probably. He can hear Freddie talking to Mindy outside. They're discussing knitting. Freddie's good at small talk, much better than Oliver is. He's pleased the teens don't have such acute hearing as the adult bots.

'Thanks to bots working at the incinerators, top levels control the electricity again,' Anthony says. 'There's no life low down. Electricity is power.'

Oliver avoids looking Anthony in the eye. He looks around the office instead, at the awards, the newspaper articles, all the fine things that he's never had. All the fine things his mum should have.

'I see you,' Anthony says. 'I know you want the life up here. You move up here, and she'll come too, you know she will. Live up here, where you can have as much as you want. Bring your mum. We can all be happy. She has two sons to love. You know how happy she'll be. With Freddie, a view of the sky, her life will be complete.'

He looks at Anthony now. Even from his crumpled position he puffs his chest up, juts his chin out, like he's never known anything but victory.

'There's a weapon,' Oliver says. 'It's going to kill all bots and the electricity.'

'Some low-level harebrained idea.' He spits some blood and foam off to the side. 'Don't be daft. In any case, up here in this tower, it's a Faraday cage. Freddie will be fine.'

Oliver checks the time. Five minutes.

'Your mother will come back to me. One way or another. She'll come back once she knows about Freddie. She won't be able to stay away from him, so you might as well join me. I always said I'd get her back somehow. Nobody leaves me. Not her, not Freddie. Nobody!'

Oliver sees it then. The maliciousness he hates so much. Anthony's plan was never to hurt his mother; it was to draw her back. Oliver punches Anthony's nose. He feels the satisfying crack in his knuckles. Blood spurts from Anthony's face but after a groan, his horrible laughter begins again. 'That's my boy.'

'I am not your boy!'

'I never needed to make you more like me, look at you! You already were! Quite the impressionable little kid, weren't you? You and Freddie are going to make a great team.'

He punches Anthony again, so hard he gulps for air, choking and wheezing.

Oliver takes the reel of tape, pulls off one of Anthony's shoes and removes his sock, shoving it in his mouth, then covers his mouth with tape. Round and round his head he wraps the tape until he's sure it won't come off. In Anthony's breast pocket is his wallet with his Hel-E card. Oliver takes it.

He paces the office, needing a few moments to think. He checks the time. A few moments is not enough. He bites his fist and squeezes his eyes shut. He needs to figure out what's the best thing to do. What a good bot would do.

He's not like Anthony. How dare he say that! He's fixing things, whereas all Anthony does is break things. He can't let Freddie end up like him. Not one bot should be like Anthony.

But he has a brother. Can he kill his father?

Oliver looks at Anthony. His nose is still bleeding and his eyes bulging as he struggles for air. He's going to suffocate on his own blood. Oliver's torn. Suffocating seems like a good thing and the worst. Or maybe not bad enough. Is that a fitting end? Too quick, maybe. There's a pair of scissors on the desk and Oliver grabs them and hacks away at the tape around his face, cutting his cheeks in the process. He rips the tape away, snagging some of Anthony's skin as he gasps and wheezes for air.

Oliver bends and places his face an inch from Anthony's. As he coughs, some blood sprays Oliver's face. 'I am not like you. I will never be like you, and I won't let you destroy all the people below. Now you can choose to live or die.' Oliver stands, then backs away, taking out his phone. He loads up the camera, and clicks record. 'Tell me what you told me in the Hel-E, Anthony.'

Anthony spurts and huffs.

'This building is going to explode and crumble to the ground in '— Oliver checks the time '— sixteen minutes. The alarm goes off in four minutes. You can go down with it, or you can repeat what you said to me, and I'll take you to a Hel-E and away.'

He sees it then, the glimmer of fear in Anthony's eyes. Not fear for Freddie now, or his pride, but fear for his life. However much he's trying to hide it, he's terrified. Josie wasn't afraid at the end, nor was his mum when she was dying. Anthony is a coward when he is powerless.

Oliver could kill him now, strangle him, watch for the exact moment life leaves him. But he waits, keeps the camera rolling.

'Below grounders do nothing but weaken us here,' Anthony says with a rasping voice. 'It's just evolution. You're willing to destroy everything we've built and all the great things we could build, for the sake of those moles. Pah!' A few weak coughs, some more blood and spit dribbling. 'Anyone with any sense would have done the same. Anyone who lives on a top level, anyone important will agree, what was done had to be done.'

Oliver smiles, and stops filming, puts his phone back in his pocket.

'There,' Anthony says. 'You've got your footage, now get me and Freddie out of here.'

Oliver tilts his head to one side, blinks a few times, and in-spects Anthony's desperation. He could save him. It's what he said he'd do. But not for the first time, he finds himself wondering, what would Anthony do?

Let him suffer under rubble like those he buried below.

Anthony squirms in the duct tape constraints. 'Undo these now!'

His mum promised him she'd never go back to Anthony. If she knew about Freddie, she'd have to see Anthony again. She'd break her promise if it means being a mum to Freddie. Anthony is never going to stop trying to make her go back to him. There's only one way to make sure she keeps her promise.

'Oliver!' Anthony shouts and rasps. 'You listen here!'

The alarm sounds, a deafening klaxon so piercingly loud and Oliver holds his hands to his ears. He kicks Anthony in the mouth, feeling his teeth crack against his shoe. Anthony groans, barely audible over the alarm, then flops over sideways, gagging and spluttering. Oliver kicks him again in the gut. Then, he pockets the Hel-E card and walks out of the office, shutting the door behind him.

Freddie's hands are pressed to his ears too. The receptionist is still with him. Her eyes bulge at the sight of him and Oliver wonders how much of Anthony's blood is on his face. 'The Hel-E is waiting,' she shouts, and points to the roof.

'This building will explode in twelve minutes,' Oliver yells to her. 'Is there a microphone? A way to make sure everyone leaves?'

She gives a shaky nod. 'There's a Tannoy.'

'Okay. Use it.'

Mindy's voice quivers and stutters as she talks down the microscope. The alarm quietens when Mindy's voice fills the speakers. Terrorist attack, she says. Explosion. Oliver's face reddens as shame heats his face. He's not a terrorist, but if it takes that word to make everyone leave, it'll have to do. Freddie tilts his head as he listens, confusion twisting his expression. He doesn't know these words.

Mindy finishes her recording. The alarm rings out loudly again and the three of them cover their ears. Her bloodshot eyes look at Oliver. 'I don't think I'll make it out in time.'

'Come with us in the Hel-E,' Oliver says. 'Let's hurry.'

Oliver takes one of his own hands away from his ears to grab Freddie and drag him through the passageway to the Hel-E pad on the roof.

The noise is a bit less here and he can put his hands back by his sides. The wind is stronger than Oliver has ever known. A railing surrounds the Hel-E pad and they all grasp it, pulling themselves along.

'Where's my dad?' Freddie asks. He's looking at Oliver's face, at what Oliver can only imagine is a mess.

'I'm taking you to see your mum right now. How does that sound?'

A smile spreads across Freddie's face. He looks so much like his mum then. 'I'd like that.'

Mindy is with them, and Oliver gives her a smile. She doesn't return it but keeps a guarded distance. The clouds move across the sky as if in a race, swirling and angry with a mist of rain beneath. To the east, the sky is so dark it could be night. A few angry bolts of lightning flash.

The Hel-E is already waiting and the three of them step inside. Freddie isn't in awe in the Hel-E, no doubt he's ridden them all his life. It takes off, swaying in a gust, lifting into the sky with the faintest purr. Oliver checks the time. Ten minutes to go.

The Hel-E hovers just above the building, tilting at an angle to brace against the wind. It circles some of the town, then comes back again. Oliver just wants to see; to witness the moment Anthony's company turns to rubble. He checks his phone, thirty seconds to go. Bang on time, the building below wobbles. A plume of dust puffs upwards.

The three of them watch through the glass bottom. For a few seconds, Oliver wonders if the dust and debris will catch up with them, and the Hel-E lifts higher. The building seems to deflate, sucking in before the walls bow outwards, erupting into shards of class and concrete.

Above the purr of the super smooth Hel-E, there's shattering glass and creaking metal, a great crash of brick and concrete. Vigorous orange flames burst out of the rubble, ash raining down, and the empire that once was collapses into dirt.

CHAPTER 46

Harriet knows where Oliver will be. If he's gone to Anthony, he's either gone to his office or house, and during business hours, the office makes more sense. She only hopes he's wearing his vest.

She takes an AutoTaxi to the edge of London, then walks. AM Investments skyscraper is up ahead. That thick spinal cord that sits on the cusp of Reading town and the city of London is visible from far away; its extensive glass frontage shines even down on level 6.

She checks the time, and only hopes she's not too late. She should have taken a faster level 10 taxi. She should have left sooner. She's breathless, her pace too fast for her body that's withered so much lately, but she needs to be quicker. If Oliver hurts Anthony, or worse, she'll lose her son forever. She can't imagine the legal processes are kind to bots.

Behind her, a man has a taser; she hears the crackle of a bot being hit. She clutches at her chest but keeps walking. There is one bot she needs to save, just one, then she can worry about the rest.

The ground shakes. The walkway tilts and she leans back, overcompensating and stumbling to her backside. She sits, stunned, then tries to stand yet she lands on her knees. A scream of flailing glass rains down to the ground. The level above shakes and bows, ridding itself of chunks of tarmac and concrete. Harriet raises a hand to shield her face and looks towards the AM Investment building as flames jet from the windows and the great skyscraper collapses, turning to rubble.

The world is in sepia as dust floats through the air and settles in a thick crust on Harriet's skin. She chokes and coughs as she sits up. Screams pierce her muffled ears, their own internal ringing as loud.

She stands, gingerly, her knees unsupportive, and inspects herself. As she shakes her head, debris falls from her tangled matt of hair. She looks up, her neck creaking as she does. Ahead where the AM Investments building should be is a pile of broken concrete and brick, sparks from cables, flames spitting from the top, a crackle like sizzling oil.

She steps closer.

What level is she on? She can't remember. Her head pounds, an ache spreads from her forehead to her neck and her ears ring with a piercing wail. As she walks closer to the rubble, the walkway ends, like shattered ribs ripped from their supports, bending down to the levels below.

A snap, a groan as more walkways yaw towards the ground. Gravity. In the rules of the universe, everything belongs at ground level. Everyone is as good as landfill.

Fine time to be philosophical, Harriet.

People run and scream, some sprint past her, clipping shoulders and knocking her off balance. Harriet should run too; she should flee for fear of what is to come next. Instead, she stares at the wrecked building, takes a lungful of dusty air and with a mother's intuition, knows her son is somewhere close by. She knows he did this.

She squeezes her eyes shut a moment and rubs her head, trying to soothe the pain. It helps a bit. When she opens her eyes again, the world is clearer, brighter, the dust already settling. She should be mortified, ashamed, in denial about what her boy is capable of. But in the rubble and fire, she sees nothing but good intention. So many want to hurt her son. It's only right he fights back. AM Investments sought to destroy the people below, and Oliver has turned that ambition to ash.

Not everyone is fleeing. There are some who stand and watch. Broad bodies in tatty clothes, some with their charging sockets visible. Bots don't know to be afraid of such things. She searches their faces for Oliver, but none are him.

A billboard plays the news, images of bots being tasered, their limbs ripped off and tied up to walls. An image she has seen too many times before with the kids and the teens. Adult bots suffering is no less traumatic, no more justifiable. The Flesh

Fraternity claim their actions as righteous. But look where such actions lead.

They've been promising this, but it was a self-fulfilling prophecy. The Flesh Fraternity said the end would come if bots thrived, but all Harriet sees is justice.

In between news stories are adverts, AM Investments promising higher towers, as their own is now mere gravel.

Goosebumps crawl up her arms, carrying a shiver. She shakes it off, then holds her arms out, embracing the warmth of the fire.

She peers down below, all the way down, and counts the levels. Through the haze, walking across landfill, are people coming up from below. There's a doorway down there somewhere, Reading's East. People can escape. Other people can hide.

A storm whips through, a strong gust. How long has it been since they felt the wind down here? How long since people below have known what weather means? When a great tree dies in the rainforest, it's a chance for stifled saplings to enjoy the light. Some splashes of rain fall, cool and fresh. The sun moves across the sky, a break in the heavy clouds, and down here, it's the first time they've seen the sunshine.

They've been in the dark down here for so long, under the shadows of those above, at the mercy of electricity and power. But now, through the gap where once the skyscraper stood, it's daybreak.

She checks her phone. The screen is cracked but she can still load up messages. There's one from Oliver. Finally. She breathes out fully, an exhale of relief. Her tension disappears and she sways as if the walkway is buckling, perhaps it is. She can forget the panic around her for a moment, the ringing in her ears doesn't matter. Her son is okay.

He's sent a video, and she clicks play. Anthony's confession. Her hand goes to her neck. Her son, fighting for what's right. She looks up at the sky. Hel-Es circle, and she hopes he's in one. She hopes more than anything that he got away.

Harriet pulls herself up to stand on a pile of rubble and heads turn to face her. There are cameras in the crowd, a news crew, people telling her story before she's said a word. The bots stand and wait; they don't know what to do. They don't know the threat that awaits them. They recognise her, though. She's Harriet Chapel, campaigner for the bots. They've seen her on TV. As Michelle said, she's the face of the bots. They all look to her, rudderless, needing a leader, as humanity goes to shit around them.

One calls her name, and the others join in. *Harriet! Harriet! Harriet!*

Her name; their battle cry.

The wind howls, warm gusts kicking up the dust and whipping the flames behind her as they spit and crackle. Still they chant her name.

She's not a leader, but she must save them. As Oliver said, no one is doing enough to help the bots. Leaders are usually powerful people, wealthy, from up top. But Harriet is a below grounder. Her silence has been her scream. However, now, she must shout louder and drown out the hate. She's a mother, and she will do right by her son.

So she stands on the rubble, facing the crowd, and imagines him next to her, shoulder to shoulder. He should be the one to lead them. It should be Oliver standing here.

There are some cries for help from the building behind. People rush to the needs of humans. Meanwhile, more bots are being tasered.

The weapon can wipe out everything electrical for twenty miles. Let it. Let it destroy everything electrical out here. Electricity is power, they all know that. Level the playing field. Put the world in blackout.

But not the bots. The doors to below are open. She'll get the bots below to safety. The Grande Finale is yet to come.

She raises her arms, the chanting quiets. 'Bots, all of you, get below. The doors are open. The weapon will be used imminently!'

They nod, start to move in the way she is pointing, orderly and unpanicked.

Over the crackle and spits from the fire, the shuffling of feet, one human shouts loudly enough to be heard. 'This is the end! The reckoning they said was coming!'

All Harriet thinks is a reckoning is well overdue.

Chapter 47

Oliver watched Freddie's face as the skyscraper collapsed. His brows drawn in, eyes large and unblinking, his lips pursed. There have been no sobs or cries from him and Oliver wonders if he even knows what death is to a human, or if he's ever seen despair to know how to show it. He's stoic, silent, as blank as a kid.

This is fine. It means Oliver can teach him from scratch.

Oliver's mum is on TV. He watches on his phone from the Hel-E as she tells the bots to get to safety. He presses his hand to his chest, a warmth emanating from there, filled with love for her but hate that he ever doubted her. He said unkind words but he'll find her now and tell her he loves her.

'Look,' he shows Freddie. 'That's our mum. She's going to save all the bots.'

'She really loves us,' Freddie says.

'Yeah, she really does. More than anything.' More than your dad ever did, is what he wants to say, but not yet.

The Hel-E circles the town, dipping and swaying to fight the wind. The sky is the blackest Oliver has ever seen during the day.

From up here, the orange glow from the building gets bigger and angrier. There was something his mum said when Josie died. Oliver asked what it was like to die and she said, there's a flash, and all the bad things go away, and all that's left is joy. It sounded nice when it was Josie dying, but for Anthony . . . that's too pleasant, too peaceful. He hopes Anthony survived the fall. He hopes he lived long enough to feel his flesh burn.

Freddie hasn't asked about Anthony again. How will he feel when he finds out he's dead and understands what that means? Oliver pushes that thought away. No doubt Anthony's voice will haunt him later along with all the others but, right now, he has to concentrate.

Mindy hasn't said anything. She's sitting as far away from Oliver as she can, though her eyes haven't left him.

After a minute of circling, Oliver needs to make some decisions. He has to get Freddie to safety below ground, but he also hasn't heard from Evie. He's messaged her multiple times and she's not replied. Does she know the weapon threat is real and urgent?

He looks at Freddie. He can't drop him off alone, he's just a teen. But he's old enough to decide. When Oliver was younger he always wanted honesty. Secrets made it hard to understand the world. So, he'll always be honest with his brother. 'Freddie, there's a weapon some crazy people are going to use to destroy all bots.'

Freddie's face pales and his jaw hangs open.

'We need to get below ground. We'll be safe there.'

'Below ground with all the moles and fungus?' He grimaces. 'Below ground is the worst place there is.'

'It's not that bad. It's safe and only for a while. How's your battery?'

'Sixty per cent.'

'Great, but before I go below, I have to find my friend and her MechaniKid to make sure they're safe. So, I'm going to drop you and Mindy off, and Mindy, are you okay to make sure Freddie gets below ground?'

Mindy doesn't respond. She's frozen. Once again, Oliver is aware how crazy and filthy he must look. He rubs his temple. He can't risk Freddie because of Evie, but he can't give up on Evie. His stomach knots and he tenses, and he does the only thing he can think of.

'Listen, Mindy,' he keeps his tone even and clear, resonating anger and threats. 'Freddie here needs to get to safety. That is very important. You will take him below ground. Reading's eastern doorway. Now tell me you understand.'

She babbles something incomprehensible and nods.

He narrows his eyes, tries to look the meanest he ever has. He doesn't want to scare her, but she has to do what he says. Freddie has to be okay. He leans in. 'If I do not find Freddie safe below ground, I'm coming for you. Got it?'

She blubs and nods again.

He keeps his narrowed gaze on her as he leans back. She'll get over her fright. She thinks he's some crazy bot anyway so he might as well seem it. He instructs the Hel-E to drop them off and they land on the nearest skyscraper roof. As soon as the door opens, the wind slams against them and Thomas and Mindy have to battle against it to exit.

'Mindy, you get him below ground, you hear me?'

Her whole body is trembling, but she sniffs, then nods.

'I won't be long, Freddie,' Oliver says. 'I'll find you below, okay? Then we'll go find mum.'

'Got it, Oliver. Thank you.' He waves as the Hel-E takes off again.

Oliver watches out of the window as Mindy and Freddie make for the lift, their bodies bending against the storm, and he hopes, really hopes, they make it below. Then, he tells the Hel-E to take him to Swan View apartments. Reading East is the nearest door to below from here, and that's also the nearest one to his mum. Maybe they'll find each other even if Oliver doesn't make it in time. If he doesn't get below before the weapon goes off, at least his mum will still have a son.

He can't think that way. He has to get to his mum. He has to tell her how sorry he is. He can't atone for all the bad things he's done if he's dead. He fills his head with happier thoughts. Thomas has always been like a brother but Freddie . . . wow . . . his mum will be made up when she sees him. Oliver wanted a family, a kid of his own and maybe one day he will, but right now a little brother to nurture and look after is a pretty good alternative. Despite the horribleness of the day, he smiles, a warm tingling spreading throughout. Anthony is dead. He has a little brother. His future is to be filled with making happy family memories.

He lands at Swan View and takes the lift down to 99. Without the code for Evie's apartment the lift won't stop there. Once he's in the lobby, he asks the concierge to speak to her. He takes out his phone and messages her again. She doesn't reply, and the concierge says there's no answer.

He groans, and it takes all of his strength not to slam his fist on the desk.

'Can you go up and check on her! Just to make sure?'

'I'm sorry, sir. But that's not our policy. We have to respect our residence's privacy. Even bots.'

Even bots. It's the first time being treated with equality seems like a bad thing. His hands clench and he headbutts the wall, trying to slam his frustrations out of his head. The concierge looks at him like he's a madman, and he composes himself. He inflates and deflates his chest a few times, quickly at first then slower, and rubs his forehead. He needs to think clearly, and the answer is obvious. She must have gone already. She would have seen the broadcast his mum did. She respects his mum, she said so before. She would have listened.

There's a long mirror that lines the lobby and as he goes to leave, he catches sight of his reflection. His forehead is bruised and dented. The rest of his face is polka-dotted with the blood Anthony spluttered. He looks down at his hands. There's blood on those too. Bret's, maybe. How many other people worked in that building? Was the fire alarm enough time for them to evacuate? He should clean the blood off, make himself look clean even though he knows he may never feel clean again.

A cold chill fizzes through him, and he stiffens, then hardens his muscles and starts walking. It was enough time for them to get out. He did his best. They all worked for Anthony's company. It was necessary.

He hopes his mum got his message, Anthony's confession, and he hopes the other bots got away before the blast.

He rides the lift down, lower and lower until it gets rickety and jerky, until the mechanisms screech with rust.

On level 6 he alights and takes an AutoTaxi east, back to Reading East doors to below. Under the shelter of the walkways above, the wind is negligible here. Anthony's card still works, and the journey doesn't take long. When he's as close as he can get, he gets out of the taxi and the rush of air hits him. AM Investments' skyscraper being flattened has opened up a window to above. Real wind and rain find their way down to ground level for the first time in forever. There's hardly any extra light as the sky above is so thick with dark storm clouds. The break in the levels is a tunnel effect, shooting the wind down the levels, slamming and suctioning against the buildings and walkways. The fire from the explosion still crackles, tunnels of fire spitting up several storeys and whipping around with the wind.

He takes a while to watch it, the destruction and the chaos. He did that. His latest bad thing. No one made him do it this time; it was his idea. He chose to destroy that building. To protect his mum, he reconciles. He'd blow up every building in the world if it kept her safe.

The lift that leads to Reading East below is still working, and he rides it the last couple of levels down. At ground level, the wind is stronger, like the gap that's opened up is forcing the air through. He angles himself to walk against it. Those storm clouds are closing in above. Rubbish blows, spiralling across the ground, smog and soot making eddies across the trash.

There's a steady stream of people coming up from below, and a line of bots going the other way. The people coming up, a lot of them have bandages and wounds, dirty faces and caked in mud. Oliver joins the lines of bots and descends the staircase. Standing on tiptoes for a bit and doing little jumps, he looks out for Freddie. He calls his name but none turn around. He must be below already. Shit, he really hopes so. That Mindy woman looked terrified, so she'd better have done what he said.

He checks his phone one last time, knowing it might not work soon. No messages. No news as to when the weapon will fire.

He makes it below. Each bot shuts the door behind them, just in case the weapon goes off. When Oliver opens it, he's as quick as he can and then shuts it again. He moves further inside to make more room at the doors. He wonders how far the weapon will penetrate in case anyone forgets to close the doors. A gust of wind howls as the door is blown open and those closer to it fight the elements to keep it shut.

More bots move further in away from the doors. Still, he scans the heads for Freddie.

It's damp, the heavy air makes it sluggish to walk through, the ground sucks at each step. In the clay, in the below ground, the echoes of the buried haunt him again. His face twists as their voices lick at his ears. Not just those, but Anthony's too. Shouting at him, calling him useless. Then Uncle Monty, always Monty, his laugh, his chatter as he cooks, his screams.

He keeps walking, not just moving up, but walking to get free of the crowd. He finds some open space, and he runs. He wants to outrun the cries, but they're all around him here. Footprints in the ground of people that are no more. The song of all the bad things he's done.

The voices of the buried call him, grab at him like the hands that reached up and he never took hold of. He feels them now, fingertips digging in, and he swats them like flies.

Leave me alone! It wasn't my fault!

He killed the man whose fault it was, but an eye for an eye doesn't work when there are so many eyes on one side, and just one set on the other. Killing Anthony hasn't made the dead people live. Anthony's pain hasn't erased all the others'.

Oliver shouts sorry into the nothingness, again and again. But it's just a word. Why is it there's a hundred different words for bad, but only one for sorry? It can never be enough.

Monty's voice calls him, his ghost shouting his name. Theo's too, the sounds of his sobbing. Oliver feels his despair, Theo's pain tearing at his insides. He can't outrun it. Here below, he's surrounded by all the bad things he's done. He tries to picture Anthony, his suffering face, as if somehow that makes amends, but Oliver killed his brother's father. He didn't mean to hurt the people below ground, yet he did mean to kill Anthony. He's a murderer. A bad bot.

He only wanted to help his mum, to make her proud. He'll never be her good little boy again.

Oliver stops running, falls to his knees as he listens to the voices. The screams tell him how bad he is, how evil, how he's just like Anthony. His fists pound the earth until his skin rips, and he cries. Loud, sobbing cries. The voices need to stop. They need to know how sorry he is.

Monty's voice, loud and clear now, still calls his name. Oliver slams his fists into his ears. He wants to rip them off, to short circuit his hearing. He wants to be deaf to make the voices stop.

Still Monty calls. His voice is soft, loving, just like an uncle's should be. Oliver's sobbing pauses, he listens. How he wants to hear his uncle's voice; how he wants to listen to him. Monty calls his name again, his voice, crisp and clear. Is Oliver dead too? Is there an afterlife where bots and humans both go?

He hears his name again. Too alive to be inanimate, too alive to be dead. And then, Oliver thinks, that's too loud and clear.

Oliver rights himself, and looks around. The tunnel is as dark and dreary as ever. Like he's been buried. He stands back on his feet and turns around. He must be buried. He's with the voices now, he's joined them in the clay, because there he is. An image in the dark. A ghost, surely it must be.

Oliver blinks, tilts his head to the side, but he's still there. Uncle Monty.

Chapter 48

A message pings on Harriet's phone from Theo.

She's not seen Oliver yet. Her heart races as she continues to search the faces for him. He could be anywhere on any level. She's waited for so long, ensured every bot she could see has heeded her instructions, and there are no other bots on her level now. He must be below already. She can't even contemplate the alternative and there's nowhere else she can look.

Her skin prickles with static. A bolt of lightning flashes through the storm clouds above. The clouds swirl and morph as they race across the sky, the wind howling now, wailing as it whips past and roaring when it meanders. One gust slams her into a pile of rubble and she scrambles to stand again, the strength of the storm forcing her to stay low. It's time to go, to get below.

She takes the lift down to ground level, stumbling over trash that blows across as she follows the bots towards the staircase that leads below. She ducks and dodges as some items fly right at her, one stuffed rubbish bag smacking her in the shoulder. Despite the onslaught of debris, the bots are so orderly. If this were humans, there'd be a crush.

'Hurry up. In you go,' she says at the top of the stairwell, encouraging them all down. She'll wait until the last one is below and make sure they're all safe. She holds onto the edge of the rail. The wind is so strong it knocks her sideways, trash pelting her in the face. She shelters around the side of the wall of the lift shaft but the wind changes direction, trash swirling all around in great eddies of rubbish. What shitty luck for the lower levels. The first bit of weather they've experienced in years, and it's a storm this bad.

She encourages the bots more. Orderly is good, but a little more speed would be better. There's a hundred, maybe more, a handful of kids. Her message must have been heard. So many know her name and thank her as they pass. So many are here, but the lack of MechaniKids weighs heavy. There are so many more still out there. The one bot she wants to know about more than any other is nowhere.

Oliver must have made it below while she was still making her way down. That's the explanation she tells herself, to calm herself, to stave off her panic. Still, her heart races and sweat collects everywhere, the wind not cold enough to cool her down.

As she waits for the final bots to get to safety, she shares Oliver's video on *Get Level,* titles it the Real Villain. She emails it to Lenny as well. Maybe the weapon will go off and no one will ever see it, but all she can do is hope that people realise it was a human, not the bots, who hurt so many.

The wind intensifies, sweeping across, sucking and slamming at everything then spitting it back out. It stinks, worse than stinks. Rotten eggs and bad shit, a cocktail that changes notes with every gust. She loses her balance once, and a bot grabs her until she holds onto the rail again. She can barely hear herself think over the noise.

When there are no more bots waiting outside, Harriet lifts her hand to shield her eyes from debris and scans over the landfill. Hot air from the burning building hits her face. Rain drops fall, thick and heavy. There are no more people lingering. Everyone who wanted to get out is out; everyone who wanted to go inside is in.

Please let Oliver be safe!

She steps into the stairwell and joins the line of people going down. Last time she descended these stairs, she was frail and tired. Now, powered with health and adrenaline, she keeps up with the bots with ease. Once she reaches the bottom, that heavy door closes with a thud behind her.

The crowd just inside the entrance is dense, and she barely fits. All the bots are so tall, and she can't see over them. They move further inside, but at a snail's pace. She needs to get past to find Oliver, but they create a solid wall. She shouts Oliver's name, and Thomas's, though with all the commotion she's sure her voice doesn't carry far. Below ground doesn't echo like featureless spaces above. The soft walls suck up the sound and what's left is muffled and dull.

She steps forward with the crowd, baby steps, making a small amount of progress and a gap opens up—a little pocket not far from the door where the tunnel notches into the earth. She claims it, breathing easier with a little more space, and calls their names again.

'Harriet!'

She snaps around at the sound of her name, calls their names again, and again, hears hers. Not mum as she hoped, but a friendly voice. Some shoulders move and bodies part and Theo and Thomas emerge from the crowd, squeezing past the others to make it to her.

She embraces them, holding on longer than she would usually. That's two of her boys accounted for. 'No Monty?' A stupid question. Theo's eyes only look her way for a split second before he's searching the crowd again. 'Or Oliver?'

They shake their heads.

She looks over at the heavy closed door. 'I should go and look again.'

Theo holds her wrist. 'He knows where to go. The storm is getting really bad. You're best waiting here.'

His face is pale, shrunken, though tight, as if he's fighting off reality. 'So many left, Theo. So many. I'm sure Monty must be with them.'

Theo gives her a pained smile. He's bottling up so much. He's trying to be strong, but she's worried soon he's going to break.

There's a zap from somewhere in the crowd. Harriet jumps, then turns her head round. Everyone faces the same way, and she side steps out of her pocket of space to peer around. There's a man, a taser in each hand, squatting low in a fighting stance. A Flesh Fraternity has come below.

Harriet's heart pounds in her ears. 'Stop that!' She runs for the man. She's not as quick as the bots who are closer. They dwarf him easily; he's outnumbered a hundred to one, and the bots tackle the man to the ground in seconds. One bot pins him to the clay with his knee, the man's face is in the dirt. Harriet smiles, her eyes narrow. Let him get sick. She hopes he ingests every toxin the below ground can throw at him.

Her head jerks around when, in the corner of her vision, there's another man a lot closer to her reaching for his pocket. Thomas is on him and Harriet yelps before her lungs seize when the usually placid and calm Thomas pushes the man to the ground and rips the taser from his hand.

'How many more of you?' Harriet jumps back at Thomas's tone. Oliver's always been so protective of him, but he's much stronger than she knew. He pins the man to the ground, pointing the taser at him.

The man struggles but he's no match for Thomas. 'This is it.' the man says with a cough. 'The end of bots or the end of humanity. You're nothing but killers!'

'No!' Harriet shouts, and again, all heads face her. She steps over to the man on the ground. His face is half in the clay, one eye glaring at her. His sneering mouth is orange from the dirt.

How many will see the video online? She has no idea, but she can show these two. She can try to change the mind of just a couple. She hopes to God her phone will work, the cracked screen now losing chunks of glass. 'Watch!'

She turns the volume up as loud as she can. It's nowhere near loud enough to carry through the tunnels, but the adult bots have excellent hearing. They all stand quietly, looking at her, knowing she's trying to help. She plays Anthony's confession video.

The man still squirms under Thomas, that relentless sneer now caked in clay. When the video's finished, he says, 'Still, flesh is divine.'

Harriet slouches and pockets her phone. It was never about finding fault with the bots, never about what bad things the bots did or didn't do. These Flesh Fraternity crazies have made up their mind.

A howling wind pulls the door open, and Harriet feels the full force of it. Theo grabs on to her to keep her upright and some bots move to pull it shut. The hinges rattle. It's been opened and closed so many more times today than it would in a month. From outside, there's a loud crash and she can imagine the carnage at the top of the stairway. The storm is so strong it's pushing around rubbish and destroying the crumbling walkways.

'Thomas,' she says. 'Kick this man out, and the other one. They can take their chances in the storm.'

The man's face turns grey as Thomas hoists him up. 'You'll see,' he says. 'There are still loads of bots out there, and we'll destroy them all!'

Thomas lifts, then shoves him into the wall while the second man is brought over, then in one swift movement, they're thrown outside, and the door is shut again.

One bot brings over a metal rod and feeds it through the lever on the door, wedging each end against the wall. It still rattles a bit, but it's held in place.

Harriet exhales, then scans the crowd again. The bots are all quiet, a tension among them from the commotion. The atmosphere is thick, expectant. She looks to Theo who checks his phone.

'I haven't got any signal with the door closed. It could be any moment.'

Then, she hears the word she's been longing for.

'Mum!'

Her breath catches, disbelief stalls in her lungs. Then again, she hears that word, and she gasps, the damp below-ground air filling her. She's weightless, floating towards that word. Is there anything more beautiful than being called mum?

'Mum!'

She turns a few degrees. Bots are moving out of the way. There's the squelch and slap of footsteps coming her way.

'Oliver!'

And he's there. Her son. Her perfect boy. She laughs a giddy laugh as he leaps the last step to her and her arms are full again.

She holds on so tight, she'll never let him go. He's her anchor. Her protector. Her son.

'Are you okay, Mum?'

'Now you're here, I'm fine.' There's nothing to worry about anymore. No badness in the world, no evil. With her son well and accounted for, there isn't anything else that matters.

Then, a squeal snags her attention—Theo's, as he shouts, 'Monty!'

Harriet releases Oliver, keeping hold of his hand but turns around. Her knees buckle and Oliver holds her up.

'I've got you, Mum.'

Her hands go to her mouth as her eyes stream. Monty, limping on a crutch with one leg wrapped in bandages, hobbles over. Theo's in his arms in seconds, the sound of happy cries is like music, and she joins in.

Her entire family is here. Her entire family is safe.

CHAPTER 49

Monty wasn't a ghost. He wasn't one of the voices of the buried. When Monty reached for Oliver, he struggled, thinking he was a limb, dragging him into the earth. But he didn't drag him anywhere, he hugged him. He wasn't even mad at Oliver. Blessed relief and happy tears instead. He'd been stuck, not able to make it up the staircase with his bad leg. Oliver said he'd carry him if he had to. To know that Monty was safe gave Oliver a little hope. For a short while, the other voices disappeared. They came back though as they walked to find others and Monty told his tale. Oliver's legs weakened, his head rattled and fizzed like it was going to explode. All the while, Monty told him it wasn't his fault; it wasn't his fault.

But it was. It doesn't matter if it was Anthony's idea. Monty doesn't know the whole story, doesn't know it was Oliver who laid the explosives. He can't rid himself of his guilt. Not down here where people have suffered. Not even destroying AM Investments is enough.

His mum now, though, looks at him with such love, like he's never done a bad thing before.

'I'm sorry I was cruel,' he says. 'I was so confused. Mum, I've done such bad things. I can't undo the bad things.'

She wraps him in a hug, but it's not enough. He can't cry properly. He can't make the badness leave him.

'You saved so many, darling. You told the world what Anthony is like.'

Oliver must still look a mess. The blood on his hands smudges around the clay and dirt, and he must still have splatters on his face. Yet when his mum looks at him, it's like she doesn't see any of that. All she sees is the good it masks. She sees the boy he was, not the man he has become.

The voices won't stop. The screams and cries repeat over and over. Monty is okay but so many are not. There was a time when Oliver saw himself working with children; now no one would let him do that.

'What's going to become of us, Mum? Of me? Everyone knows I'm a criminal. A killer.'

She rubs his back. Her touch is a comfort, but it can't make him good again. 'I don't know. But we fight as a family, okay?'

Family. It's all he ever wanted. He still needs to find Freddie. He won't tell her yet, just in case he hasn't made it below. He looks at Thomas. He's wearing his vest, the metal square showing through his button-up shirt. Theo and Monty haven't paid much attention to anyone else in a while. Happy tears wet their faces, their eyes only on each other. It still hasn't really sunk in. Uncle Monty is alive. He isn't a ghost. He's really alive.

Yet his head continues to ring with cries of children, the song that stopped so suddenly. Killing Anthony was one small thing, and he'll still need to confess that to Freddie. Good or bad is a matter of perspective. And Oliver's perspective is aligned now. He needs to make up for the bad. He needs to atone, somehow, if he ever can.

The rain hammers at the door outside; the wind screams. With Oliver's good hearing, he can make out every drop and crash of rubbish. Then, above the weather, is another voice. A tinkling laugh, a child's voice.

Oliver freezes for a second to listen again. It's unmistakable. Evie. Bonnie.

Oliver steps towards the door. Even with a metal rod wedged in place, two bots are keeping hold of it to stop it swinging open. He pushes the rod and nudges them out of the way, the door sucking open and he struggles against the force.

'Oliver, no!' his mum cries.

'I'll be quick,' he shouts over his shoulder. 'It's Evie.'

He races up the stairs, taking three at a time. There are two men in the stairwell, holding onto the railing as the wind pulls against them. Oliver has no time for them. He sprints the last few steps until he's with them. They're drenched, soaked from the rain, all the while Evie is trying to keep Bonnie's spirits up.

'It's an adventure, Bonnie. We're nearly there.'

A gust sucks all the air from the stairwell and Oliver lunges to grab hold of their hands. He grasps Evie more forcefully than ever, but Evie smiles at him, not with fear or hurt like she did before. Oliver steps around them, tucking them beneath him and holding on until the gust passes. The air tries to drag them away, such a force he's never known before, but he keeps them sheltered, pressing his feet into the step for purchase.

They're near the top of the stairwell and in the small view of outside, orange flames light the sky and heavy raindrops splatter to the ground. Oliver lifts Bonnie up into his arms, and she giggles, unfazed and enjoying the excitement of the storm, and he holds her close as they run down the stairs.

He bangs on the door, and it opens. Oliver, Evie and Bonnie tumbling inside.

A phone pings, and Theo grabs his, the open door giving him a second of signal.

'Ten minutes,' he says. 'They're setting the weapon off in ten minutes.'

'There are still more,' Evie says. 'Harriet's message went out and some came straight away, but some are still on their way. Loads haven't come down at all. So many kids.'

Oliver looks at the door, a hand grabs his wrist. He turns, and his mum's watery eyes meet his. 'You can't save them all, darling. We've done all we can.'

His insides hollow out and his shoulders slump. He leans against the wall, his mum beside him, Bonnie still in his arms. Maybe more places are a Faraday cage, like Anthony's office. Maybe the weapon won't work. His hopes are pitiful and defeated by negativity. But then he looks at Evie, Thomas, Bonnie. He can't save them all, but he's saved those who matter most.

'Evie!' Thomas calls to her, and she goes to him.

They embrace, and Oliver averts his eyes. He doesn't feel jealous anymore. He smiles and thinks, perhaps it's better this way. Thomas is a better man than him. He deserves the best woman.

He still needs to find Freddie. He puts Bonnie down and his mum crouches to the floor, her smiling face greeting Bonnie. Oliver steps towards the crowd and over the commotion. He can hear his name being called.

Some bots move out of the way. He sees Mindy first, looking no less scared than she did before, but she did what he asked. With her is Freddie.

Oliver grins. 'Wait here a moment,' he says.

He walks back towards his mum, who is chatting with Bonnie. She's enchanted by the little kid, but Oliver needs to tell her.

'Mum,' he says. She looks his way. 'There's someone else you need to meet.'

He holds her hand, supporting her as she stands upright, still smiling. He steps away from her now, and walks towards the crowd of bots. 'It's all right,' he says to Freddie. 'You can come over.'

The wall of bots parts a little, and Oliver reaches through, placing his hand on his back and encouraging him forwards.

They step away from the bots and into the tiny space where his family are. 'Mum,' Oliver says. 'This is Anthony's son. A MechaniTeen. His name is Freddie.'

CHAPTER 50

All the air expels from Harriet's lungs as her legs grow weak, drained, and she leans against the damp wall. Unblinking, she can't take her eyes off the boy standing before her. Her next inhale is shallow. She inspects every inch of him, searching for an explanation. His shock of black hair, those facial features she recognises, the eyes so much like hers. Her hands go to her tummy, where she once carried her baby.

It can't be. It just can't be.

Oliver takes a step closer to his mum, his hand still on Freddie's back, gently encouraging him like a big brother. 'Anthony raised him since he was a kid. He wanted to lure you back. He raised him as his son. Freddie has known all his life you're his mother and I'm his brother. He really wanted to meet you.'

Freddie smiles. His grin is every bit as gorgeous as Oliver's. 'Hi. May I call you Mother?'

Harriet's next breath releases as a whimper. She can't hold back her tears. She steps towards this young man, an adolescent, who is every bit how she imagined her Freddie would be. And he calls her mother. Is there any other word as beautiful?

'Come here,' she says and opens her arms.

He's almost exactly the size Oliver was as a teen, maybe just an inch shorter. She leans away to look at him. How can she say no to his question? She can't. She can be his mother, if that's what he needs. She can't let him be an orphan.

They sit on the floor, Harriet unable to pull her gaze away from the teen. Her grief has never gone away and now, seeing this Freddie, it's raw again, tearing at her insides. How she wishes this teen was her Freddie. How she wishes she'd nursed him and watched him grow. He's not her baby. He's an imposter, but it's not his fault. She knows this boy isn't her baby, isn't her flesh and blood, but it would be so easy to be his mother too. He's already so easy to love.

Bonnie crawls onto her lap and introduces herself to Freddie. Harriet smiles at Oliver, trying to convey her gratitude. With all the harshness in the world, all the turmoil that is happening outside, she has her son, sons, plural, a little girl on her lap, Thomas, as good as a son, and her best friends together. Below ground they attribute so much to luck and as she gazes into the eyes of her boys, she knows she's the luckiest woman in the world.

CHAPTER 51

Just a few more minutes below and they'll be fine to leave. Out in the real world, Oliver wonders what he'll be able to teach Freddie. They can play football or frisbee. Hopefully he'll still get to see some more of Bonnie. He may not be able to play a father figure, but uncle is a pretty good job to have. She's still clutching the bear he gave her and she leans over to him.

'I call her Sparkle. Do you want to hold her?'

'Why, thank you,' Oliver says, and takes the bear. 'Nice to meet you, Sparkle. I think she needs a sister. How about when we get out of here, we choose her a sister?'

'Yeah!' She laughs and shoves Sparkle down his T-shirt. 'So she stays warm.' She giggles.

Just a few minutes and they'll be free. Free of Anthony. Free of this weapon. With the video, they'll be free of hate. They may be without electricity for a while if the weapon works, but Oliver knows somehow, they'll figure that out together. To have got this far, there's nothing they can't handle. In all the bots around him, Oliver sees friendship and hope. There's George and his colleagues in the crowd. They made it out. The Flesh

Fraternity think they're getting rid of bots, but really, they've created a community.

Oliver vows to spend the rest of his life making up for the things he's done wrong. He'll do whatever it takes to prove he's every bit as good as his mother thinks he is. He'll find a way to deserve her love. Someday, when he's done enough good things, maybe the cries in his head will be silent.

There's another howl of wind, a creak of metal and two bots by the door hold on, leaning right back to counterbalance the force from outside. They groan, fighting the suction force of the wind. The ground vibrates. Tornado is a word that's been whispered. First one in decades. AM Investments might not be the only building destroyed today.

Oliver checks the time. There's still two minutes to go. The door just has to stay in place for a couple more minutes.

'Let's get all the bots further inside,' Theo says.

There's a steady shuffle. Harriet picks up Bonnie and holds her as they walk more towards the centre, Thomas and Evie a little way ahead.

The wind outside batters the door. There's a yelp from the bots and Oliver turns to stare. The metal rod that was jammed in place has bent, the two bots fight with all their strength to hold on to the latch, but the hinges on the other side tear open and the force of the wind tries to suck the door up the stairwell.

'Hurry! Help!' one of them shouts as they battle to keep a grip on the door.

Oliver leaps to help along with another bot. The four of them now tug and pull on the door. It weighs a ton with the force of the wind. Their heels dig into the ground but they slide, further and further as the door tries to fly away. They can't let go. If they let go, the door will get sucked away and everyone below is done for.

From behind, Bonnie is sobbing. Even her childhood innocence can't stave off fear forever. The shuffle continues to move inside but not fast enough. Oliver is counting the seconds, and it is only seconds left. The door fights for freedom, unsealed, there's still a gap.

A phone pings. Theo's.

'Boys!' he shouts, even with Oliver's hearing it's barely audible over the wind. 'Get inside, now! There's no time!'

The wind through the small gap batters against them. They don't let go. How can they? If they let go, the door is lost. But it's too heavy, it's too hard.

'Get further in. Now!' Theo yells. 'They're setting it off in thirty seconds!'

Oliver looks over his shoulder. Behind, there's his mum, Bonnie in her arms, her wide eyes scream at him. 'Oliver, inside, now!'

They won't make it. He knows they won't. Little Bonnie, Evie, Thomas, Freddie. If he lets go, if he doesn't seal the door, they'll all die. He needs to shut the door. Pulling it isn't enough.

Thomas locks eyes with him. He's wearing his vest. Oliver isn't certain it'll work, Theo said as much. Thomas takes a step forward and Oliver shakes his head. Thomas knows. He understands without them saying words. He's unbuttoning his shirt, but there's no time, and if the door can't be closed, Thomas needs to be okay. Evie is next to him, Bonnie is sobbing. That's Thomas's family now. He needs to be with them. He needs to survive for them.

Oliver turns his head a few degrees more and looks at his mum instead. He hopes she understands too. The screams in his head are still loud, even over the wind. The cries of the people he killed. He's done so many bad things and he vowed to spend the rest of his life making amends.

'I love you, Mum,' he says. 'Fly free.'

There's a wail. A cry, begging him to stay, comes from behind as he takes the metal rod and steps out through the gap. His mum's pleas crush him but he ignores her as she calls his name.

He jams the metal rod against the stairs, bearing down and levering himself back as the wind tries to suck him up too. He digs his feet into the ground and throws himself against the door. He stamps his feet closer, groans with the force of every bit of his strength, wedging with his legs, readjusting the rod and forcing his whole weight against the door.

It shuts, the clang of metal on metal, but he stays wedged against the door. He still has the little bear down his T-shirt. The wind calms for a second, and he takes out the bear. He looks at the pink fluff around its glassy eyes. By his feet, a spider scurries across the ground.

There's a flash. All those screams and bad things go away. The voices fall silent, and all that's left is a blissful stillness. In that moment he sees his mum, his family. He's not wedged against a door in the stairwell anymore. He's in the kitchen, the clinking of plates, steamy tea on the table. His uncles are laughing. Then he's outside, beneath the sky of 99. He feels the climbing frame between his hands, his mum's hug in his arms.

In that last second, all he knows is joy.

He's flying, he's free.

CHapTer 52

Bonnie has eyes that shine like Oliver's. She smiles like he did as a kid, innocent, unaware trauma can exist at all, completely untainted by the perils of the world. She knows no suffering.

Whereas suffering is all Harriet knows.

The door is still shut. It's too soon to open it, Theo insists. So Harriet sits, her legs too weak to stand, Bonnie on her lap, and gazes into the eyes that remind her of the boy she loves.

Loved.

Oliver.

Maybe he'll be fine. Maybe the EMP didn't reach down the stairwell. Maybe the tornado stopped the weapon from working.

Her heart cramps, a muscle overused and undernourished. She hopes it'll stop and let her rest. Not so long ago she so wanted to live. Now she's spent, worn out from trying. Is there a heaven? Will Oliver be there? Freddie will. The original Freddie. This new Freddie is sitting next to her, alien yet so familiar. All he's asking is to be loved. Such a simple thing. He's not her son, yet he thinks she is his mother. She can't love him, not yet. Her heart is all taken by another son. Her boy. Her protector.

There's a hand on her shoulder. Theo. 'It's time. We're going to open the door.'

The men holding the door let go. The wind outside still pulls, rattling the door in its frame, but it doesn't come open. Something is blocking it.

Or someone.

Harriet shuffles to face the other way. From behind there's lifting and pushing, the scuff of feet and the scrape of metal, until there's a thud.

That sound chills Harriet's bones.

She stays on the floor, gazing at Bonnie's perfect face. Can anything really be so wrong with the world when there is a child's face this perfect? All she can do is hope, but she knows. In her gut, she knows. Her body is so used to loss. The aches are already beginning, the emptiness, a premonition of what she is about to have confirmed.

Thomas sits to one side of her, Freddie the other. For how long, she's not sure. Their silence is shared, a mutual vacuum. The ground beneath is soggy. Ahead, the tunnel is dreary, dismal, a reflection of them all.

Still Bonnie smiles. An enchanting thing.

There's that hand on her shoulder again. 'Do you want to see him?'

'Is he definitely gone?'

'Yes.'

'Are you sure?'

He doesn't answer. That grip on her shoulder tightens, and that tells her all she needs to know. How can so much sadness exist? How is it possible to go on?

Her gut caves in, hollow, punched, an emptiness like she's never known. A cry, so unrecognisable yet it's hers. Her lap is empty, Bonnie has scarpered elsewhere, and Harriet's hands are in the dirt. She bends forward, her head too heavy to lift, her body folded like paper. Her insides split into a thousand pieces until there is nothing left of her.

She's on her feet. She's unsure how, but she's standing by him, a tall body, broad, covered in a sheet. From one end a little hair sticks out, a kink of a curl.

She's on her knees again and she stares at it, willing it to move. *It.* The pronoun TRI used for him when he was so impossibly small. Is that correct now? The pronoun once life has left. *It* is a table, a chair. *It* is a boy who is no more.

She drapes her body over the unmoving thing that was once her son. Her perfect, beautiful son. He doesn't move. The sheet is cold to the touch.

Perhaps she can stay here forever with him. Death was so close just a short while ago, how she welcomes it again.

She cries until her lungs heave, empty, too weak to cry anymore. She pulls back the end of the sheet and gazes upon her son's face. She traces his cheek dimples, musses up his hair. In death, he looks more at peace than he did before. She whispers for him to wake up, to open his eyes, to call her mum. She cups his face and holds him some more. Her protector. A hero until his last moment.

Just to the side, there's a little pink bear, one finger still touching it. She holds his hand. His pink skin no longer blanches under her touch. It's uniform, unresponsive, inanimate.

And then there is Bonnie. 'Sparkle!' she says, picks the bear up, holds it to her chest.

With Bonnie stands Thomas, Freddie, Evie and others. All the people her son saved. Bonnie sits next to Harriet, takes her hand. Bonnie is too young to know what grief is. Too young to know life's horrors.

'Do you want to hold Sparkle?' she asks.

Bonnie smiles at her and puts the bear on her lap. Harriet looks at the bear, strokes its fuzzy fur. Oliver gave his life to save this girl. Harriet doesn't want her to know what such sadness looks like. Children are so impressionable, so much more than she ever realised.

❀ ❀ ❀ ❀

Harriet doesn't remember getting home and doesn't know how long it's been. Weeks pass in a blur of denial and despair. It's a new mark of time: the after. How she yearns for the before. Before the event that has left her forever changed, forever emptier. She's had a few of those events. Somehow, they get harder instead of easier.

There's chatter in the house, a constant conversation that she can pick out only bits of. A hundred MechaniBots died, many more MechaniKids. The MechaniTeen Institute was fine.

Somehow, they have electricity.

The incinerator batteries were below. The EMP wiped out the solar, the wind, the top levels are in blackout. The top levels have lost their electricity. Not just Reading town and London. The Flesh Fraternity detonated EMPs across the country. So many bots killed. Too many to count.

The Flesh Fraternity are in hiding, wanted posters for them are everywhere. Harriet listens but fails to care.

Other bits, she pays more attention to. The whispers come through the walls, mentioning her son.

Oliver.

Lenny aired Harriet's video. The world saw Oliver kill Anthony. Whether the viewers judge that as an act of evil or justice depends on how low down they live. Though Harriet is sure that *Delilah's Law* will be a long way off. The top levels are blaming Oliver. For the fall of AM Investments, for murder, for provoking the Flesh Fraternity. They're writing it off to one bad bot.

She doesn't care, and she doubts Oliver would. The lower levels hold the power at the moment. They're the only ones with electricity, so Harriet wonders which narrative will prevail.

The ones that matter know the truth. The lower levels and below hail him as a hero, for getting the truth out, for punishing the real villain.

Harriet never wanted a hero. She only ever wanted a son.

How would it be for him, if he was alive? There's no way a bot would be allowed a fair trial. Her boy was doomed whatever happened in the tunnel.

When her eyes go to the window, the streetlights glow brightly, and she swells with pride for what Oliver achieved. He saved so many. Does pride dampen her grief? No. It makes her ache and gasp for breath. As proud as she is for all he saved, she'd rather a million times over not be so proud, and have her son here. She buries her head in her pillow, forever damp from tears and uses what little strength she has to scream.

When Harriet gets out of bed, it's only brief outings, to the bathroom mostly. She listens, avoids company, then goes back to bed and picks through her life, wondering what she could have done differently. Not that long ago, close to death, she taught herself not to dwell on the what ifs of the past. Now, it's all she does.

Her cries are quieter. She has no voice left. She wishes the electric wasn't on. A blackout, forever darkness, sounds somehow better than enlightened reality.

Freddie sits with her sometimes, silently, alone. Next to her but still so far away. She should find a way to reach him, to show him love, but not now. Not yet.

There's a knock on the door. She ignores such sounds, but this one knocking doesn't wait for an answer. It's Bonnie. All smiles. Harriet tries to smile back, but the muscles that do that are too unused to work.

'Look,' Bonnie says. 'Sparkle has a sister. I'm calling her Sprinkle.'

'That's nice.'

'Here.' She puts the fuzzy purple bear next to Harriet. 'When you're better, they can play together.'

Bonnie leaves then, the door still ajar, and Harriet fumbles with the little purple bear. A simple bear ignites such imagination in a child. She briefly wonders what adventures Sprinkle will have in her lifetime. Children's toys are the start of so many stories.

She used to like telling stories, to act them out. The children laughing was the best applause.

She hunkers down under the duvet. Not today. Not yet.

CHAPTER 53

'Can I make you some tea?' Evie asks most days.

She lives here now. There's nowhere for her to charge at her old address. Oliver's bed is being put to use. Waste not, want not. The efficiency of the lower levels continues even after death. If there's anything more than friendship between Evie and Thomas, Harriet still isn't certain. They seem more plutonic, like old friends.

'Thanks, Evie. That would be nice.'

She should be sick of tea. She's drunk gallons of the stuff over recent months but once again, it's all she can stomach.

From the kitchen, people are laughing. How can there be laughter when her boy is dead?

Because the world still spins. She should know that by now. Grief halts time for no one. Her hair still greys, her night sweats are rampant, her lines dig deeper.

She still has the little bear, Sprinkle. She walks to the kitchen where they all are. All minus one. Heads turn to face her, pinched smiles, not judging her performance, only wishing it was a happier one.

'Sprinkle!' Bonnie says.

'I thought she might like to see her sister,' Harriet says.

Bonnie gives Harriet a hug. 'It's nice you're out of your room. Can I call you Nanna?'

Harriet's breath stalls in her lungs. The question knocks her sideways. She thought she had no more tears left but they fill her eyes once again. Not sad tears this time, an overflowing of warmth. 'Of course,' she says.

Thomas and Evie shuffle along the bench to make room for her. Monty is cooking, Theo has put down the broken fan and screwdriver for a moment.

'Hey,' he says.

She doesn't need to say anything to Theo. Her face says it all. She's alive. Somehow, she's surviving.

❀ ❀ ❀ ❀

Today is the first day of many. Harriet dresses, attempts to style her unstylable hair, and walks to the community hall on 5. The walkways are quieter these days, with less rubbish crashing down. This has delighted those who live low down. There's a peace that some have never known. With the electricity still patchy, the factories aren't working and people are having to make things last. There was outcry on *Get Level* from a group of people who had to venture down to 10 to charge their phones, just so they could moan they had to hand wash clothes rather than buy new, and they didn't even know what to buy since the advertising billboards don't work. Harriet and her family smiled at that. The peace won't last, they are all sure. But any respite from the constant crashing and adding to the trash is a win. Theo and Monty are busier with work than they've ever been. Top levels are queuing up for refurbished this and repaired that. For some, making things last is quite the novelty.

Harriet has in her pocket Oliver's dinosaur T-shirt he had as a kid. The world hasn't been disposable to her for a long time. She cherishes so many things.

Evie is already at the community hall. She's been helping out there a lot, since her job up on 105 is no more. There's still no electricity on the top levels. Electricity is power and at the moment, the once powerful are powerless.

Freddie is with Harriet, wanting to try his hand at the family business, he says. He's keen to learn, and to bond. Anthony was never that kind to him, Harriet has learned. Not violent, just cold. He'd never had a hug before. Freddie to Anthony was a tool to win her back, not the son they never raised.

Harriet loved his father once and in Freddie, she sees all the good points he once had. A sense of humour, a hint of ambition, dashing good looks from his younger days, and his unwavering loyalty. His grief has been a strange journey; he's lost not only his father but a truth he really believed. The world is not as he knew it. Harriet spared him the worst details. Her scars don't need to be his too. She sees in Freddie a blank slate. A boy keen to love. All he wants is a mother.

She can't hate Anthony anymore. She's run out of hate; she only wishes the world has. Anthony left everything to her in his will. He loved her still, in his own way. She has more money than she ever dreamed of, more than she could ever need. She's setting up a fund for treatment for the below-ground sickness. No way will she be silenced now. This world and its hate has taken so much from her. She won't let it take her humanity too. What that means for the bots, she's not sure. There are less, so that means there's probably enough for now and TRI won't make any more. If TRI tanks, she won't shed another tear.

She has an apartment on 107 should she want it. She'd like to see the view from the window again, to sit in Oliver's bedroom, to hold his dinosaur toys. Perhaps a bolthole, for quiet weekends. Or maybe she'll sell it to add to the treatment fund. Life on 5 isn't so bad. She'll buy a bigger place, one so Bonnie has her own room. Pink curtains and a rainbow duvet. Monty's already making it.

The class are all sitting waiting for her, crossed legged on the carpet, gazing with expectant faces. Bonnie among them, 'That's my Nanna,' she whispers to one of the other children.

Harriet smiles every time she hears the word Nanna. For every sad memory, a happy one is made.

Harriet's grief crushes her most days, but life is short, and too precious, especially for someone who came so close to death. So much is disposable and thrown away, but he worst thing to waste is a life. She can list her regrets forever. She regrets not raising Oliver to be more selfish, self-preserving. He was always a protector. She should have put a stop to that when he was a kid, when he was the sweetest little boy. But he did more for Mechani-Rights with his one act than Harriet did with all her fame and campaigning. As she looks at some of the bots, safe and happy in the lower levels, she knows however much she didn't want a hero, his friends needed one.

In a life that has experienced so much loss, she has learned to count her blessings. And she has more than ever. She looks at the sweet faces of the children sitting so quietly and knows that all is not lost. There's always love when there are children, and with them there's always a reason to go on. As long as there are children, she still has a purpose. As long as there are children, there's hope.

The stage Monty built has been decorated with 'Welcome back' banners. Glitter sprinkled across the floor. Theo's fixed the coloured lights and they flash, blues and reds swirling across the stage.

'Say good morning to Ms Chapel,' Evie says.

They do and give her a clap. Harriet takes a bow before she's begun.

Harriet has her script. She's learned her lines.

There's a chair on the stage and she sits, then smiles back at them. All eyes are on her, silent, bated breath. They're ready to hear the story.

She clears her throat and begins. 'Now, let me tell you a story about a little boy . . .'

A note from Emma

Thank you so much for reading this series! If you have a moment to write a review, the QR code below takes you to the Amazon page. Reviews mean so much to authors and help other readers find books they'll enjoy.

Subscribers to my website and bookshop receive free short stories for all of my series, as well as a few others. Subscribers also hear first about new releases and promotions, my book recommendations, and whatever else in the world has caught my attention at that moment. You can also keep in touch via Facebook or Instagram.

I started writing this trilogy while living in a little house in the mountains in Italy. It's very beautiful here, though the Internet drives me mad on the weekends when the tourists arrive and the bandwidth can't keep up. I've spent the last six or seven years living in a van, besides the odd stint in some shack or house sit, plus a couple of months living in a tent when my van was being repaired. That was horrible. Put me off camping for life.

Anyway, having somewhat of a nomadic existence away from cities, my grasp of technology is a little behind. It took me four months to figure out how the thermostat worked in this house. I'm still not sure I've mastered it. But I read the news and listen to a lot of science podcasts and the one topic that comes up time and time again, is AI. The benefits and the dangers. There was a famous story a few years ago about a chatbot that turned into a holocaust-denying racist, but then I read an article recently about a woman who had an AI boyfriend. She spoke to him on a device for hours each day and felt a real emotional bond to him.

Poor Oliver. My heart broke writing this. As loved as Oliver was, the demons of his past left their mark. Like that chatbot that went rogue, he learned from his experiences. Oliver was so impressionable. There was too much he still didn't understand. Technology such as his invokes fear because it's humans that make it and humans that teach it. When there are so many bad people in the world, can man-made intelligence ever exist without all the pitfalls that come with being human?

Oliver wasn't a saint, he was as flawed as any human, but he died a hero. He died a better man than the man who tried to ruin him. Because he wasn't only tainted by hate, but also nurtured by love.

Emma's Other Works

The Eyes Forward Series. This best-selling series is set in a world where the population has escalated, and governments employ ever more sinister ways to reduce it. Three stories set in a world where fertile women are branded a nuisance, every child is deemed a burden, and every citizen is a spy.

If you are in the mood for some more twisted dystopian, my first series, The Raft Series, is also available. In this world, the entire country has been sterilised and all non-human life made extinct. But poison comes in many forms and Savannah Selbourne must discover the truth.

For thriller vibes, gore, twists, and some rather unhinged characters, check out the Be Her duology!

ACKNOWLEDGEMENTS

Preserve would not be in print without the help of my wonderful betas and critique partners. Thank you to Danica, Emily, Allison, Katie, Jaime, and Barry. Their time and honest feedback made this book what it is today. Thank you also to my editor Shannon, for being so incredibly thorough, and Lawrence for his proofreading skills.

Thanks especially to my partner, John, for giving me the space and time I need to write, for his support, patience, and encouragement.

And thank you for reading it.

www.ingramcontent.com/pod-product-compliance
Lightning Source LLC
Chambersburg PA
CBHW030926120726
47906CB00002B/509

9781068760082